The Proud
and the
Prejudiced

Colette
Sancri

The Proud and the Prejudiced

A Modern Twist on Pride and Prejudice

Colette L. Saucier

Southern Girl Press

First Southern Girl Press Edition, December 16, 2014

A portion of this narrative previously published as
All My Tomorrows, Copyright © 2012 Colette L. Saucier
ISBN-13: 978-0615657387
ISBN-10: 06156573

Southern Girl Press ISBN-10:0986371807
ISBN-13:978-0-9863718-0-6

DEDICATION

To my muse.

CHAPTER 1

Alice flipped through the yellowed pages to the beginning of the dog-eared novel.

The Edge of Darkness
Chapter 1

It was raining when I awoke that Sunday morning. I knew immediately because of the click-click of the drops hitting the awning Daddy had put up that summer to shield my window from the sun's burning rays. It was autumn now, and when I looked outside, the brown, orange, and gold leaves of the trees in our backyard were drenched and sleepily waving in the breeze.

We didn't have carpeting, and the floorboards were cold on my bare feet. After climbing down the stairs, I pretended to be a tightrope walker, balancing myself on single floorboards all the way to the kitchen. Daddy was sitting in "his chair" reading the paper and smoking his pipe. I always loved the smell of his burning tobacco, but when Tad, my older brother, would sneak a cigarette, its stink made me sick.

Tad was thirteen, and that wasn't his real name, which was George. He had read "Tad" in some book and liked it better than being called Junior because he had been named after Daddy. But now my two front teeth were missing, and when I said "Tad" it came out "Dad." This could make things confusing since sometimes no one knew who was talking to whom, but it wasn't all the Toothfairy's fault. Tad's voice sounded a lot like mine, due to his age, and he called our father simply Dad. Mommy said she'd be glad when her children could speak normally.

Mommy was wearing a pink Sunday dress and a stained white apron as she peered into the oven. When she turned around and saw me, her lips pursed up as if she had eaten a lemon. "Lexie, look at you, walking around barefoot on this cold floor." I looked down at my dirty little feet and then back to my mother's eyes. "You're sick enough as it is. Now you get back to bed."

Then Daddy said without taking his eyes off his paper, "Let her stay. Her room gets so cold, the warm oven will do her good." He hadn't gone to church that morning. He had stayed home because of me, but he tried to get out of going to church as much as Mommy would let him anyway.

Mommy felt my face for fever. I always loved the way she smelled, no matter what. I liked it on special occasions when she put Émeraude on her wrists and behind her ears, but today she smelled like bread, and I knew she'd been baking. This was my favorite smell since I was the one to get the heel off the loaf fresh from the oven. Mommy told me to sit down and she'd fix me up some breakfast. Tad came in from outside. He was already filthy from playing with the neighbors, and his oiled hair was messed up.

"What'd you do with your church clothes when you changed?" Mommy asked without turning from the stove.

"I haven't changed yet."

Mommy looked at him, and her face turned red. "George Andrew Hayward, Junior! You march up those stairs right now and take a bath so hot that when you come down you'll be steaming! And you're not going out again today!"

"Mom!"

"Don't you raise your voice to me, young man! Now march!" She pointed her finger in the direction of the living room, and Tad sulked off.

Mommy's face was sweet even though she frowned. Her face relaxed when the kitchen door closed behind Tad. She and Daddy met eyes and then she turned back to my breakfast on the stove.

Mommy and Daddy had some sort of secret communication system. They seemed to have an entire conversation with just one glance. I asked Mommy about it one day. "You'll know someday when you marry the right man."

I sat in the chair next to my daddy's with my feet on the seat and rubbed my shins to warm them. Mommy placed a bowl of steaming oatmeal before me and stirred in some sugar and milk, and I ate it. It was a typical Sunday at our house, just like so many others.

Daddy had brought a TV home a couple of years before. It was black and white and kind of dark. When we first got it, we thought if you were watching a show and left for a while, when you came back the show would still be on. Even Daddy was surprised when we found out the show was over. Tad would always get a pillow from his bed and stretch out on the rug in front of the TV. Daddy would yell at him because he'd keep squirming his feet. Usually he fell asleep there on the floor, and I remember thinking how big his rear end looked.

That night we watched Walt Disney. When Tad fell asleep, Daddy carried him up the stairs. Daddy was a very strong, big man. Mommy told me once that the reason she married him was because he was so much like her father, and I wondered if I would marry a man like Daddy someday, too.

Grandpa had been like a private detective or something. I once saw him on the front porch picking at a bullet hole in his chest, cleaning it with a knife. Grandpa must have had quite a life. I heard Mommy tell our neighbor Mrs. Mahaffey that he had been married to an Indian woman called Jess a long time before he met my grandmother, and before that he had been married to a woman named Sarah who died from taking too much aspirin.

He and the Indian woman had had a son named Homer. Not much was known about him, but Mommy said she remembered when she was little, a boy named Homer came to stay with them until he was caught stealing and was sent away. Jess had been murdered, shot in the head. I heard Mommy say that some people thought Grandpa had done it, but he wasn't convicted. I don't think he did it.

When we were older, Tad told me that Grandpa wasn't Mommy's real father. Gram had been married once before to a much older man.

4

He said when Gram was young, she turned up pregnant one day, and her father – a coal miner – threw her out of the house. That didn't make much sense to me because, after Gram's mother had died in some botched operation to keep her from having another baby, Gram had been taking care of all her younger brothers and sisters. Gram had been one of ten children, but Kate had been stillborn, Victor died when he was six from a spider bite, and Ivan had been killed by a train. I guess Gram's father decided he'd rather take care of six children himself than let Gram stay there with a baby.

After Gram left home and had my aunt, she met my mother's father. He had been in his fifties even then, but he married her in spite of Aunt Eunice. Gram then had Aunt Sable and Mommy, but her husband was older than her own father. When he got sick and was bedridden and couldn't work, they took in a boarder to help with the expenses. Tad said it was a well-known fact that Gram and the boarder were having an affair, but I don't know how he'd know that. After her husband died of cancer, Gram married the boarder, and that was my grandpa.

It was about midnight that Sunday when Tad came into my room and shoved me until I woke up.

"What's goin' on?" I asked him sleepily.

"Come on," he ordered. "The house is on fire." He was so calm, I didn't half believe him. He took my hand and pulled me out of the room.

I glanced at Mommy and Daddy's room, but the door had been swallowed by flames. I remember I started screaming then. The smoke stung my eyes and made me cry, even before I started crying for real, and the heat scorched my skin. I screamed even through my coughs, and Tad picked me up and ran down the stairs. The mirror on the wall had turned black, and the hardwood floors were changing colors.

Outside, Mrs. Mahaffey cried as she wrapped a blanket around me. I stopped screaming and stared at the house as it was engulfed in flames. I guess I was in shock. The thing I remember most about standing out in the wet grass that night was the smell – a horrid, putrid smell that made me ill. Little did I know it was the smell of burning flesh.

And my life would never be the same.

Reality interrupted fiction with a light rapping on the door. Alice set her tuna salad sandwich on the neon green nylon baggie on her desk and dropped her mother's ragged paperback in the bottom drawer next to her purse.

"Come in."

The door opened, and Eileen's head popped in. "Hey, Mrs. Jellyby is here. Peacock wants the cast and crew on the hospital in ten."

"I wonder if this is it." Alice rubbed her temple in anticipation of the inevitable headache.

Eileen – in full make-up, scrubs, and white coat – pushed in and closed the door. "That bad, huh?" To Alice's non-answer, she sat down. "What will you do?"

"Go back to New York, I guess. I don't really see myself collaborating with a bunch of Hollywood writers. You?"

"I think I'd like to try films, as a character actor."

"Why character?"

"Come on. I'm no Giselle. I don't have 'the look.' I think I would find more satisfaction playing interesting characters than always being the leading lady's best friend."

"What about stage? You could come to New York with me."

"And not have the option of a second take? Never!" She laughed. "Plus, I like L.A. It grows on you."

Alice took another bite of her sandwich before tucking it away. "Yeah, like a fungus," she said as she chewed.

"Well, I'm still going to try to talk you into staying. I'll miss you too much if you leave. Who will I have to split a bottle of Malbec with me?"

"That's what video chat is for, and then we each get to have our own bottle."

Alice and Eileen were the last to arrive at the hospital set, and their appearance quieted the buzz of the others gathered. All eyes turned to Mrs. Jellyby, and Alice immediately knew one thing by the slight upturn at the corners of the producer's mouth and her bright floral-print dress: the soap had not been cancelled.

"Thank you for coming so quickly," Mrs. Jellyby began in a quivering falsetto that carried across the soundstage. "I have important and exciting news. As I am sure you are all aware, this has been a tough year for *All My Tomorrows* from a ratings and affiliate sponsor point of view. After thirty-seven years, the very survival of the show has been at risk.

"Today the network demonstrated its unwavering support for *All My Tomorrows* with a new addition to the cast."

Uh-oh. In a split-second, Alice's mind ran over all the concurrent storylines and where a new character would fit in. *I wonder if it's too soon since her fiancé's death for Sienna to have a new romance.*

"Peter Walsingham will be joining our family next week!" Mrs. Jellyby grinned and clapped her hands.

Alice cursed her own heart for skipping a beat at his name. What she would have scripted as a "collective gasp from the crowd" led into applause by all but herself and Mr. Peacock, who met her eyes across the set with a quick nod. An actor from film and primetime meant a leading role. All the scripts would have to be rewritten.

"Giselle, I don't think you will mind sharing love scenes with Peter." *Bingo.* To Mrs. Jellyby's pronouncement, Giselle smiled and blushed as the other's laughed.

Even though Alice had a lot of long nights of rewrites ahead of her, she knew the excitement of Peter Walsingham provided a much-needed relief from the pall that had settled over the soap since sweeps.

"And perhaps, just perhaps, we can convince him that he wants to stay on with us." Mrs. Jellyby waded in with the others, and from where Alice stood, she sounded like she was cooing.

"What do you think?" Mr. Peacock asked Alice after making his way across stage to her side.

"I think Sienna has recovered quickly from Blaine's death."

The director grinned. "Time is relative, especially on soaps."

"So how did you manage *this* coup?"

"I had nothing to do with it. You know Walsingham was just killed off on *COD*? That was at his request. Said the publicity from his relationship with his co-star was disruptive on the set."

Alice raised her eyebrows. "I'm surprised they didn't let Winnie Johnson go instead."

"They didn't want either one of them to go. Even negative publicity is publicity, and they thought having off-camera lovers brought in more viewers."

Alice scoffed. "I'm sure his *wife* will be relieved to hear it."

"I think that's one of the reasons he wanted out. This has been a big drama itself. It was not an amicable break."

"With the wife or the show?"

"Both, I think, but I meant the show." Mr. Peacock pulled out an electronic cigarette and sucked on it. "They killed him off so he couldn't come back, and the only way they agreed to let him out was if he finished off his contract here."

Shit. "For how long? Mrs. Jellyby is smoking crack if she thinks he will stay on. Will he be here for a full story arc? We can't have sweet and innocent Sienna having a fling. She can't sleep with anyone unless they are *violently in love.*"

"He'll be here until July when he has to go on location for some movie, then he'll be back for three months after the Olympics, although Mrs. Jellyby thinks she can convince him to stay."

Alice wished she smoked, if for no other reason than to have something to do with her hands – and she did still think it looked cool – but she figured it would be silly to start smoking with a fake cigarette. "I still don't like it. The viewers are not going to like her hopping into bed with someone without falling in love with him first. Even having a known adulterer cast in the role could tarnish her reputation in the eyes of some viewers. When 'Hollywood's Bad Boy' married 'America's Sweetheart,' they thought he had reformed."

"Who knows? It might get us new viewers."

"We're talking backstory, character development, romance, conflict. And where am I supposed to send him in July?"

He laughed and put his cigarette back in his pocket. "You'll think of something. I have faith."

"I need a Xanax," she said as he walked away.

The Edge of Darkness
Chapter 2

Marlene Hollingsworth had known my mother since they were little girls. They had both been born and raised in Joplin, Missouri, as I had been for my six years although I had been born while Mommy and Daddy were staying in New York. Mommy and Marlene had been best friends in school and stood up with each other when they each got married right after Pearl Harbor. During World War II, Daddy had to go to Fort Robinson in Little Rock for boot camp, and Mommy went, too.

Mommy lived at a house as a boarder since Daddy had to stay on base, and to pay for her room, she worked at the dime store. One day after she had been standing on her feet for hours, a customer was rude to her. She started crying and all she wanted was to go back to Missouri.

Like a miracle, Marlene and her husband Molly walked into the store right at that moment. They packed her up and took her back home to Missouri.

The war moved people around a lot. When Daddy was stationed in Louisiana, Mommy went with him, and she didn't see Marlene again until Daddy went overseas. After the war was over, Marlene and Molly and Mommy and Daddy bought houses down the street from each other and were best friends all over again. They even both had little boys about a year apart. Then Molly went into politics, and first he and Marlene had moved to a bigger house in a finer neighborhood, then he took his family all the way to Washington, D.C. Mommy and Marlene would write letters, but they didn't see each other again until I was three. That was when Marlene had wanted to come home for Christmas, and Mommy and Daddy invited them to stay with us. Their son Anthony stayed in Tad's room, and their daughter Annette stayed with me, but I don't really remember it. After that visit, Mommy and Marlene stopped writing, and we never saw them again. Until now.

Marlene and Molly were divorced now, which I didn't really understand then, and she had gotten their house in Alexandria, Virginia. She lived there with her daughter Annette, only a few months older than I, and her son lived in Georgetown with his father.

After Tad and Anthony were born, Mommy and Daddy had drawn up a will stating that Marlene and Molly would become the legal guardians of Tad and any subsequent children should anything happen to them, and Marlene and Molly had done the same for their children.

That's why after the fire, Tad and I went to go live with Marlene.

I really liked Marlene; she was like a movie star. She let us call her by her first name. She always wore her blond hair in a tower on top of her head. She wore tons of eye make-up and bright red lipstick and nail polish. She puffed at a cigarette she held in a long holder. She had fancy clothes and mink coats and one that she said was beaver. I liked it best. Her black poodle Jake had a fluffy hairdo and painted nails and always stayed by her side, and she would feed him the olives from her martinis. Sometimes she would pour some of her morning coffee into the saucer and put it on the floor, and he would drink it. She said he might have a hangover from eating too many olives. I think Jake liked it best on the mornings when Lillian, the maid, brought donuts and Marlene would tear a piece off and put it in his coffee.

The house had a huge party room with plush white carpeting and twin blue-silver sofas and a low, round glass coffee table. Trees and plants filled the room, and the bar was always in full supply of liquor. When Marlene would sit on one bar stool, her poodle would climb onto the other and sit on his hind legs while she fed him. Behind the bar, an enormous mirror covered the wall, and the other walls were papered with a blue, Victorian print. This was my favorite room in the house, though I rarely was allowed in. It was the first time I had ever seen a crystal chandelier.

Annette and I had a marvelous time together at first. We had tea parties for her dolls and looked through Marlene's fashion magazines. A stone wall about four feet high surrounded the enormous house, and we would walk on it pretending to be trapeze artists. This had been my idea. Since they had carpeting, we couldn't balance ourselves on floorboards, so the wall was an adequate substitute, except I was always afraid I would fall and break my neck. Annette's brother Anthony would visit occasionally but not enough for him and Tad to become good friends.

I started going to school with Annette after Thanksgiving. With the exception of the fire, I had never been so scared in all my life. For one thing, in school Annette completely ignored me and only played with her friends. For another, Tad and I were separated since our schools were not co-ed. I didn't know if I would like going to an all-girls school, and I wanted to be with Tad. Ever since the fire, Tad and I had spent more time together, just the two of us. Sometimes we would talk about Mommy and Daddy since everyone else acted like they never existed. I had my own room, but at night I would climb into Tad's bed just in case there was a fire. None of the luxuries in my new life could compete with the comfort he gave me.

Alice sat just offstage perusing the new script when Peter Walsingham arrived with his entourage, and she was relieved most of the cast and crew were at lunch. Even the few crewmembers there gawked and whispered to one another. Alice peeked up at the newcomers then fixed her attention to the script on her lap, although she couldn't help it if they were in her peripheral vision. *Damnit, he's just as beautiful in person. And Winnie Johnson just as gorgeous. And*

thin. Naturally, he would bring his *paramour* with him to the set. She willed her heart to stop racing, reminding herself that by all accounts this guy was a misogynistic dick. *A dick named Peter – ha!*

Winnie walked around the set touching the furniture and mantle. "I have never seen anything so cheap in my life. And this is supposed to be your home?"

"Not if I can help it," Peter said in *that* voice.

"They must have spent the money for sets on the cameras. Why do they need so many?"

"It'll be fine; you'll see," the other man said, his voice lively and excited. "It really is a great show – and you'll be working with Giselle Meyer!"

"Who the hell is that?" asked *the* voice.

"Oh, c'mon, Peter, you must know her! She's incredible. You see, years ago she was going to be a nun, but before she took her final vows, Damien declared his love for her, but then he was in a terrible accident and had amnesia –"

"Jack," Winnie said, "don't tell me you actually watch these soap operas!"

"Only *All My Tomorrows,* but it's really good."

Alice suppressed a smile. She liked this Jack person.

Peter huffed. "I consider that highly improbable, but I won't argue with you. What's done is done, and I am stuck here. They wanted to punish me and have succeeded, but what I won't stand for is portraying some former character raised from the dead. Ridiculous."

"Not dead, actually. Just lost at sea."

"It's another man's role. I feel like an understudy. Even in this pitiful excuse for a drama, I should be able to develop my own character."

At that, Alice glanced up and right into the eyes of Peter Walsingham. Her own eyes widened at having him stare at her from across the set. And why was he gawking at her? At first she didn't turn away because of shock, but then, since he evidently had no intention of breaking the eye contact, she continued out of sheer stubbornness. *I suppose he believes his fame and movie-starness intimidate me. Well, he's right, but he doesn't have to know it.*

"But you get to bring back Tristan!"

Peter broke the gaze and turned to Jack. Alice smiled. *Ha! I win! I win a staring contest he had no idea we were having.* Her smile faded and she returned to the script.

"What is with these names? I'd rather play Tristram Shandy."

The reference surprised Alice. *At least he's not illiterate.*

"Tristan is Clarissa's brother. You'll like working with Eileen Seaver."

"Yes, that's another thing. I have seen her picture. No one in his right mind would believe she and I could be siblings."

"Perhaps you got all the looks in the family," Winnie said, returning to Peter and Jack.

Alice slammed the script shut, but the sound of paper slapping together was far from satisfying. *So, he is too handsome to play Eileen's brother!*

"If you have issues with the script," Jack said, "why don't you discuss them with the head writer. I'm sure she—"

With a humorless laugh, Peter said, "I doubt she could write her way out of a paper bag."

That is it! Alice jumped down from her chair and marched toward her office. *I could certainly have written a better comeback line than that!*

CHAPTER 2

The Edge of Darkness
Chapter 5

Marlene legally adopted me when I was fourteen, since I had been with her longer than my real mother. Although she never came out and said anything, I think Annette resented it. Before then, Annette and I would be best friends at home, but she would completely ignore me at school, as if she had no idea who I was. Once we had the same last name, though, she couldn't pretend I didn't exist. Instead, she joined the other girls who teased and taunted me.

My appearance at that time could only be described as ugly. I had stringy red hair like yams, and my face was broken out from the chocolate that also contributed to my weight problem. I spent all my free time reading, studying things not needed for school and feeding my imagination. The main reason, I suppose, was because I didn't have any friends.

Annette generally led the attacks against me, which I didn't understand since we were sisters –

although she made it clear to everyone that we were not "real" sisters. Of course, she was pretty and popular, and that's what the popular girls did. They said I was weird, and they said it so often I began to believe it myself.

By then I knew I wanted to be an actress, and I decided to practice the craft immediately. I would regale my classmates with terribly untrue tales, not so much to get their attention but more to see if I could fool them into believing me. Sometimes these falsehoods went too far when they actually *did* believe me. All the mean girls would talk about parties and going out, so I told them about a wild party I had attended, in my mind. I fictionalized a guest list, entertainment, hors d'oeuvres, and the hostess all in intricate detail. After hearing my story, some of the girls relayed it all to Sr. Theresa, the principal, and I was summoned to her office.

"Some of your friends are worried about you. They said you attended some sort of hippie bacchanal."

"If they are the ones I think, they are no friends of mine. I did no such thing."

"But they all heard you talking about the party."

"For some reason, they don't care for me – at all. I wouldn't doubt that they all got together and made up this ridiculous story just to turn you against me." At this point, I turned up the histrionics and even managed to make myself cry. "And you believe them! Of all people, I thought I could trust you. Why do they hate me? They are trying to ruin my reputation, and I have never once served then an injustice!" The nun believed me. Or maybe she believed Marlene, who could have verified that I had not spent a single night out of her sight.

I think Marlene, Mother now, might have chosen that time to adopt me because Tad had gone away. He still lived with us while he went to college at Georgetown, but as soon as he graduated, he was drafted. I knew as much as I could about Vietnam, and I was against the war even before the Marines took Tad. I prayed every night that he wouldn't be sent overseas.

Molly was a Senator now, and he used his connections so Tad could stay in the States as long as possible. I still never saw him, though, since he was stationed in California. I figured Molly had used those same connections to keep his own son out of the war altogether and couldn't help but resent them both for it, especially when the inevitable happened.

Almost a year after he had been drafted, Tad was standing in the kitchen when I came down before school.

"Tad!" I ran into his arms as he lifted me off the ground. "What are you doing here?"

"Can't a guy come and see his little sister every once in a while?"

"You better believe it! I've missed you so much."

"Me, too. You haven't been out drinking and carousing, have you?"

"Of course." We laughed, and I caught him up on any new things since my last letter as we walked into the living room and sat on the sofa. "And how is everything on the base?"

He averted his eyes. "Um, fine."

"You still haven't explained your unexpected appearance."

"I'm here because I have to talk to you." He glanced at his watch. "But you'd better get to school."

"No, we can talk now. I have first hour free today anyway. You can't expect me to spend the day imagining the worst."

He looked at me then. "Lexie, it is the worst. I'm going. They're sending me to Nam."

"No. No, they can't! What about Molly?"

"There's nothing he could do. He arranged for me to come here first to see you, but he couldn't do anything else."

"It's not true! It's not true! They can't send you!" I was screaming, and tears flowed down my cheeks in rivers. He held me close, but he couldn't stifle my hysteria. My screams had awoken Mother, and she and Annette came running into the living room. "You just can't go!" I pulled out of his arms and fled to my room.

I know he tried to cheer me up while he was there, but sometimes just looking at him made me cry. I couldn't believe my own brother was going to Vietnam. A few days later at the airport, Mother left us alone to say goodbye.

"Don't worry, Lexie. I'll be back in thirteen months."

"That's over a year."

"It will go by quickly. You'll see. I want you to stay as busy as possible and not think about where I am so the time will pass faster."

"What if something happens to you?"

"Nothing is going to happen. Don't worry." He kissed a tear under my eye. "But I want to talk to you about something I think you should know."

We sat on a couch in the airport, and he took both my hands and looked into my eyes. "Lexie, after Mama had me, she and Dad really wanted another baby – more than anything in the world – but I gave her a hard time in the delivery room. The doctor said it would be dangerous for her to have another baby, but she didn't care. She wanted a baby, and so she got pregnant."

"Why are you telling me this?"

"She got pregnant, Lexie, but it was a difficult pregnancy. She miscarried in the seventh month, and she had to have a hysterectomy."

As what he said came together in my mind and I started to make sense of it, I began to cry. "Why are you telling me this now? You said nothing was going to happen to you."

"They still wanted a baby. So they adopted you."

I shook my head back and forth. "No. No, I don't believe you."

"It's true, Lex. I went with them to New York to get you."

"So then who is my real mother?"

"I don't know. She was a young actress in New York, but I never knew her name. And they fixed it so your birth certificate had Mama and Dad's names. I don't even know if they went through an adoption agency."

"I suppose that explains why I love acting."

He wiped at my tears with a handkerchief. "I'm sorry to tell you like this."

"I…I don't suppose it matters. I mean, I was adopted by Marlene anyway. Does she know?"

"I don't think so. You know, something happened a long time ago between Marlene and our mother that made them stop being friends. I think Mama would have told her if she wanted her to know."

"I just wish you weren't telling me now

because I know why you're telling me."

"Lexie, nothing is going to happen to me, but just in case, I thought you had the right to know."

Then they called his flight and he kissed me goodbye. "I love you, Alexandra."

☼

"Come in," Alice said without lifting her eyes from her book.

"Mrs. McGillicutty, we need to talk about –"

At the sound of Peter's voice Alice raised her head, and he broke off. She scowled. "Mrs.?"

"It's you," he said, frozen in the doorway.

"Not if you are looking for *Mrs.* McGillicutty. Why would you presume I am married?"

"I – well…with a name like McGillicutty, I assumed…"

"So you assume every female McGillicutty emerges from the womb married?"

The shock from recognition fell away as his face relaxed. "No, of course not. I apologize if I offended you, *Miss* McGillicutty."

She pointed at a chair with her pen. "Alice will do. You have something to discuss?"

He closed the door and took the offered seat. She was too pissed off at him to be star-struck, and she had prepared for this conversation.

"I saw you on the set," he said. "I assumed you were an actress on the show."

"You assume quite a lot, Mr. Walsingham."

"Peter. You can call me Peter."

"What an honor," she said. "Now, why are you here?"

"Yes. About my character. Tristram."

"Tristan."

"Tristan. Right. I don't want that role."

"Oh? And why might that be?"

"He was lost at sea and declared dead. The premise is ridiculous."

"No, it isn't; it happens all the time."

"Like when?"

"Well, there's *My Favorite Wife; Move Over, Darling*; Gilligan."

"That's fiction. I mean it's not realistic. Besides, *Move Over, Darling* is a remake of *My Favorite Wife*."

Although amused at his knowledge of old romance movies, she would not let it divert her. "Realistic? So you really are a war veteran slash forensic pathologist who will not rest until he avenges the murder of his wife? No wonder you embodied your role on *COD*."

He smiled at her. *Oh, dear Lord, he's smiling at me.*

"I take your point," he said, "and thank you for the compliment."

She rolled her eyes. *Shit.* She *had* complimented him.

"Regardless, I feel uncomfortable portraying a character that belonged to another actor. Should I be watching tapes of his performance? I should have an original —"

"I am surprised you care so much, Mr. Walsingham. With our cheap sets and implausible plots, we both know even appearing on a daytime drama is far beneath you."

He stared at her, the smile now gone, replaced with...nothing – his face completely blank.

She let a few moments of silence pass between them before she spoke again. "Listen, you are here for a limited run. I do not have time to create a new character and develop a new romantic storyline with Sienna. Tristan already has a backstory and a previous relationship with Sienna that I can work with."

"Was that before or after she went into the convent?"

"Before. I think. I don't know; that was before my time. We have researchers in charge of continuity." When she stood up, he did as well, and she walked around the desk. "I am sure you can understand why it needs to be that role. Forget the previous actor – you've been 'changed by the sea.' Make the role your own." She opened the door and stepped back to invite him to leave.

A crease formed between his eyes flicking back and forth between her and the doorway.

"You shouldn't frown like that; you'll get wrinkles between your eyebrows."

He ignored her. "Do you think viewers will believe that Eileen Meyer and I could be brother and sister?"

"Why? Because she's a neurosurgeon? I'm sure they will just assume she got all the brains in the family."

She took advantage of his confusion to usher him out and close the door. Then she leaned back against it and blew out a full breath.

CHAPTER 3

The Edge of Darkness
Chapter 7

The summer before my junior year of high school, I went through a tremendous metamorphosis. My face cleared up, I had my hair cut and styled, and I lost all the weight. With a surge of confidence, I knew this year would be different.

Although our high school was also all-girls, we were close to an all-boys school and served as their sister school. We cheered for their sports and had co-ed clubs. That year, one of the first things I did was join the drama club and audition for *Godspell*. Even though I only got a part as an understudy, I had never been so thrilled in my life. I might not be performing, but I had been chosen over so many other girls. And for the first time, I had friends – lots of them – and the cast and crew spent all their time together when we weren't in school.

I worked hard on *Godspell*. Not only did I

have to do all of the duties of an actress, in learning lines and blocking, but I also worked on the tech crew. But with the excitement and fulfillment of working on the production, the work didn't bother me at all. Plus I was the envy of my classmates because I worked with Sean Hooker, the heartthrob of high school. I hated to admit it, but even I had a bit of a crush on him. Besides being the most gorgeous senior on the boys' campus, he was a professional actor, working on plays outside of school and even commercials, which made him completely irresistible.

I understudied for Lisa, and she frequently missed rehearsals, so I had to work closely with Sean in several scenes. I couldn't help feeling shy around him. I tried to treat him like all the other actors, but he would look me right in the eyes and I would melt.

After opening night, I hugged the others in the cast, but to Sean I only offered my hand. I refused to let him believe I was another co-ed in love with him. It had gotten to the point where one day at tech, Sean was forced into seclusion by ninth-grade girls who found out he would be there that day. To my surprise, Sean rejected my hand and pulled me into a bear hug. I, being a consummate actress, hid my state of shock well, even as my heart raced, and said, "Congratulations! I'm so glad it went well!" He silently released me and walked away.

After the next performance, I took the offensive and placed my hand on his shoulder and said, "Congratulations," just as a woman from the audience came up and started commending his performance.

I removed my hand, but Sean stuck his out to

me, and I had no choice but to take it. He held my hand tightly and then took it between both of his and rubbed it, never taking his eyes off the lady. I was totally bedazzled. But then something caught his attention. He dropped my hand and walked away, leaving me to talk to the woman. I came to the conclusion that, since I didn't throw myself at him like all the other girls, he was being kind of a tease. That killed the crush.

A lizard lived outside my bedroom window. Every morning when the alarm woke me, I would see his silhouette on my shade as the rising sun shined in. On this particular morning, my lizard did not appear.

That day a Marine came to our door. Tad was missing in action.

"Nobody ever died from a trifling little cold."

"She's burning up!" Alice gawked up at Mrs. Jellyby, her hand on the forehead of the near-delirious Giselle, slouched beside her on the sofa of the set for the living room. "And, by the way, people *do* die of colds every day, if they are allowed to develop complications."

"But the rehearsal!" cried Mrs. Jellyby. "The scene is not that long."

"I...I can do it," Giselle said, but wooziness pulled her back against the couch even when she tried to sit up.

"Forget about it," Alice said. "It's Friday. Rest this weekend and get well. The rehearsal can wait until Monday."

"*Monday!*" Mrs. Jellyby shrieked the word as

though a rodent of unusual size had just run across the set. "We can't begin with delays. What will *he* think?"

"Who?"

Mrs. Jellyby peered around before tilting her head and speaking low to the sofa. "Peter Walsingham."

Alice crinkled her forehead and curled her top lip. "Who gives a shit? Giselle is sick!"

"I just don't want him to get the wrong first impression."

"Oh, believe me: he already formulated his first impression."

Then, *the voice* from the movie screen boomed from behind them. "What's this about first impressions?" Peter sauntered toward the set with his hands in his pockets and Winnie and Jack two paces behind him.

Mrs. Jellyby wrung her hands together and sputtered over her words. "I-I am so sorry, Mr. Walsingham, but we may have to postpone today's rehearsal."

Alice rolled her eyes. *Why the hell is she apologizing? She's his boss!* "Giselle is burning up with fever and needs to go home and rest."

"Oh, no!" Jack ran around Peter to the sofa and sat on the other side of Giselle, taking her hand.

"What does this do to the production schedule?" Peter asked and pulled his hands from his pockets as he stepped onto the stage, standing at the corner of the sofa.

Alice had to twist her neck to look up at him. "We still film on Monday. You'll just have to rehearse earlier that day." Heat rose in her cheeks when their eyes met and he wouldn't release the hold.

"Pro…probably only one once-through before filming."

"Isn't that enough? I know my lines."

She turned around to face him. If they were going to do this staring contest bit again, she didn't want to get a crick in her neck. "It's more about blocking, camera angles, and pace. Today's rehearsal was more for *your* benefit. Giselle could do this in her sleep, but you've never done a soa- a daytime drama before." If he took offense, as she halfway hoped, he did not let it show.

"I am dreadfully sorry for the inconvenience." Although Mrs. Jellyby's whimpering nauseated Alice, at least it drew Peter's attention away from her.

Peter flaunted his hand in Giselle's direction. "The girl is clearly ill," he said, annoyance raising his volume, his voice echoing off the fake walls. "If this rehearsal is intended to assist *me*, can't someone stand in for her? I'm sure this isn't the first time something like this has occurred. That's why they invented understudies."

"I…I…" *Mrs. Jellyby – finally at a loss for words!*

"She's in no condition to drive," Jack said. "I'm going to take her home." He and Alice stood and helped Giselle to her feet.

"No," Giselle said, "you don't need – "

"It's no problem." Supporting her with an arm around her waist, Jack escorted her off the stage.

"Winnie," Peter said. "You should go with them."

Winnie, who had been standing back watching this scene with crossed arms and a bored frown, said nothing, but her gaping eyes and mouth spoke the defiance she would not voice.

"She may need a woman's assistance." Peter

noticed Winnie's eyes flash to Alice. "Alice can't go. She's working. You're not doing anything. Go help Jack."

With a huff, she stomped after Giselle and Jack as they hobbled out of the soundstage.

"Now, let's get on with it," Peter said far more like a director than a movie star. "Where is Mr. Peacock?"

Peacock had been sitting away from the stage, perusing the script and eating a sub waiting for this particular drama to conclude, so he had his mouth full when his name caught his attention.

"In the conservatory with the candlestick?"

Even though Peter spoke in so authoritative a tone as marked his self-importance, Alice turned her back to him and jumped off the stage before he could see her grin that threatened to break into laughter.

"M white ear." Mr. Peacock garbled his words through the sandwich in his mouth as he arrived at the set.

Alice opened her script to the scene and put it into the hands of a *clueless* technician. "Here, Jeff. Go stand in for Sienna."

Jeff popped another Funyun in his mouth, without having swallowed the one he had been chewing, wiped his hand on his jeans, and nodded as his eyes scanned the page. As he walked to the set, Alice took her seat behind the cameramen where she could see the monitors mounted from the ceiling.

"All right, everyone." Peacock stood in the center of the set and clapped his hands, assuming control as Mrs. Jellyby wandered off in defeat. "Places! Now *Tristan*," he said to Peter, provoking an eye-roll. "You will start at this spot." He pointed down at a marker. "Then when Sienna turns around, she'll start walking, you'll follow her and stop on that marker. Got it?"

"Why would she turn and walk away from me during this emotional conversation?"

"That's…that's how we're going to try it. It's just a rehearsal, so we can see how it works. *Sienna*," Peacock said, turning to the trim young man in jeans and a t-shirt, still wearing his headset. "You will stand on this marker." Then he pointed to places on the script in Jeff's hand. "You will turn around here…then you will walk to your next marker starting here. Got it?"

Jeff nodded. "Yup." With all the time he had spent watching the production, he probably knew the setup better than Peacock.

"OK, then." Mr. Peacock scampered off the set and sat in his chair beside Alice, eyes on the monitors. "Action!"

Jeff (in complete monotone) – It has been a long time Tristan since you went away.

Tristan – I know. *Too* long.

Jeff (in complete monotone) – I began to be afraid you would never come back again people did say you were lost at sea but I hoped I hoped it wasn't true

Tristan – They were right, Sienna. It's true, I have been lost, lost in my own head. I had to find myself before I could come back to you. But now I *am* back.

Jeff (turns around; in complete monotone) – A lot has happened in Valley View Bay since you went away you know Lucas is married now do you remember Damien he was in a terrible accident

Tristan – A lot has happened to me as well. I want to show you that I have changed –

Jeff (walks away; in complete monotone) – Yes I hardly recognized you.

Tristan – But I want to show you that I have changed on the *inside*. Being at sea, traveling the world...

Jeff (stops on his mark; in complete monotone) – No one has to run off and join the merchant marines to change people themselv—

"Cut!" Peacock hopped off his seat and over to the stage. "Tristan, what're you doing? You are supposed to follow Sienna when she walks away."

"Why would Tristan go after her?" Peter asked, his tone tight. "Clearly *she* is not receptive to him yet. He's a merchant marine, for Christ's sake. He would wait until her wall begins to crack before making a physical move toward her. Why does he have to follow her now?"

"Because if you don't, you're not in the shot. We need you both on camera." Peter had no argument to counter that logic, so Peacock walked back to his seat, where Alice had her forehead down in her hand to hide her suppressed laughter. "Now let's take it from 'It has been a long time Tristan since you went away.' And action."

Jeff (in complete monotone) – It has been a long time Tristan since you went away.

Tristan – I know. *Too* long.

Jeff (in complete monotone) – I began to be afraid you would never come back again people did say you were lost at sea but I hoped I hoped it wasn't true

Tristan – They were right, Sienna. It's true, I have been lost, lost in my own head. I had to find myself before I could come back to you. But now I *am* back.

Jeff (turns around; in complete monotone) – A lot has happened in Valley View Bay since you went away you know Lucas is married now do you remember Damien he was in a terrible accident

Tristan (walks toward Sienna) – A lot has happened to me as well. I want to show you that–

"CUT!" Alice couldn't recall Mr. Peacock ever expelling such a long exhalation of frustration as he marched back on set. Peter walked around Jeff to meet him. "What was that? Sienna hadn't started walking away yet. You need to stay on your marker."

"If I have to follow her, I think it's more natural to follow her when he says he wants to show her."

"It doesn't matter what you think! You're not the director!"

Peter released a puff of irony and shook his head then spoke through clenched teeth. "I stayed in the shot, didn't I?"

"That's not the point. The camera was focused on Sienna. Are you this difficult with all your directors?"

"If you mean do I give them my opinion based on my study of the character, yes!"

"No wonder you were fired from *COD*."

"I wasn't fired – I quit. Listen, this is never going to work. I can't do this scene with that kid. He can't act worth a shit, he's just reciting the lines, and he smells like onions!"

Jeff lifted his hand to his mouth, huffed on his palm, smelled it and shrugged.

"It's a simple scene. You start on your marker, you walk to that marker, you stand on the marker. Sometimes you talk; sometimes you listen. I would read Sienna's lines for you, but I need to watch the monitors. So can't you put your acting abilities to work with Jeff?"

Peter turned away from Peacock, and his eyes landed on Alice. *Oh, shit.* She leaped from her chair to run to her office and make her escape.

"Miss McGillicutty."

Double shit. Her shoulders fell as she turned toward the set, her eyes downcast.

"Can't she stand in for Sienna?" he asked Mr. Peacock. "She must know the script – she wrote it."

"She prefers to watch in case she wants to make

adjustments to the dialog."

"I would think she would be able to do that even better if she's acting it out."

"Alice," called out Mr. Peacock. "Would you mind standing in so we can get out of here sometime tonight?"

She dragged herself to the set passing Jeff, who offered her the script, but she waved it away. She narrowed her eyes at Peacock giving him her best evil-eye, which he ignored, then took her mark.

"OK, we're going to take if from the top. You know where to start. I'll call out the rest of the blocking." Once back in his chair, he said, "Action."

Sienna (nervously, eyes averted) – It..it's been a long time, Tristan. Since you went away.

Tristan – I know. *Too* long.

Sienna (meets his penetrating gaze) – I began to be afraid you would never come back again. Then everyone said you were lost at sea, but I hoped. I hoped it wasn't true

Tristan – They were right, Sienna. It's true, I have been lost, lost in my own head. I had to find myself before I could come back to you. But now I'm here.

Sienna (turns around, nervously fidgeting) – A lot's happened in Valley View Bay since you went away. You know Lucas is married now. Do you remember Damien? He was in an accident and –

Tristan – A lot has happened to me as well. I want to show you that I have changed –

Sienna (walks away; Tristan follows) – Yes, I hardly recognized you.

Tristan – No, I want to show you that I have changed on the *inside*. Being at sea, traveling the world, it's a humbling experience…

Sienna (stops on her mark)

"Tristan," Peacock's voice bellowed from the shadows, "you keep walking until you're about a foot behind Sienna.

Sienna (stands on her mark, Tristan walks toward her) – No one has to run off and join the Merchant Marines to change, Tristan. People themselves alter so much, there's something new to be observed in them forever.

Tristan – Have *you* changed, Sienna?

Sienna – Of course. I'm not that naïve girl you abandoned anymore.

Tristan – I wasn't leaving *you*.

Sienna – I was just collateral damage.

Tristan (places his hand on her upper arm) – I never meant to hurt you. What I did was selfish and without a thought to anyone's feelings, how my actions affected others. I was ruled by my temper and resentment toward my father. I couldn't forget his vices or his offenses against me.

Sienna – But even when he died, you didn't come back.

Tristan (turns Sienna to face him eye to eye, grasps both her arms, pulls her closer to him; emotionally) I never claimed to be perfect. I have my faults, but I want the chance to redeem myself in your eyes. I want to prove that I have become worthy of your love.
(He lifts his hand to her face and strokes her cheek with his thumb.)

Sienna – (*gasps! This is not in the script!*)

Tristan – (peers into her eyes) Can you give me that chance?

Sienna (*trembles under his touch*) – Hu-How do I know you won't leave again?

Tristan – (lowers his hand to hold her neck, where he can no doubt feel her pulse racing, and rubs his thumb along her lower lip) I won't make promises I can't keep. But you can't have such an attachment to this place. You couldn't have wanted to stay in Valley View Bay forever.

Sienna – (*closes her eyes, melting from his ministrations, her breathing accelerated; raspy*) I…I don't know what you mean.

Tristan – (places his hands on either side of her head, raising her face, waiting for her to look up at him) If I leave, I'll want you with me.

Sienna (*wonders if he's been sucking on a butterscotch, reminds her of butterscotch schnapps sweet in her mouth, sending a river of warmth through her and pooling below her belly; realizes he is leaning in as if...as if to kiss her! - widens her eyes; yells*) – CUT!

Peter did not step away or release her, so Alice repeated, "CUT! CUT! CUT! CUT!" and pulled away from him, although he still held her with his gaze.

"You're quite the actress, Alice," he said, dropping his voice so only she could hear.

Her heart racing and breathing ragged, heat flooding through her, burning her face, she stormed off the set and straight to Peacock. "Why the hell didn't you call cut? Why didn't you call out stage direction?"

"I thought what you improvised was perfect."

"This was not in the script!" When Peter's footsteps stopped behind her, she spun around on him. "Mr. Walsingham, it is obvious you cannot take direction, but you have to stay on script."

"I didn't change any lines."

"You know what I mean. A stroke on the cheek after your last line – that's it! Tristan is not supposed to kiss Sienna for two more episodes."

"But he didn't kiss her."

"Well, that was too damn close. I don't want to see that on camera."

"My apologies, Miss McGillicutty," he called after her as she rushed to the safe haven of her office. "I promise, Tristan won't do it again."

She slammed her door, leaned back, and dropped her head against it, closing her eyes and craving butterscotch schnapps.

CHAPTER 4

The Edge of Darkness
Chapter 10

I didn't cry for Molly when he was killed in a car accident; I cried for his family. I hadn't seen Anthony since his high school graduation. Then he had gone off to Harvard. His father lived just long enough to see him pass the bar exam.

Tony, as he preferred to be called now, moved in with us right after Annette and I graduated from high school. He had been taken on at a law firm in the area and needed a place to stay while he figured out where he wanted to live. He was tall – six two – with light brown curly hair and big blue eyes. I was scared to death of him. I barely spoke to him until two weeks after Molly's funeral, and then just to say hi. I didn't feel like his sister, and I'm sure he did not feel like my brother. Even he and Annette didn't act like brother and sister – nothing like Tad and I.

Annette left a month after the funeral for Radcliffe to get settled in before the semester started, and I was relieved. She and I had tried to keep our distance throughout high school, but we never could get along after Mother legally adopted me.

I hadn't decided what I wanted to do now. My grades were good, and I considered college, but I still thought I wanted to try it as an actress.

I wanted to be closer to Tony, especially since his father had just died and his own sister, or our sister, had gone. I was just so frightened of him. Something about him scared yet intrigued me. When he occasionally joined Mother and me for dinner, I never could think of anything to say.

Molly's death had left Mother terribly distraught. I suppose, in spite of her male houseguests, she never stopped loving him. The next thing I knew, her friends had packed her up for New York, and she had a ticket on the QE2. Once she had gone, I rarely saw Tony at all, which was fine with me. He worked and stayed at his end of the hall while I hung out with my friends and stayed in my room.

Ben from high school called me one day. I hadn't seen him since he had graduated two years before, but I still remembered he was a good kisser. He was home from college and looked me up. Ben picked me up at two, and we went to a movie. I enjoyed having his arm around me again as we watched the film. Then we went to his parents' house for dinner as we had so many times before, and it was as if we hadn't been apart for two years.

I sat close to him in the car on the way back home as the radio played softly. He had his arm around me, and we kissed at each stop sign. Then he detoured off to park by a lake and turned off the engine, leaving the radio on. Ben turned to me and wrapped me in his arms. We started kissing and lay down. After a while, the steering wheel got in the way, so we moved to the backseat.

It felt so good having him on top of me, kissing me. He kissed my neck as his hand traveled up and down my leg. His lips ran over my breasts through my blouse. I felt strange all over. He lifted me to kiss me harder and used his hand to hold my mouth in place. He kissed my neck and then my breasts and smothered himself between them.

He kissed me hard again and then just held me. "I love the way you feel," he whispered. I started unbuttoning my blouse. "What are you doing?" he asked.

"I don't know."

Ben kissed my breasts and pushed his nose into my bra. "Am I crushing you?" he asked between embraces.

"No," I whispered, out of breath.

"Would you like to crush me?" He pressed his lips against mine. "Do you want to get on top? I want to see if I can hold you just as tight," he kissed me, "feel you just as much," he kissed me, "and kiss you just as hard."

We rolled over. "Oh, I can feel you much better this way." He moved his hand up and down my leg, going higher each time and hiking up my skirt.

"I like it better the other way," I said.

When we switched again, he became more aggressive. Then I realized our position and jerked my legs together. "It was just beginning to get fun," he said and resumed kissing me.

The radio announced it was ten-thirty. "I better get you home," he whispered and pulled me up but didn't stop kissing me. Then I buttoned my blouse, we got in the front seat, and he drove me home.

Back at the house, I knocked on Tony's door. "Yeah!" he yelled through the door.

I stuck my head in his room. "I'm home, and I'm going to bed."

He was reading in bed. "All right. Good night."

"Good night." I closed the door, and Ben and I slinked to my bedroom.

We were stretched out on my bed and had gotten about as far as we had in the car, with my blouse unbuttoned and him on top of me, but this time I didn't pull my legs together.

My locked door burst open and splintered, and Tony flew in like a raving maniac. "You get your ass the fuck out of here!"

Ben jumped off of me and the bed, and I sat up with my shirt opened. I stared at Tony as Ben disappeared. Then Tony and I shared a moment of eye contact before he walked out, closing the door behind him.

"You aren't going out again until Mother comes back."

"But that's not fair! She might not be back for weeks!"

"I don't give a fuck what's fair! After last night, you're lucky I don't send her a telegram right now."

"I don't know why it matters to you anyway. I'm eighteen. Why do you even care?" He didn't say anything. "Are you going to tell her?"

"I don't know what I'm going to do." He stormed out of the room.

I hated him. He was trying to ruin my life. Why did he hate me so much?

A few nights later, I was in my room talking to Ben on the phone when I heard a car drive up, and I looked out my window. Tony was walking toward the house with a well-built blond.

"He is such a hypocrite," I complained to Ben. "Sure – 'Do as I say, not as I do.' I hate him!"

After we hung up, I was reading when the doorbell rang. I thought it was kind of late for someone to drop by unannounced, but I knew I better answer it since Tony was "entertaining." I pulled on my robe and went to the door.

When I opened it, two Marines were standing there. They said something, but I didn't hear. First I was numb and silent, staring at them, and then I was screaming. In a flash, Tony was there. I was still screaming – I couldn't stop – and he grabbed me and hugged me against his bare chest. I was shaking violently with tears streaming down my face. He and the Marines spoke a few minutes, then he closed the door, and I clung to him and cried as he kissed the top of my head.

All of the screaming had made me weak, and he had to support me as we walked toward the stairs. Then I just collapsed in his arms, and he picked me up and carried me up to my room and laid me on the bed. He sat next to me and caressed my hands and face with an empathetic look on his face and so much sadness in his eyes. He tried to brush away my tears, but they were coming too fast and too strong. He kissed my hand. "I'll be right back."

45

His girlfriend had gotten out of bed and was standing in the hall. "You better go home. I'll call you a cab," he told her. "My brother's body was just found in Vietnam, and I need to take care of my sister."

After that, I barely noticed their whispers in the hallway. When Tony came back, he kissed me on the forehead. "Try to go to sleep," he said, looking into my eyes.

I felt like a little girl again, taken captive by sudden trauma and seeking refuge in a warm heart. He was good to me. He was being a brother, I thought. I licked my lips, and they tasted salty from Tony's perspiration. Even in the midst of my sorrow, I knew it was the sweat from his lovemaking, which my screams had interrupted.

When I awoke the next morning, I rolled over and found Tony sitting in the chair next to the window staring at me. "Good morning," he said softly. The sunlight was shining through between the curtains and lit his face, and he smiled with the sweetness of a cherub. "Did you sleep well?"

"I don't know. I was sleeping," I said, then thought how stupid it sounded. Suddenly I remembered, and I burst into tears.

Tony came and sat on the bed next to me and cradled me in his arms. "Shhhh, baby. It's all right." But we both knew it wasn't.

His hands supported my head as I sobbed on his shoulder. He rocked me in his arms and tried to quiet me, then he leaned back just enough to wipe away my tears. He kissed my forehead and placed kisses on my cheeks. I don't think either of us realized what was happening until it had already happened, but Tony gently placed a kiss on my lips. He looked into my eyes and then kissed me again.

The kisses were not passionate but so very tender and sweet. He laid me back on my pillow and stared deeply into my eyes as he brushed his fingers over my hair. Then we started kissing again, and I realized I was no longer crying and my sobs were somewhat stifled. I lifted my hands up to his shoulders and held him while we kissed, more loving than sensual.

Then Tony sat up and caressed my cheek. "Are you ready to get up now?" I nodded, and he helped me out of bed. "Go wash your face and come down, and we'll have breakfast."

As he walked out of my room, an overwhelming amount of guilt came over me. The news of Tad's death had only come the night before, and here I was kissing Tony. Was I trying to replace him in my heart?

Tony stood from the table as I walked into the kitchen. "Lexie, I want to apologize for…for what happened upstairs. I took advantage of your grief and tried to relieve my own through you."

I slumped in a chair beside him. "I'm sorry. Here you have just lost your father, and I'm putting another burden on you."

"It's a burden I willingly accept." We sat quietly for a while, lost in our own thoughts and misery. "Lexie, let's start over. Let's put our sorrow behind us and just focus on the future."

"But that's so hard to do. It's virtually impossible for me. Tad was my brother. I can't just ignore this loss I feel."

"You can if you try."

"You don't understand."

"But I do. I do perfectly. I know how close you and Tad were after your parents were killed, but my father and I were a team. I worshipped him. I've had a few weeks to come to this realization, but even though we will never have them in our lives again, we will never lose the memories."

"I know he was missing in action, but I never let myself believe it. His death was so sudden."

"And my father's murder wasn't?"

"Murder? I thought he died in a car accident."

"Didn't Mother tell you?"

"No."

"My father was trying to get a bill passed that would increase the oversight on some union activity to keep organized crime out of it. He died on his way to the vote. They've kept it out of the press while they investigate, but his car had been tampered with. His brake line had been frayed."

"I…I don't know what to say. I had no idea. I'm so sorry. I wish there were something I could do."

After a moment of solemn silence, he looked at me and said, "There is. Join me. Join me in my efforts against this grief. It will only control our lives if we allow it to."

I looked at him and realized how much pain he had in his eyes. "I will try. That's as much as I can promise."

After her debut as an understudy, avoiding Peter on the set had proven easier than Alice anticipated. In fact, Alice would have had a difficult time getting to Peter through the throng of admirers. In addition to Mrs. Jellyby and the string of gophers, make-up girls, and catering staff seeing to his every need, Winnie Johnson spent as much time on the set of *All My*

Tomorrows as she did her own show in the neighboring soundstage. The only time Alice had any contact with him at all occurred when he sought her out in her office, which he had been doing with increasing frequency, to provide his input on her script based on his "character study" of Tristan.

"I wonder if the summer hiatus means Winnie will spend more time here or less. When does she film *COD*?" Alice asked Eileen as they stood smirking at Peter surrounded by his harem. He smiled his thanks to a girl handing him a cup of tea, and she turned red and practically melted at his feet as Winnie looked on with arms folded across her chest and disgust on her face.

"It's different on a weekly series. Peter said he was impressed by how hard everyone works here and the fast pace."

"Oh, don't tell me he's hooked you, too."

"No, of course not," Eileen said, "but he's not as bad as you think."

"I know he is a serial womanizer who thinks he is too good for all this. And you didn't see how he made a fool of me when I stood in for Giselle. Constantly coming into my office to discuss 'Tristan's motivation,' as if he gives a damn. This is like summer stock to him. Do you think he takes any of this seriously?"

"Maybe not at first, but I think he does now. He was so upset with Peacock the other day when he wouldn't let him have a retake because Peter knew he could 'do it better.'"

Their laughter drew Peter's attention, and when their eyes met, Alice feared she had become as red as the young girl. She turned away.

"I have to admit he has wanted to discuss Tristan's character with me a lot for someone who thinks the role is beneath him."

"He does seem to be in your office a lot."

"Yes, but usually only to find fault – in the plot, in the dialog, with me in general. Of course, he might just be seeking refuge in my office. Even *he* might want to get away from his groupies on occasion. But he is still a misogynist. And he destroyed his marriage to 'America's Sweetheart' to be with Skinny Winnie."

"I'm not so sure about that."

"Then why didn't they deny it when the paparazzi found them holed up at his mountain retreat?"

"I thought you didn't read the tabloids!"

"I don't, but they're kind of hard to avoid when the headlines are screaming at you in the checkout line."

"Well, they may have had an affair then," Eileen said, "but I don't think there is any affection between them now – at least not on his part. He seems almost as annoyed by her coming here as you do. And he was willing to go through a lot to get away from her."

"Oh, yes, the horror of daytime television." They laughed again, and again he turned his attention from an animated Mrs. Jellyby to them. "I think he knows we're laughing at him," Alice said as he held her gaze. Then she focused past him to where Giselle sat in close conversation with Jack Hartz, who had turned out to be Peter's agent.

"Look at those two."

Eileen followed her line of sight. "Talk about star-struck. Jack follows her around like a lovesick puppy."

"He's lucky she hasn't fallen head over heels for Peter like all the other females here."

"Yeah, that's one co-star Peter's unlikely to get into bed."

"And she's the only one having love scenes with him. A shame if he has this reputation as such a ladies' man and it turns out he's a terrible kisser."

This time when they laughed, Peter got out of his chair and had come to stand in front of them before Alice even realized he was walking toward them.

"I don't know what's going on over here, but it is clearly more entertaining than anything being said over there."

"Don't tell me you are bored with your groupies," Alice said with a grin. "Perhaps we could have a new batch flown in."

He kept his eyes on her and tapped his finger on his chin as if seriously considering it. "Mmm…I don't think that will be necessary."

Alice wanted to think of a witty reply but still hadn't come up with anything when Giselle walked up to them with Jack just behind.

"Alice, Jack is having a get-together Saturday afternoon," Giselle said. "We wanted to see if you and Eileen could come."

"I can't," Eileen said. "I'm going to my mother's for the weekend."

"How 'bout you?" Jack asked Alice.

"I-uh-a party?"

"Just a few friends over, hang out by the pool, fire up the pizza oven."

"I'll be there," Peter added.

Alice returned her attention from Jack to Peter. "Do you mean to deter me, Mr. Walsingham?"

"I certainly hope not, Miss McGillicutty."

She smiled but took a step back and prayed she wasn't blushing. *Does he have to look at me – with his eyes?* "I'll have to let you know. I need to figure out where to send Tristan in July."

Alice walked back to her office with Giselle quick on her heels. "Alice, please come on Saturday. I don't want to go by myself."

"Kind of last minute. Did you ask Jack to invite me?"

"No, of course not. He only just decided to do it a few minutes ago while we were talking about his house."

"How did Peter know about it?"

"He didn't. He couldn't have."

"Then why did he say he would be there?"

Giselle shrugged. "He probably assumed Jack would invite him."

"He does assume a great deal."

"Alice, please come. I really like him. He says he's going to invite some of his clients, and they are all A-listers. I'd be the only one from soaps."

"You shouldn't let that bother you. Not only are you more beautiful than anyone on screen today, your co-star is Peter the Great."

"You know what I mean. I need a friend there."

CHAPTER 5

The Edge of Darkness
Chapter 13

After another amazing day of museums and picnics, we came home one evening to a dark, quiet house. It had been raining, and we were both sopping wet and giggly from singing in it. Even though it was still summer, I was chilly from being wet, so Tony lit the gas fireplace while I got us some towels.

"I don't know how I would have made it through the last ten days without you," I told him as we sat in front of the fireplace to dry off. "I hope your firm doesn't mind you abandoning them."

"No, they understand, although they might not recognize me when I go back."

I knew what he meant. "When I first saw you after all these years, I was scared to death of you. It was as if there was an icy aura, a coldness surrounding you. But now it's gone. Now you're warm." He looked warm, too, sitting next to me in the glow of the fire.

He rubbed my cheek with his thumb as he stared into my eyes. "That coldness was grief, and you have given me the strength to overcome it."

"How could I when I have been grieving, too?"

"Because I had to come through for you. It wasn't enough to come through for myself. You gave me a reason to be strong and not allow it to overwhelm me, or it would have conquered you."

"You don't think this grief would have passed on its own?"

"Maybe, but after how long? It would be horrible to waste any length of time in tears, even a moment, because life is so precious, and we never know when it could be taken away."

I leaned over and kissed him on the cheek. "I think you're wonderful."

Tony caressed my cheek. "I think you're beautiful."

Our lips came together tenderly at first, like that morning in my bedroom, but then more passionately. As the kisses continued to deepen, he brought me slowly down onto the rug. Then we smiled and he lay beside me, and we turned facing each other. We kissed until I was dizzy and felt like I was in a dream.

He rubbed under my chin and down my neck, and his hand traveled down to the opening of my blouse. "I want you, Lexie. You have no idea. I want you so bad, it's driving me crazy."

I didn't know what I wanted. I knew I was falling in love with him. We had spent every waking hour together since we heard of Tad's death, and the better I knew him, the more I cared for him. Still, it was all moving so fast. I understood what he meant about every moment being precious and how quickly it can be taken away, but I had never been in love before – never made love before.

I took his hand and brought it to my lips, kissing it and nuzzling it, trying to tell him what I could not bring myself to say - that we needed to slow down because I wasn't ready. I hoped he would understand without me speaking the words, which I was afraid he would take as rejection. I guess he didn't get the message. He took his hand from mine and brushed it over my hair, then he started kissing me again.

I wasn't kissing him back, and he noticed. He wrapped me in his arms and rolled on his back so I was on top of him. He held the back of my head and pressed our lips tightly together. I tried to resist, but as if my lips had a will of their own, I started kissing him back.

His hands followed my frame from my shoulders down my back and to my thighs. He rolled me over onto my back and kissed me deeper. He ran his hands over my body until they met at the snap of my jeans. Once he had unzipped them and put his hand inside, I wanted him, too. As he touched me, I couldn't believe the waves of sensation he poured over me. He yanked at my wet jeans to pull them down, and I wiggled to help him. He kissed up and down my neck and nibbled my ear as he unbuttoned my damp blouse, then he kissed the tops of my breasts above my bra.

As he fondled me and kissed my mouth again, words, poetic phrases raced through my mind. I felt the passion flaming through me like the fire beside us. He unzipped his jeans and pushed my legs open, and then I felt him against me. I wanted him; I wanted him so bad.

Just as we were about to join, a car drove up, its headlights flashing a stream of light across us through the window. "Dammit!" he said. "Who the hell could that be?" He wrestled with zipping up his pants and then helped me redress, then we stood up and started for the door.

Before we made it that far, the door opened.

"Mother!" Tony did not hide his shock or his annoyance.

"I'm back, my darlings!" She walked in with a chauffeur behind her with the luggage. "I tried to get here as quickly as I could as soon as I received your telegram. I wish you would have sent it when you first found out." She paid the chauffeur and dismissed him.

"Why didn't you call?" Tony asked. "We could have picked you up from the airport."

"I did. No one answered. Where were you two?"

We looked at each other. "At dinner," he said.

"So you two have been getting along then? Have you become better acquainted?"

"Uh, you might say that."

"I'm so glad to hear it. I would hug you both, but you look like something the cat drug in. I'm exhausted from that transatlantic flight. Unless there is something we need to discuss tonight or talk about the arrangements, I think I'll retire." Neither Tony nor I spoke. "All right, then. Good night, children."

"Good night," we sang after her as she climbed the stairs.

I turned to him. "Good night, Tony. Thank you, for everything."

His face looked crushed. "Lexie, you're going to sleep?"

"Yes. I think I better. I'll see you in the morning."

He kissed me again and sent chills down my spine. He took me in his arms and held me tight. "Sweet dreams. Dream of me."

Having capitulated to the pool party scheme, Alice settled into the lounge chair under an umbrella with a strawberry margarita and her paperback, ready to read and relax. Giselle and Jack were at the far end of the pool smiling at each other; Peter, of course, had Skinny Winnie attached to him with no intention of letting him wander away; and none of the other guests acknowledged her existence. *Perfect.*

The next morning, Tony and I decided it would be better if we were not open about our relationship until after Tad's funeral. I guess we were afraid of how Mother would react, and we didn't want to add more to this stressful time. But more often than not, our feelings would shine through. Although neither of us had said it, I knew we were in love. We would steal a kiss or a touch here and there and kiss whenever we had a moment alone.

Soon after the funeral, Mother was back to being her old self again. Her hair was freshly blond, and she began having visitors again. It seemed her grieving for Molly, and for Tad, had passed.

One morning I was awoken by Tony's soft kisses on my face. I opened my eyes and saw him sitting beside me without a shirt on. He crawled under the covers close to me. His body was warm, and I wrapped my arms around him as he kissed my neck and ran his hand over my nightgown. He reached the hem, and his hand traveled up my thigh. Once he touched me, I knew I was ready.

"Lexie, I –" Mother said as she came in the door but broke off and gaped at us. Tony and I sat up immediately. "What is going on here?" Tony and I looked at each other. "Oh, my God! Oh, my God! Oh, no!" She ran crying out of the room, slamming the door behind her.

"Jesus shit," he said. "Again, her timing is impeccable."

"What are we going to do?"

He stood up from the bed. "Well, at least now she knows. No matter what she says or how she feels, she isn't going to come between us. I don't understand why she is so upset. At least this way, she wouldn't have to hassle with in-laws."

It took a few seconds for the term "in-laws" to register. "What?"

He sat back on the bed and took my hands in each of his. "That's why I came in here this morning. I thought it might be easier for Mother to hear that we're engaged and not just screwing. I know it's quick, but I know I love you and I want to be with you. So will you marry me?"

I hugged him, hard. "Oh God, Tony. I want to be with you, too. But you're right. It is quick. Can we...can we talk about it a little more? I mean, I'm only eighteen. Mother thinks we're having sex now anyway. Can we talk about it later?"

We came apart. "Sure. I understand." He tapped a kiss on my lips. "I'm going to go talk to Mother."

As I dressed, I could think of nothing but his proposal. I hadn't even decided what I wanted to do with my life. Becoming an actress was probably a pipe dream, but I thought I'd like to try. I just didn't want to lose Tony in the process. Perhaps we could have a long engagement.

I could hear them screaming at one another from the top of the stairs. As I got closer to the kitchen, I was able to make out the words they were yelling.

"Did you have intercourse with her?"

"Mother!"

"Did you have intercourse with her?"

"That is none of your Goddamn business!"

"I would say if my children are having sex, it is very much my business!"

I walked into the kitchen, and they both turned to me. "Lexie," said Mother, "leave us alone. Anthony and I need to discuss this."

"No!" Tony said. "She has every right to be here. It's her life!"

"Well, I'm her mother!"

"And I'm her lover!"

"So it is true."

I could feel my face turning red.

"Lexie, please leave Tony and me for a while. I just need to talk to him about some things alone." She dug into her purse on the table and pulled out a wallet and her car keys. "Here. Take this and go shopping, or go to a movie. Just give us a couple of hours to clear the air."

With the keys was a hundred dollar bill. "I don't need this much."

"Take it. Go get some new clothes. Besides, I

didn't bring you back anything from my trip."

Tony took another hundred out of his wallet and stuffed it in my hand. "Here. Buy yourself a whole new wardrobe."

"But –" I started to argue, but he placed a finger on my lips.

"Shhh…We both want you to take the money, and neither of us will take 'no' for an answer."

"Uh, thank you."

"Goodbye, Lexie," Mother said.

Then, to my mother's vocal disgust, he pulled me close and kissed me ardently. "Bye, Lexie," he whispered in my ear. "I'll see you in a little while, and we can finish what we started."

I knew I was blushing, so I left quickly.

I was hungry, so I stopped at a diner for breakfast and then went shopping, but being alone with my thoughts just made me anxious. I went to a movie, but my mind kept wandering back to the house wondering what was going on. Finally, I could take it no longer.

When I got home, the house was dark and seemed empty, deserted. At first, I thought, "Oh, my God. They've killed each other."

I called out that I was back, but no one answered. "Tony!" No reply. I went upstairs and knocked on his door, but he didn't say anything, so I opened the door. His room was a wreck, and all his clothes were gone.

I started running around the house, crying and calling his name. I found Mother in the party room.

"Where is he?"

"Gone." She had been drinking, and her face was a mask.

"Gone? What do you mean gone?"

"He's packed up and moved out."

"Where did he go?"

"He didn't say. Here." She handed me an envelope with my name on it in Tony's writing, and I ripped it open.

Lexie,

I love you. More than you'll ever know. More than I even knew until this moment when I have to let you go. That's why I have to leave. I know I could not stand being near you and not be able to touch or kiss you. I don't even know who I am any more, but I know that I love you. You gave me my life back.

With all my heart,

Tony

I stared knives at Mother that were probably as piercing as my voice. "What did you do? What did you say to him? Why did you make him leave?"

"My darling Lexie." She extended her hand to me, but I wouldn't take it. "Please sit down." When I sat beside her, I could tell she had been crying. "Tony is your brother."

"So what if legally he's my brother?"

"No, he is your brother."

"Not by blood."

"Yes. By blood. I had an affair with your father. Your mother and Molly didn't find out about it until years later. That's why she would never speak to me again, and why Molly divorced me. When I was with your father, that's when I became pregnant with Tony. You and Tony have the same father."

As she had spoken, I started to cry, and now I was near hysterics. "What have you done? What have you done!"

"I had to tell him. It broke my heart to tell him, he loved Molly so much. Now to learn he wasn't his father. But I had no choice. It's incest."

"Mother, it wasn't incest!"

"Haven't you heard what I've been saying? Please calm down and listen to me. You are half-siblings, and that is incest."

"But I was adopted!"

"I know, but your real father is Tony's real father."

"No! My real parents adopted me! The Haywards adopted me!" I fell onto my knees on the carpet and held my head in my hands as I sobbed."

Once she finally made sense of what I had told her, once she knew the truth, she said, "Oh God, what have I done?" She leaned over and rubbed my back. "I'm so sorry, Lexie. I'll go find him. I'll bring him back."

And then, the laugh: Winnie's whinny broke the trance evoked by the melodrama on the page as two shadows fell across Alice.

"What are you reading, Alice?" When Winnie said her name, it always sounded like an insult.

"Just a book," Alice said without glancing up.

Winnie leaned in closer to read the title. "*The Edge of Darkness.*" She laughed again. "So you must be one of those women addicted to romance novels. I suppose that makes sense since you write for a soap opera."

Alice sighed then, gritting her teeth, lowered the

book to face Winnie – in a bikini too tiny to deserve to be called swimwear – and Peter looking down on her. "I take great pleasure in reading many kinds of books." She hoped her smile appeared as insincere as Winnie's. "I'm not going to try to read anything serious while drinking a cocktail at a pool party where I am sure to be interrupted."

"I wouldn't know. I never read romance novels."

I doubt she ever reads.

"I remember that book," Peter said and extended his hand for Alice to hand it to him. He held her place with his finger and skimmed the frayed back cover. "My mother had this." He handed it back opened to her page.

"This belonged to my mother," Alice said. "I just happened to come across it when I was going through her things."

"I'm sorry. She passed away?"

Alice nodded. "Almost a year now, but it took me awhile to be ready." For once she wished she could see his eyes but couldn't with them hidden behind sunglasses.

"How is it?"

"Not too awful. Kind of over-the-top. The author could have used a thesaurus. And a copy of *Strunk & White*."

"Well, I'm sure back then novels were nothing like the trash that is coming out now," Winnie said. "Nothing compares to the erotic romances published today."

"Henry Miller might disagree," Alice said, and Peter laughed. "How about you, Winnie? What kind of books do you like?"

While Winnie fumbled for an answer, Peter sat on

the lounge chair next to Alice's, much to her chagrin.

"While we wait for Winnie to select a favorite from her extensive library," he said, "why don't you tell me what you read when you are not likely to be interrupted?"

Is he making fun of Winnie? She squinted at him from behind her own sunglasses. *What is he up to?* She considered answering *Ulysses* but decided it sounded too pretentious, so she answered honestly. *"The Red and the Black."*

His eyebrows rose over the top of his glasses. "Stendhal?"

"Why do you sound surprised?"

"That's serious literature for anyone, let alone someone who…"

"Who writes for a soap?" She tried to keep her hackles in check. "I could just as easily be surprised that you even know Stendhal. After all, actors are usually presumed to be empty-headed." She couldn't resist a slight nod in Winnie's direction, but Winnie had her eyes on Peter with a pout on her lips. "So, Mr. Walsingham. Pray tell, what is your favorite book?"

After a moment's thought, he said, "I can't say as I have a favorite." Before Alice could tease him, he continued. "I like Stendhal, Balzac, Proust. But I also like Conrad."

Who the hell is this guy? Genuinely impressed, Alice said, "You certainly know your French literature. And then Conrad. I like him, too, particularly *Nos* –"

"Nostromo."

"Yes."

"That would be my choice."

"Do you agree with him? No one is incorruptible?"

"Alice," Winnie said, and Alice would have sworn Peter winced at the sound of her voice.

"Did you think of a book?" Alice asked her.

"Alice, you must be burning up in that-that mu-mu." She waved her hand over Alice's long white swimsuit cover.

"I am actually quite comfortable, but thanks for your concern."

Ignoring the interruption, Peter said, "You are obviously an intelligent woman, and I can always tell in the scripts which lines came from you. What are you doing wasting your time writing for a soap?"

This time, the hackles would not be suppressed. "I could very well ask you why you waste your time acting."

"It's hardly the same thing."

"True. I actually write something original, while you recite someone else's words."

He stared at her, or at least she thought he did, for what seemed like several minutes but couldn't have been. Finally, he said, "You're right."

"Alice, come for a swim with me," Winnie said, and they both gaped up at her.

"Uh, not right now, thanks." *What the hell? Why doesn't she ask her damn boyfriend to swim with her and leave me alone?* Until that afternoon, Winnie had never spoken to Alice, and now she pretended they were the best of friends.

The sounds of laughter and splashing then drew their attention to the end of the pool as Jack lifted Giselle and dropped her into the water.

"Giselle is such a pretty girl," Winnie said. "It's a shame she'll never have a career outside of soaps."

"What makes you say that?" Alice asked. "Lots of actors get their start in soaps."

"Perhaps, but she's been on that show too long for it to be a start."

"Unfortunately, that's true," Peter said.

Alice set her book aside before she ripped it apart. "Well, you're on the soap now, Peter. Wouldn't that be considered a step backwards? Are you now doomed to a career on daytime television?"

"I already have an established film career, with another movie this summer. No one would think I have taken the role out of desperation or because I am at the end of my career. Most people in the industry see this for what it is – a power play by the network. For a soap opera actress like Giselle to begin a film career, she would need connections that she doesn't have."

Alice jerked herself up and tossed her book down. "Come to think of it, I am feeling kind of hot. I think I *will* go for a swim." With that, she yanked off her swimsuit cover, threw it onto the lounger, and headed toward the pool.

"A one-piece?" Winnie asked with a laugh as if shocked by the very idea.

"Yes, Winnie, some people actually buy swimsuits for swimming."

As she dove into the deep end, Alice knew one thing for certain – Peter Walsingham would never kiss her friend again.

CHAPTER 6

Peter crashed into her office with such violence the door hit the wall.

"Are you out of your fucking mind?"

"Uh – Door. Closed. There for a reason." Alice had never seen him so angry before – not even on screen – with his eyes bulging and his nostrils flaring and his fist twisted around what must have at one point been the script – and it pleased her immensely.

Her calm manner only provoked him, and he threw the mutilated script on her desk. "Are you insane?"

"If you do not calm down, I will have to ask you to leave."

He turned away and ran his fingers through his hair, possibly pulling some of it out in the process. "This is spite, isn't it? Is this because of what I said about soaps and Giselle over at Jack's?"

Yes. "Don't be ridiculous." When he faced her again, she knew she was smirking, but she couldn't help herself.

"I won't do it."

"You have no choice."

"It's incest, Alice!"

"No, it isn't. Tristan and Sienna haven't slept together."

He began pacing the short distance from one side of her office to the other. "But I kissed her."

She rolled her eyes and sighed and hoped she appeared bored with his tiresome behavior. "So did Luke."

"Luke and Laura?"

"No, Luke Skywalker. He and Princess Leia kissed, and no one cared when they – Hey! How do you know about Luke and Laura? From *General Hospital*?"

"So my mother-er-Tristan's mother walks in while I am kissing Sienna and then announces that I am the product of her affair with Sienna's father?"

"How do you know characters from *General Hospital*? I thought you didn't know anything about soap operas."

He threw his hands in the air. "Would you forget about Luke and Laura!"

"You're the one who brought them up. And you were the one who thought no one would believe you and Eileen were brother and sister. Well, there you have it – you have different fathers. Would you sit down? Watching you walk back and forth is giving me a crick in my neck. It's like watching a tennis match in slow motion."

He closed the door and sat across from her, piercing her with his stare. *Damn his eyes. Huh. Maybe that's where that expression comes from.*

"Why are you doing this? I am supposed to be the romantic lead."

"We both know you think this is beneath you. You will be gone before the end of the year. Plus you're getting ready to go off and film a movie in Tabora."

"Toronto."

"Whatever. The show needs a strong storyline going into the Olympics so viewers will want to come back. Sienna needs more than a story arc. She needs a husband. She has never even been married. If this show is going to survive after you leave, I need something I can build on so maybe she can get married next year."

She was relieved when he finally broke the gaze. He tapped his finger on her desk like Morse code and pulled his top lip with his bottom teeth.

"Won't I be devastated by this?"

"Of course. You should read the rest of the script. This is the perfect reason for you to go away for a while and get your head together. You were in love with her."

"But the man I always believed was my father –"

She waved his words away. "You never liked him anyway. He's the reason you went out to sea in the first place."

He rubbed his hands over his face, inhaled deeply, and exhaled fully. "Can I at least gouge out my eyes?"

"You didn't sleep with your mother. You kissed your sister. And your half-sister at that."

He groaned. "Can I at least throw up?"

"Only projectile vomiting will do. If you can vomit at will, I'll be happy to write it in for you."

He looked at her and smiled. "You would. Wouldn't you?"

No, no. This isn't right. He should not be smiling.

"Do you need syrup of ipecac?"

The Edge of Darkness
Chapter 14

For weeks, Mother tried to find Tony. He had not gone back to the law firm, and no one there had spoken to him. She even hired a private investigator, but it was as if he had vanished into thin air. I could only imagine what he must be going through. To find out that the man he loved and admired his entire life was not his "real" father, and then to think that he had come so close – millimeters close – to having "intercourse" with his sister, I worried he might be on a downward spiral back into the despair he had tried so hard to conquer.

I couldn't stay there anymore. I was doing nothing with my life but wallowing in my own misery. I decided to go to New York – the city of my birth – and follow in my biological mother's footsteps and become an actress. I wanted a fresh start and said goodbye to Lexie and began using Alex. Mother didn't want me to go, but after I convinced her it was not because I couldn't forgive her (although I couldn't help but be angry) she accepted it. She helped me get settled in an apartment in Chelsea and a job as a hostess at one of the most elite restaurants in Midtown Manhattan.

I had been living in New York about six months when I realized I was totally, madly, passionately in love – with the city itself. Oh, yes, I had become obsessed with the skyline and the bright lights of Broadway just as so many other young actors had before me; but I even loved the grime of Times Square, and the Punks of CBGB. Once again, I had walked into an entirely different world.

Now well-established in my new world and lifestyle – auditions by day, the restaurant by night – I finally got my first part, the role of Louise in an off-off-off-Broadway production of *Gypsy*. I still had not gotten over Tony, and I asked Mother if she had heard from him every time we spoke. Only time heals wounds of the heart, and Tony had taught me that time was too precious to waste on tears. Perhaps this attitude allowed me to submit so easily to infatuation.

One evening at the restaurant, I had worn my best dress because we had been told a VIP would be dining with us that evening. For this, I loved my job. I relished the idea that someday I could tell my children that I had met a duke. They need not know he was eighty-seven and barely spoke to me. I had always aimed for an exciting life, even as a child.

Wearing my low-cut, ritzy, satin red gown and wearing some of Mother's jewelry, which she had sent and refused to take back, I felt sophisticated and kind of sexy. No, *very* sexy. About eight o'clock, a handsome, tall gentleman, perhaps forty, with dark hair and eyes and a sensuous smile walked in.

"Hello," he said quizzically in a strong British accent as his eyes traveled slowly from my shoes up to my face.

"Good evening. May I help you? I'm Alex Hollingsworth, your hostess."

He took my hand in his and brought it to his lips. "A pleasure, Miss Hollingsworth. I do hope it is Miss."

I smiled. "Yes, it is."

"Then would you think me forward if I asked you to marry me?" I tried to laugh off my blush but managed to giggle like all of my nineteen years. He still rubbed my hand in his. "All right, if not marriage, what of dinner tomorrow night?"

"I'm sorry, I can't."

"Lunch?"

"I'm afraid not."

"Then come to my hotel with me tonight, and we shall share breakfast in the morning."

I smiled and shook my head. "I'm sorry."

"Why are you rejecting me like this? Can you not see I have fallen completely head over heels in love with you?"

"We are not allowed to privately associate with our guests."

"Then I shall have you fired."

"I really couldn't see you then!"

"Why not?"

"I'd have to look for another job."

He released my hand and looked away. "James." He called for Mr. Caine, the manager and my boss, who hurried over to us.

"Yes, sir! How good to see you again. I hope everything is to your satisfaction." Mr. Caine practically fell over himself wanting to please this man.

"Thank you, James, everything is perfect." Then he eyed me. "Although I do have one complaint."

"By all means, sir, how can I help you?"

"I have become entranced with this young woman who refuses my invitation to dinner because she is under your employ."

"Well, yes, sir, that is the policy. Of course, rules are made to be broken. The young lady has my consent, though it is her choice."

"Thank you, James. You have made me a terribly happy man. That is," he turned to me, "if you will accept."

"I…" I didn't know what to do. I looked to my boss for advice, but he had already walked away.

His hand came to my face and turned my head back to him. Before I knew it, he kissed me! I was so stunned, I couldn't respond. I couldn't even decide if I was offended or thrilled.

"I shall pick you up at eight tomorrow."

"But I'll be working."

"I shall take care of it. I hope you will wear something as lovely as the dress you have on this evening."

I felt light-headed, as if in a trance. "I…I don't even know your name."

"Robert. Robert Wallace."

"Robert Wallace," I repeated. Then it hit me. "Robert Wallace? Your grace, we have been expecting you."

He stepped close to me so our faces were only inches apart and grasped my arm, firm but not harsh. "Dammit, don't do that," he said in a low voice. "No matter what my title is, I am just an ordinary man who desperately wants you."

I decided. I was thrilled.

The next night had to be one of the most wonderful in my life. He picked me up in his limousine, where we drank champagne and I had my first taste of caviar. Then we went to dinner followed by dancing. When I thought the night was coming to an end, he brought me to Rockaway where we sat on the beach drinking champagne.

He had quizzed me almost non-stop through the evening, and I told him everything about losing my parents and moving to Virginia. I told him about Molly being killed last year and Tad being found right after. He went from being sympathetic to horrified as I related my tale.

"When did you come to New York?"

"About six months ago."

"Why did you decide to make the change?"

What could I tell him? The truth would be too painful to speak and too shocking to hear. "Please, I'm bored talking about myself. Could we change the subject?"

He stretched out beside me, reclining with his head braced on his hand, and looked up at me. "You never once mentioned love. Haven't you ever fallen in love? Has there never been anyone special in your life?"

The pain bubbled up from deep inside me. "What is it you want from me? Why are you always throwing love in my face?" I could feel the cynicism flowing through my lips.

"Ooh...you are quite young to be so bitter." He touched my hair gently. "You have answered my question. If this is not the right time for me to become involved with you, just tell me."

I couldn't stop the tear that slowly fell down my cheek. "You understand. Don't you?"

"I understand more than you will ever know."

He moved his hand from my hair down to between my shoulder blades and pushed me down into his embrace. He kissed me, gentle at first but then deeply, and his lips were as sensuous as they had first appeared. I had forgotten how wonderful it felt to be held this close, to feel a man's breath within me. As we lay there in the sand, his hand began to roam, and I pulled away.

"Is it the wrong time?"

"No, actually, the timing is perfect. I'm just not used to moving this quickly."

He rubbed his finger along my jaw. "Of course, my sweet Virginia girl."

☼

Alice walked down the hall aligned with doors emblazoned with the names of the soap stars, headed to Eileen's dressing room, and had no intention of, yet couldn't help overhearing Jack talk to Peter with his door ajar.

"So I heard a bunch of the cast is going to eighties night at this club in West Hollywood. Are you going?"

Alice came to a halt in the middle of the hall and squeezed her eyes shut speaking softly to herself. "Oh, please say no. Oh, please say no."

"Eighties night…in West Hollywood? You cannot be serious," Peter said, and Alice offered up a silent prayer of thanks. "I cannot think of any more deplorable waste of an evening."

"Come on; it'll be fun. There'll be dancing, and it would be good for you to get better acquainted with the other actors."

"If you are planning to go, then I am certain it is because my new *sister* will be there."

"What? Oh, well, yeah. Sienna, I mean Giselle said I should come. Don't tell me you're still pissed off about that."

Alice strained to hear, even squinting as though that would help, but Peter didn't respond to Jack's last comment.

"You know I hate to dance," he said, "especially to eighties music. That has to have been the worst decade in the history of music. And why should I become acquainted with the other actors on this *soap opera*? I'm only here temporarily."

Alice jumped when Eileen burst out of her dressing room and yelled her name. *Shit.* She hoped Peter and Jack didn't figure out she'd been eavesdropping.

"Oh, yes, it's ladies night," Eileen sang out, "and it's eighties night. Yes, it's eighties night, and the mood is right." She came up beside Alice, with arms raised and snapping in time to her improvised song, and bumped her hip against Alice's, and Alice had no choice but to bump back.

As Eileen continued to sing, melding her own lyrics into a medley with "we need the bump – gotta have the bump," Alice laughed as they bent their knees and bumped harder until Peter's door opened wide, and he and Jack stepped out into the hall just in time to see the tail end of their performance.

"So I gather you'll both be there tonight?" Jack asked.

"Wouldn't miss it!" Alice's words rolled out with her laughter. "You coming, Jack?"

"Yeah, Giselle invited me. Sounds like fun."

"So, Miss McGillicutty," Peter said, amused skepticism in his tone and flickering on the corners of his mouth, "you enjoy this eighties music."

Alice flared her eyes at him in challenge. "Sure, why not? Eighties music is awesome. I might even dress up like Madonna."

He tilted his head and arched his eyebrow. "With a cone bra?"

"No, that's nineties Madonna. I'm talking about eighties Madonna, with the lace gloves and rosaries."

"I think Madonna is *in* her eighties by now."

"It's just for fun. I guess you wouldn't understand."

Jack glanced at his watch then tapped Peter on the shoulder. "We need to go if we're going to pick up Winnie."

"Yes," Alice said. "You wouldn't want to keep Winnie waiting. I'll see you tonight, Jack," she called out over Peter's shoulder.

"I'll see you there as well," Peter said before turning to go, and a chill rushed over Alice. Then Peter looked back at Eileen. "Oh, and, by the way, it's 'We Need the Funk' – not bump – and it's from the seventies, not eighties." Then he walked away, with Alice stunned, speechless, and frozen in place.

"C'mon, Alice," Eileen said. "We need to go, too."

"Crap! Why the hell is *he* coming? I specifically heard him tell Jack that he hated the eighties. He called it a 'deplorable waste of an evening.' I can't believe he'd change his mind."

Eileen smiled at her friend with brows raised. "Oh, can't you, now?"

"What are you talking about?"

"Mmmhmm. Go ahead, play coy with me. He changed his mind when he found out you were coming."

Alice rolled her eyes. "Don't be ridiculous. He despises me for turning him into Sienna's brother. The only time he even speaks to me is to criticize. He has nothing but contempt for me and everything to do with the show."

"If you say so," Eileen said, her intonations like

notes on a xylophone.

"For an actress, you don't sound very convincing."

Duran Duran poured out from the glittering dance floor as Eileen and Alice walked in to the nightclub, late as usual. Most of the cast and a few members of the crew were already there and had claimed several tables near a large circular booth. Where *he* sat. With *her*. Winnie had her arms crossed and stared away from, well, everything, petulance painted on her face as heavily as her make-up. The flashing lights danced on the sweat beaded on Peter's forehead, and his expression dripped with boredom as he scanned the room. Then his gaze landed on Alice, and their eyes locked. She hated her own circulatory system for rushing blood into her cheeks. *Damnit, does he have to look at me with those movie star eyes?*

Eileen freed her from his spell by seizing her arm. "Alice," she yelled over the music but directly into Alice's ear, making her cringe. "Let's go get a drink."

"Yes!"

Jack and Giselle were chatting together at the bar when she and Eileen walked up, and they stood and hugged as if they hadn't just been together a few hours before.

"How has the music been?" Alice asked them. "Have you been dancing?"

"Yeah," Jack said. "The DJ is good. All eighties dance music, as you'd expect."

"You missed 'Holiday,'" Giselle told her.

Alice shrugged. "That's not one of my favorites. I'll wait until 'Get Into the Groove' or 'Like a

Prayer.'"

"So I hear you're quite the Madonna fan," Jack said

She shook her head then ordered a Jack Daniels & ginger ale from the bartender. "My mother – *huge* Madonna fan. I guess I kind of inherited it from her. I uh…" The bartender handed her a plastic cup full of ice with a splash of tan liquid. She focused on her drink as tiny prickles of emotion moved up the back of her nose to behind her eyes. "It, uh, makes me feel close to her. Funny how even happy memories can make you feel sad."

Jack ran his hand up and down her arm. "I'm sorry, Alice."

She forced a smile on her face and shook her head before tears could gather in her eyes. "No, I'm fine!" She drank down the contents of her drink, which amounted to about three tablespoons. "I am just ready for a few more of these and a song I can dance to."

Perhaps it was kismet, or maybe the spirit of her mother intervened, but as Alice finished her second drink, the opening strains of "Like a Prayer" began, and all four of them squealed with wide-eyes as if they'd just won a trifecta, and they ran out onto the dance floor. They jumped up and down, shaking their hips and clapping during the refrains, she and Eileen leaning against each other singing, "I'm down on my knees" through their grins; then they lofted their arms above their heads, waving them through the foggy air with the precision of ballet dancers during the slow verses.

This segued into the Eurythmics' "Missionary Man," and Alice danced with wild abandon, knowing she couldn't dance worth a damn but not giving a shit. Then she caught a glimpse of Peter, sitting alone – *Where had Winnie run off to? Gone to* powder *her nose?* – in the booth watching them.

She screamed in Eileen's ear. "Why did he even come if he's just going to sit there and pout all night? He's just here to draw attention to himself and make the rest of us feel uncomfortable."

"Who?"

"Who do you think? Peter." She motioned in his direction with a subtle jerk of her head.

"What do you care, right? Just ignore him. He's not even bothering you."

Maybe that's what was bothering her. *No! No, no, no, no, no, no, no!* "He's sitting there just watching us."

With a playful glint in her eye – or maybe it was just the mirrored ball overhead – Eileen ran her tongue over her teeth. "Maybe he likes to watch."

Alice gaped at her and grinned then slapped her upper arm. "You naughty, naughty girl!"

"Ouch!" Eileen rubbed her arm. "For what it's worth, Giselle said he's staying in the booth so he *won't* draw attention to himself. There are enough people here not from the show that he'd probably be swarmed with groupies taking pictures with their cell phones."

"Then I wonder why he came at all, if just to be miserable." Rick Astley's voice droned through the speakers. "Ugh. I hate this song. I'm going to go to the bathroom then get another drink. Can I get you something?"

Eileen shook her head, and Alice scootched her way through the crowded dance floor – *Really? For Rick Astley?* – and went to the ladies room before heading toward the bar.

Peter got to the bar just as she did. "Can I buy you a drink?"

"It's ladies night. My drinks are free."

His eyes wandered over her Culture Club t-shirt and jeans then back up to her face where they remained. "I thought you said you were going to dress like Madonna."

"Jack and ginger," she said to the bartender. "I said I *might*. I couldn't find my rosaries. Misplaced after years of disuse."

"You, sir?" asked the bartender.

"Double Jack on the rocks," he answered without turning away from Alice.

"So, Peter, are you having *fun*?"

He nodded. "I am enjoying myself."

"No place you'd rather be instead of *wasting* your time here?"

"Well, I guess I could think of a few places I'd rather be."

"OK. Name one."

He stared at her from over his cup as he sipped his drink, penetrating her with his eyes, setting butterflies off flittering in her tummy. She pushed her drink away; she'd obviously had too much.

"Well?" she prodded.

"All right. I would like to be with my daughter."

"Your daughter?"

"Yes. I don't get to see her often. She's amazing. I suppose all parents think that of their children, but in my case it's true," he said with a teasing smile. "So smart. She would love you."

Me? She flinched, surprise wrinkling her brows. "Me? Why would you think your daughter would like me?"

He leaned on his elbow on the bar. "I don't know. I suppose because of your feisty McGillicutty spirit."

Alice almost did a spit-take but managed to suppress her laughter. "Oh, yes, the McGillicutty spirit."

"Unfortunately, she wants to be an actress like her mother. Turn into another Hollywood Barbie doll."

"Like her mother? And her father's occupation has nothing to do with it?"

He smiled. "Touché."

Then the electro-beat of Dead or Alive thundered through the club, and Alice's eyes closed and mouth opened as she jumped up. "Oh my god, I *love* this song!"

He kicked back his Jack and set his cup down on the bar. "Come on. Let's go dance."

"Listen, I didn't say I liked this song to get you to dance with me. I am fine dancing with my friends."

He held his hand out to her. "I know that. Dance with me anyway."

His words mixed with the tempo of the music to send a tremor through her. "I know you hate to dance – and you hate eighties music. You probably don't even know this song."

"Yes. I do." He leaned over and spoke in her ear, that sultry voice from the silver screen carried on his warm breath against her neck. "'Come Home With Me.'"

He pulled back and she shivered, the blood that had infuriated her earlier now having deserted her, leaving her skin tingling.

Then a voice behind her. "Peter!"

Saved by the dumbbell.

Peter brought his hand up, squeezing his forehead as he released a ragged sigh. "What is it, Winnie?"

"I have never been so annoyed. I'm sick of this place. And I'm tired. Can't we leave now?"

"Actually Miss McGillicutty and I were about to—"

"No, you two go on," Alice said and removed herself from between them.

"Alice, wait."

"Thanks, Peter. I know you were being polite; but, really, I don't need a dance partner. Winnie needs you to take her home." Then she skipped off to the dance floor and away from him, in time with the frenetic beat of the music.

CHAPTER 7

The Edge of Darkness
Chapter 16

The duke appeared at rehearsals one day and presented me with a single red rose.

"How did you know where to find me?"

"My dear lady, that is one of the privileges of having power, money, and royal blood." He leaned forward and gave me a kiss, which probably would have lasted much longer had I allowed it. I had to admit, the duke had been quite understanding and gracious about my desire to take things very slow. "Will you join me for lunch?"

"I'd love to," I said, and I meant it.

Over lunch, he asked, "Why didn't you tell me you were an actress?"

"I guess for the same reason you didn't at first tell me you are a duke. I didn't want you to judge me by my title."

"I don't see the connection."

"Most people see actors as failures or

dreamers or bums unless they become a star."

"Oh, my dear, you are already a star in my eyes, even if you weren't an actress."

I blushed and grinned. "You always know exactly what to say."

After a fabulous lunch, he took me back to the theatre and said, "I'll see you tonight."

"I can't. I have to work."

"I'll take care of it."

"Robert, I have to work."

He tapped my nose. "You are certainly no bum." We kissed goodbye, more than once, and parted without settling if we would see each other or not.

I did see him that night, but rather than as a date, as a member of the clientele. I felt sorry for him eating alone under the gold murals, and when it wasn't too busy, I walked over to talk to him.

He stood as I approached and had me sit on the wall side of the table next to him. "You look absolutely radiant this evening."

I smiled. "So do you."

"Ha, ha! Aren't you the charmer!" I found him rather charming, with all the chivalry of Middle Ages' knighthood. The waiter eyed me when he came to the table and set a steak in front of the duke, which he began carving. "Darling, I must leave for Britain tomorrow."

"What? Why?"

"My love, that is where I am from. Ashes to ashes, dust to dust. I must return from whence I've come." He set down his silverware and brought one hand to lift my chin to look into my eyes. "England is my home."

"So," I said with a cry in my voice, "that's the end of us?" I knew my tone exaggerated my feelings. Although I certainly found him gallant and I had enjoyed the brief time we had had together, I couldn't say I was crushed by his leaving.

"That is why I wanted to speak with you." He took my hand in both of his, kissed it, then rubbed it against his cheek. "I want you to come to England with me."

I was in too much of a state of shock to hide it. "What? But we barely know each other!"

"Alexandra, I do love you. I know you don't want to believe me, but I do. Please say you will."

"I...I can't." I pulled my hand away.

"Why not?"

"I have a play to do."

"You do have an understudy."

"You don't understand. Acting is everything to me. It's my life." I might have sounded overly-dramatic, but I wasn't acting. "I could never make you happy because I would be an adulteress. I am only faithful to my art – it is my only love." I thought the speech rather good for being improvised.

"I see. Then I shall stay here with you so you needn't leave your one true love."

I worried about what he might expect from me if he stayed. "But what about ashes to dust? Returning to your homeland?"

"My darling, I would give any price for you."

"Why?"

He slammed his palm on the table. "Because I love you, Goddammit!" Everyone in the restaurant turned and looked at us, and he leaned toward me and spoke in a low voice. "Can you get that through that actor's head of yours? Do you think I go after every woman I meet like this? You are special to me. I refuse to let you go."

I found his words both flattering and disconcerting. "But I would feel guilty if you gave up your home for me."

He took my face in his hand. "You are not forcing me to do anything I don't want to do. That is not within your power."

God, help me, I prayed. "You…you just don't know me well enough. Once you do, you will see you don't love me. You couldn't possibly love me now."

"Don't tell me how I feel, Alexandra. I love you, and nothing will change that."

"Nothing?"

"Nothing."

"Then go. Go back to England. If, in one year, you feel the same, come back for me. Then I will know your love is strong enough to last."

He looked mournful. "Why are you doing this?"

"Because I have loved and lost, and I'd rather never have loved at all."

"He really did hurt you."

"He really did."

"I shall go. I have caught a beautiful butterfly and would love to have her near me always, but I must love her enough to let her go so she may be happy."

He walked out without even kissing me goodbye, leaving behind his twenty-dollar steak. A part of me hoped he would come back in a year, but I refused to let it show.

"Come in."

Her door opened to Mr. Peacock escorting an extremely attractive man grinning broadly. "Alice, I wanted to introduce you to Rich Dover. He's been cast as…What's Sienna's new man's name?"

"Raife," she said, walking around her desk.

"Haven't we already had a Raife?"

"I – I don't know. I'll look into it. Nice to meet you, Mr. Dover."

He took her offered hand and shook it between both of his. "Rich, please. Glad to be here."

"You look familiar. Where might I have seen you?"

"I've had small parts over the years. A murderer here, a victim there. You are probably most familiar with my film work. Co-worker, secondary friend. Before that I had become quite well-known as 'Party-goer number 3.'"

She chuckled. "Well, I do hope going from films to soaps isn't too much of a disappointment for you."

He shook his head. "I am happy to be acting. The rest is just geography."

"That's a refreshing attitude. I guess you know you're going to hit the ground running, starting tomorrow. Raife's role is important right from the beginning."

"So I'm coming in as Sienna's lover?"

"Well, eventually, but first you do have to meet. You are going to find her crying in church because she just found out the man she's been dating is her brother, so you will be there to comfort her." *I wonder if it's too late to change his role to a duke!*

"And I'm a priest?"

"Not yet. You're in the seminary."

He listened and nodded as she went over his role

and never once complained about the implausibility. *Yes, he will do nicely.*

Alice walked out to the set with Rich and Mr. Peacock to introduce the new Raife to his co-stars.

"Everyone," Mr. Peacock said, "this is Rich Dover. He will be Sienna's new...whatever."

"Eloquent as ever," Alice said, which was the last anyone said before a crash in the corner diverted everyone's attention to Peter.

As they all watched in stunned silence, Peter glared at Rich then stomped across the soundstage and out the door, which would have slammed with a terrific racket had it not had a pneumatic closer. Instead, with excruciating slowness, it came to rest against the jamb with a whisper. Then all eyes turned to Rich, who stood frozen in place, as white as a ghost.

"I take it you two know one another," Mr. Peacock said.

"I thought I was taking his place."

"You are with Sienna," Alice said, "but he's still on the show."

Beads of sweat had formed on his upper lip, and he wouldn't meet her eyes. "As you may have guessed, he and I are not friends."

She frowned. "I don't anticipate that you will be having any scenes together. And he's leaving the first week of July to film a movie and won't be back until after the Olympics."

That seemed to reassure him, and he smiled at her and blotted his mouth with his sleeve. "Sorry. You wouldn't know it to look at him, but he has a vicious temper."

"Actually, I have been on the receiving end of that

temper."

"I'll let you finish the introductions," Mr. Peacock said to Alice and, with a pat on Rich's shoulder, excused himself.

"So you've been a victim of the famous Walsingham temper, too," Rich said with a smile that reached his eyes, fully restored to the man she had met in her office.

"Well, I wouldn't exactly say I was a victim, but I have seen it in action. He and I are not on friendly terms either."

"Really? Then we'll have to exchange stories."

"Oh, absolutely!" she said and laughed.

"How about Saturday night? Dinner."

She blinked back her surprise and shook her head. "Are you asking me out on a date?"

"If you have to ask, then maybe I'm doing it wrong." His eyes flicked to her mouth then back again. "I'm sorry. Of course, I should have known you'd have a boyfriend or fiancé or something."

"No, no, there's no one. It's just..." *Just what? You idiot. This gorgeous guy just asked you out! Plus, Peter hates him, so that's got to be a plus.* "Yeah, sure. I'd like that."

Alice hadn't been out on a *date*-date since she wrote Blaine off the show and out of her life. When she had broken things off with him, she thought he would have been more professional than to ask to leave *All My Tomorrows,* and she decided then not to become romantically involved with any of the primary cast again. Now here she was, breaking her own rule with yet another boyfriend for Sienna. *Well, it's just one dinner. I'll just wait and see.*

Alice liked this part, the getting-to-know-you dance where all the stories are new and there's no history of hurt feelings hanging just overhead. They talked and laughed and drank, and ate dinner in there somewhere. She earned his laughter when she told him about Peter throwing a fit when he found out about the brother-sister twist, but she omitted the precipitating events leading up to it.

"He is not thrilled to be on a soap as it is," she said.

"Oh, I imagine he thinks soap operas are beneath him."

"You do know him, don't you? So what's his problem with you?"

"We were working on a film together last year – would have been my largest role, possibly a break-out. I *displeased* him, and the next thing I know, I'm off the picture."

"What did you do to offend him?"

He stared into his wine glass as he rolled it between his hands. "I can't think it's a good idea to discuss one woman when I am out with another."

Her eyes widened and her chest rose with a swift intake of air. "You fought over a woman?"

"Not exactly. I didn't know it at the time – especially since he was married – but after the story broke about him and Winnie, I realized that was why he got rid of me. I had something he wanted."

"You and Winnie Johnson were together?" That did cause him to drop a notch in her estimation.

"That's just it, see. We had only gone out a few times. I have no idea if it would have developed into something, but he made sure it didn't."

"I can't believe he got you fired from the movie."

"He's the star. I don't have any proof of it, but I think he has kept me from getting work in primetime, too, at least on this network."

"I knew he was an arrogant, womanizing ass, but I had no idea he could be so vindictive. Well, at least *COD* is on hiatus. Winnie had been hanging out at the set all the time – *that* would have been awkward."

Rich gulped down the rest of his wine. "Well, let's not let him dominate our evening. I'm sure we both have more interesting stories."

"Agreed."

After dinner and several nightcaps, Rich brought her home and walked her to the door.

"I-uh-I'm not going to ask you in. I had a great time, but I don't think we should…"

"I understand. I don't think we should rush into anything either, but I'd like to take you out again, if that's OK."

"Yes, I'd like that. You have my number."

They stood under the light over her door smiling at each other until he touched her cheek and pushed some hair behind her ear, leaned down, and brought his lips to hers. Sweet, moist, and tender.

He pulled back and ran his finger down her face to her bottom lip. "I'll call you?"

She nodded and said goodnight. Once inside, she set down her purse and kicked off her shoes when her cell phone began to vibrate. She didn't recognize the number, but she answered anyway.

"Hello?"

"Hey, it's Rich. I was wondering if you were busy Wednesday night."

☼

Sienna – (still sniffing) Thank you. You have been so kind to me, Father..."
Raife – No, not Father yet. I am a religious Brother.
Sienna – (slight laugh) Yet another brother.
Raife – Just call me Raife.
(Tag Sienna smiling)

"Cut. Print."

Mr. Peacock's words were followed by a buzzer and the crew stepping away from the set as Alice and Jack walked toward Rich and Giselle, respectively.

Rich met Alice with a grin as he tugged off his clerical collar. "So how long do I have to wear this thing?"

"Well, Giselle cannot be the only reason that Raife doesn't become ordained. That wouldn't look good if she came between you and God. We have to make it clear that you are not cut out for the clergy."

He leaned closer to her. "I'm sure I can convince you that's true."

She smiled up at him and at the pleasure she found in flirting. That was the other problem with the script. Each time she began writing a romantic scene for Raife and Sienna, she would picture Rich with her instead.

She caught a form from the corner of her eye and glanced over. Peter glowered at them from off set with a pronounced frown.

"He really does hate you," Alice said. "Every time I look up, he is glaring at you. If he keeps creasing his eyebrows like that, he's going to get wrinkles."

"I'm surprised he can move them at all with all

that Botox."

She faced Rich again when she giggled so Peter wouldn't know she was laughing at him. Suspect, perhaps. "Do you really think he uses Botox?"

"This is Hollywood. I was about to go out for a cigarette. Join me?"

"I didn't know you smoked."

"Occasionally. Do you?"

"No, but I-uh-was thinking of starting."

"Starting? You're kidding."

"But with electronic cigarettes."

They both began giggling then, and Rich glanced at Peter before taking her hand. "Come on. I'm tired of Lord Voldemort staring me down."

"Alice," Peter called out from his make-up chair. She stopped and faced him but didn't approach. She refused to be summoned to join the bevy of females floating around him. As soon as he seemed to realize that, he stood and walked to her with script in hand.

"Is there something you can do for me, Mr. Walsingham?"

"Uh...yes. I wanted to discuss this scene I have with my sister. Clarissa."

She released an aggravated sigh. *Now what?*

"Could we speak somewhere more private?" he asked. "Your office perhaps?"

She shrugged and led the way, and he closed her office door behind them. She faced him with her arms folded across her chest.

"So what's the problem now? The plot? The dialog?"

"No, I've given up on that. I was just thinking that this is momentous information Tristan is sharing with Clarissa. I don't think he would discuss it with her in a hospital cafeteria."

"We've had too many scenes in her living room already. She's a brain surgeon; she has to spend some time in the hospital."

"But even to discuss the script, I asked if we could speak in private. She is a neurosurgeon. She should have her own office at the hospital."

He did have a point. "We do have a doctor's office around here somewhere. This is really going to piss off all the extras in that scene."

"Maybe we could start in the cafeteria and move to her office. Here, let me show you." He opened the script and handed it to her and then, coming behind her to read over her shoulder, pointed out the section. "We could go ahead and keep all this..."

He spoke low, his breath against her ear, and his nearness disconcerted her. Her already-tiny office continued to shrink around them. *Is he sniffing my hair?*

Focus! "And, uh, right here she could say something like, 'We should discuss this in private. Let's go to my office.'" He smelled good. Under the aromas of make-up and hairspray and soundstage, she could detect a spiciness that reminded her of pumpkin pie yet somehow masculine. Warm and familiar, like holidays at home.

"Yes, exactly," he said softly against her neck.

She started then turned around to face him and took a step back. She waited for her heart to start beating again before speaking. "I...um...I like it. I'll talk to Mr. Peacock." When he didn't make a move to go and continued to stare, she asked, "Is there something else?"

"Yes. I wanted to apologize for my behavior the other day. I shouldn't have stormed out like that. I'm lucky my fit didn't go viral on the Internet."

"OK."

"There's no denying Rich and I have a history, and his appearance took me by surprise."

"He was quite shocked to see you as well."

"Do you know him? Is that how he got the part?"

"I have nothing to do with casting. You should know that. I hadn't met him before that day."

"Well, you've certainly become friendly with him quickly," he said, his tone turning sharp.

Her mouth dropped open, and she shoved the script into his chest before walking around to the other side of her desk. "I am friends with many members of the cast. And you're one to talk! You've become *friends* with your harem pretty fast."

Peter took a deep breath in preparation for his retort, but then he just exhaled and shook his head. "I don't want to argue with you, Alice. Just keep in mind that people are not always what they seem."

"Thanks, but I think I figured that out some time ago."

CHAPTER 8

The cast and crew gathered together at the hospital set stared at Mrs. Jellyby – slight smile, bright dress – as if doubting the veracity of her speech.

"And thanks to the rise in ratings during sweeps, ALL of the affiliates' advertisers have renewed!" As the cast and crew cheered, she raised her voice to add, "And we owe it all to Peter Walsingham!"

More like the network executives who forced him here. Alice watched Peter standing on the far side of the set to see how he reacted to the din of excited appreciation now aimed at him, but he just stood there with the beginnings of a smile at the corner of his lips, his eyes turned in her direction.

"I think this calls for a celebration," Mr. Peacock said over the noise.

"A party," someone suggested and others agreed.

"It would have to be this weekend," Mrs. Jellyby said. "Our guest of honor must leave us next week, and we cannot celebrate without him."

As the others bounced around ideas, Peter walked to center stage next to Mrs. Jellyby. "I would like to offer my home for the celebration," he said, evoking unanimous shock as well as flustering Mrs. Jellyby.

"But, no, you're the guest of honor."

"If I truly am responsible for this, then I should take responsibility for the celebration as well." He faced Alice when making this illogical pronouncement, as if it were her decision.

The crew called out requests like children planning their birthday party.

"A band!"

"No, there's no time to book one."

"I think a band can be arranged," Peter said.

Why does he keep staring at me like that? She decided to up the ante. "What about an eighties cover band." *Let's see him pull that out of his ass.*

He smiled at her. "As you wish."

After a quick knock on her door, Rich came in before she could respond.

"Where were you?" she asked. "You missed the big announcement."

"I heard – great news!" He stepped around the desk and sat on the edge of it next to Alice.

"I suppose you also heard about the party. Are you going to come even though it's at Peter's house?"

"They did say all the cast and crew were invited, and that includes me. Why should I miss out? It's his problem, not mine." He leaned over and brought his lips onto hers before she could protest against kissing at work. "See you tonight?"

She nodded, and he kissed her again. *Oh, what the hell.* Then he stood up and walked out, closing the door behind him.

That night after their date, Alice and Rich stood

once again under the lamp over her front door.

"I don't suppose I make it across the threshold tonight?"

"No, sorry. Maid's day off – the place is a mess."

"Hmm. So when do you think the maid will come clean?"

"Not sure yet. She's new, and we're taking things slow."

He stepped closer, putting his hands on her waist, and kissed her, pulling gently at her lower lip with his teeth and awakening every nerve in her body.

"So," she said, "you're definitely coming to Peter's party, I mean, the cast party?"

"Of course. But I'll have to meet you there. I have to drive out to Malibu to help a friend move some stuff."

"But you will be there."

"You think I would miss an opportunity to see Lord Voldemort's castle?"

She closed her eyes as they kissed again, and at his lips' urging, she opened her mouth. She put her arms around his neck, and his tongue touched hers. *Peter.*

Her eyes flew open. *Peter? What the hell? Why would I think of Peter while I am kissing Rich? I really like Rich. And I can't stand Peter. It's probably because we were just talking about him. Yeah, that's it.*

Her confused brain distracted her from her present situation until a hand on her breast alerted her to the tongue in her mouth, and she broke the kiss and stepped back to face a red-faced, panting Rich.

"Wow," he said. "That was some kiss. You sure I can't come in?"

Uh-oh. "Sorry, not tonight. Goodnight," she said

as one word and escaped behind her door before he could react.

Alice would not describe Peter's house in the Hollywood Hills as a castle – more of a palace. Palatial could be the only word appropriate for the tastefully decorated mansion. She tried not to gawk up toward the high ceiling and around at the expanse of marble tiles and all the rich furnishings, which brought to mind the Bellagio. She had arrived late, since she came alone and wanted to ensure at least most of the others would already be there; and when no one answered when she knocked and rang, she had let herself in only to stand by herself on the other side of the door. She could hear music in the distance but not clear enough to determine the direction.

"I had begun to think you wouldn't come."

Alice turned to Peter's voice behind her. "I...uh. Sorry." *Why am I apologizing?*

"I was afraid that...well, you *did* come. If you'd like to leave your things in the cloakroom, I'll take you out to the others."

"Ah, well, aren't you the perfect host. Don't you have a butler or something?"

She dropped off her purse – *Really? A cloakroom?* – and he walked with her through a maze until they arrived at a large room filled with guests spilling out to the pool area. Peter grabbed two crystal flutes from the tray of a passing waiter and handed her one of them.

He touched his glass to hers with a ting. "Congratulations."

She sipped then asked, "Why are you congratulating me? You have achieved what you came here to do, or rather what the network sent you to do."

"No, the novelty of having me on the show might have brought in a few viewers, but it's your storylines that kept them hooked. I still think they are ludicrous," he said with a smile, "but clearly you know your audience. So here's to a team effort."

He touched his glass to hers again, and as she drank, the music caught her attention. At first she had thought a DJ must be out there, but now she could see the stage on the far side of the extensive patio. He had done it – an eighties cover band.

"The band," she managed to sputter out. "How?"

"You said that was what you wanted."

She lifted her eyes to his, and something about them disturbed her. She suddenly felt nervous, as if she had lost something, or there was something she had forgotten to do.

Her breathing grew labored as she took another sip, bringing his focus to her lips before returning to her eyes.

Butterscotch schnapps.

Then she remembered. *Rich.* As late as she had arrived, he must already be there. She scanned the room but didn't see him.

"Are you looking for someone?" Peter's tone had taken an edge since his toasts.

"Yes, is…is Eileen here yet?"

Peter drank the rest of his champagne in one swallow. "Yes, she's by the pool. I'll show you."

"No, thanks. I'll find her."

She rushed in among the other guests, often being

forced to stop to greet her co-workers and their dates or mates. The pool had lilies with candles floating on its surface. A few people were dancing on the patio out by the band, with tiny white lights strung over the makeshift dance floor. He had done it all at a moment's notice; and with the beauty and perfection he had arranged here on Earth, she would not have been surprised if he had ordered the stars twinkling in the black sky as well. *Must be nice to have that kind of money.*

One thing she did not find, however, was any sign of Rich. Eileen waved to her from beside the bar.

"I've been wondering when you'd get here."

"I just walked in the door. Have you seen Rich?" Alice asked, still searching through the guests. "Could he be dancing?"

"No, I don't think he's here yet. I was just out by the band and didn't see him."

"I thought he'd be here by now."

"Maybe he didn't want to come since he and Peter are not exactly friends."

"No, he said that was Peter's problem, not his."

"You're really into Rich. Aren't you?"

"Well, yeah! He's a hottie! Don't tell me you're interested in him."

"I could never go out with a guy with the last name 'Dover.'"

"Why not?"

"What if we ended up getting married? Then I'd be Eileen Dover."

They both erupted with laughter, which Alice stoked by adding, "Too bad he doesn't have a brother named Ben!" Alice almost choked on the remainder of her champagne and took a full glass from the bar.

"Alice, listen. I need to talk to you about something. Well, this probably isn't the right time or place."

Alice turned her full attention back to Eileen. "That doesn't sound good. Let me finish this glass, and then I'll be ready to hear it." She drank most of it down and then studied her friend.

"I got a part – in a film."

"Eileen, that's great!" She smiled broadly and pulled Eileen into a hug. "That calls for more champagne! So tell me about it."

"It's a small part, but I do have lines and lots of screen time."

"What's the role?"

Eileen glanced down at her glass then back to Alice. "It's as an old hag."

Alice burst out laughing. "I know you said you aren't as beautiful as Giselle, but you're certainly no old hag!"

"They'll use make-up, silly, and this could be a great opportunity for me."

"I know. It really is wonderful. So when do you need to be on set?"

"I have to be in Louisiana by the end of the month."

"Louisiana in August. Ech. At least that's during the Olympics so I don't have to send you off to a medical convention or something."

"Well, that's the thing I need to talk to you about. I don't want to come back."

Alice thought she must not have heard correctly. "What?"

"I'm leaving *All My Tomorrows,* Alice. I need you to write me out."

"Shit – how long do you have to be on location?"

"It's not just this film. I really want to give this a shot. I've been giving it a lot of thought ever since it looked like the soap was going to be cancelled. Don't hate me for saying it, but I don't want to spend my entire career on a *daytime drama*."

"Of course I don't hate you. I feel the same way. Don't you dare repeat this, but I do want something more. As long as you don't kick me out of your life, I want you to have everything you want."

"I would never let you out of my life. In fact, I wanted to see if you would come with me on location."

"Louisiana in August? No way. Not happening. You might have to suffer for your art, but I don't."

"I've been so worried about telling you. I'm sorry you have to change the storyline."

"Well, I'm sorry, but I will not kill you." The bartender stopped mid-pour at Alice's declaration. "I refuse to kill you off, just in case you want to come back. Peter's leaving, so you can go visit him to spend time with your devastated brother, and while you are there, you meet the man of your dreams." *Speaking of which...* "Now I have to find out when Rich is getting here."

Alice set off on the journey to the front of the house, stopping only to speak to Jack-and-Giselle – they were joined at the hip, after all – and with a few missteps along the way. She finally retrieved her purse from the "cloakroom" and pulled out her cell. A text.

> Still in malb not gonna make it sorry
> prob better not to spoil the party by
> pissing off vold

She would have thrown the phone across the marble tile except she really liked the case, but she did shove it back into her purse with great force. *That's it. I'm going to go.* Except she had not eaten much all day, and the three glasses of champagne had gone straight to her head.

"Fuck it." She tossed her purse down and marched toward the party. She barely knew this guy; she was not going to let his non-appearance prevent her from having fun with her friends – really the only family she had.

Alice had not counted how many glasses of champagne she'd had, but it must have been quite a few to get her out on Peter's patio dance floor. She had to admit, the band could imitate just about any song from the eighties like a New Wave mynah bird. In fact, although she didn't know whether to credit her friends or the upbeat music or the champagne – perhaps the combination – she could not remember the last time she'd had so much fun, not even in West Hollywood. She and Eileen and Jack and Giselle were hopping around frenetically under the stars and twinkling lights to some song she didn't even recognize but that sounded like eighties pop.

After ten or more fast songs in a row, the music stopped, and a saxophonist came into the stage lighting. As the opening riff for "Careless Whisper" began, Jack-and-Giselle again became a unit, and a cameraman took a laughing Eileen into waltz position.

Alice turned to leave the dance floor and stopped just short of walking into Peter. Before she understood what was happening, he had taken her hands and tugged her toward him.

"Where's Winnie?" she asked.

He furrowed his brow and peered at her through squinted eyes. "Why would she be here?"

He stepped forward as she resisted. "I've been dancing – I'm all sweaty." She was, too. Her blouse clung to her chest, and her scalp was drenched.

"So am I." He traced her face with his eyes and pulled her into his arms.

Her arms were trapped against his damp chest, so she had no choice but to circle them around his neck; but that only brought their bodies closer. They barely moved, their feet somehow turning them in a sluggish rotation, reminding her of slow dancing in high school. A tingly numbness enveloped her. She surrendered to it and laid her head against his shoulder, and he tightened his hold.

God, she loved this song. Her mother had it on almost all of her playlists. The singer sounded so much like George Michael, or perhaps the champagne improved his performance. With her eyes closed, she released a full, deep sigh. *Only one thing could improve this moment.*

As if he had read her mind, Peter pulled back ever so slightly and lifted her chin with his forefinger then brought his mouth down upon hers. Nothing sweet and gentle here. He claimed her mouth with fierce passion, and she reciprocated. Their lips moving together as they continued their semblance of a dance, her body pressed against his, converged to send a charge of electricity coursing through her. He pushed his fingers through her wet hair, pulling her mouth even closer as his tongue collided with hers. He stopped even pretending to dance then, focusing all effort on the mutual plunder of their mouths.

The song had not ended when he pulled his face away. Confused, she opened her eyes and found him gazing at her intensely. The second refrain came to an end; only then did he release his hold on her hair. Taking her hand, his other arm still around her waist, he led her away from the others and into the house while the saxophone continued to play.

As soon as they entered the dark silent room and the door closed behind them, he had her against the wall and his mouth upon hers. She couldn't get enough of it – she never wanted his mouth to leave – and she wrapped her arms around his neck to prevent its escape.

He must have felt the same way because, even as he began to unbutton her blouse, he never broke away, never released her lips to trail soft kisses down her throat or nibble her ear or any such nonsense. She wanted to consume him and to be consumed in return. He felt good, he tasted good, he smelled good. She had already kissed away the saltiness of sweat from his lips, but his scent of spice and lust still teased her. Their chests rose and fell in rapid synchronicity. Although he had unbuttoned her blouse with care, he exercised no restraint with his own, pulling it apart as buttons jumped into the dark. He opened the front closure of her bra, but he did not bring a hand to her breast. Instead he laid his hands against the skin of her back, pressing his bare chest against her breasts so she could not imagine how he could hold her any closer. And never once did his mouth cease its relentless assault.

They kissed in this manner for some time until she could think of only one way to bring him closer, and she could feel his desire as well. As if by instinct, she parted her legs, and he pressed himself against her. He set her on fire – she yearned for him, burned for him, but only he could extinguish the flame. Her heart raced, and she couldn't catch her breath until she thought she might suffocate. Only with all her strength could she take her mouth from his to gasp for air. He panted as well and dropped his head against her forehead.

"Alice." Her name had never sounded erotic until spoken with his breathless voice.

His voice. *Peter. No, no, no.*

"Wait," she said, bringing her hands to his shoulders and pushing him back an inch, but she kept her eyes squeezed shut. *Oh, no. I am one of them – one of his groupies.*

"Alice. Be with me tonight. I have to go to Toronto tomorrow, but –"

"Oh, no." She extricated herself from his embrace. *A one-night stand. I almost became one in his long string of them.* She blessed the darkness of the room that concealed her blush and her nudity as she fumbled with her clothes.

He reached for her, but she recoiled from his touch. "What is it? What's wrong?"

"This – all of this. This is a mistake."

"Alice, don't say that."

When he took hold of her arm, she jerked away. "Stop! I-I'm sorry. I've had too much to drink. This should not be happening. I didn't know what I was doing."

He switched a lamp on just as she finished buttoning her blouse, but she had missed one in the process and had to begin again.

"Look at me," he commanded, and for some reason she obeyed.

She couldn't believe how delicious she found him, the strength of the attraction with his shirt open, his breathing still heavy, his mouth...She looked away.

"It's him, isn't it?" A hostile edginess sharpened his tone.

"Who?"

"Rich. I saw him, in your office, kissing you."

"Oh, *now* I see what this is about!"

"What *what* is about?"

She did face him then, prepared for the challenge. "You and Rich. You could have any other woman, but you cannot stand for him to have something that you don't."

"Is that it, Alice? Does he *have* you?"

"That is none of your business!"

"Are you sleeping with him?"

"That is *really* none of your business!"

She turned and strode with purpose to the door and out into the hallway with him right behind her.

"Listen to me – you need to be careful with him."

"Says the half-naked man who was just ravaging me!"

"You didn't seem to mind. In fact, I would say you–"

She interrupted him with a primitive sound – half-growl, half-groan. "Stop following me! I am not one of your bimbettes!"

She marched on toward the sounds of the party in progress and turned into a lounge-like room, quiet except for Mrs. Jellyby's voice reverberating from the sofa where she sat pontificating to a weary Mr. Peacock.

"You've seen how he is with her," Mrs. Jellyby said, oblivious to the presence of Alice and Peter just inside the room. "She has him wrapped around her little finger! You know the people he represents. He will get her a movie deal before the year is out – mark my words! And once Giselle is in films, just think what that will mean for the show!"

Mr. Peacock noticed them then. "Alice? Is something wrong?"

Alice could only imagine how she must look to them – her hair a tangled mess, her face a chafed wreck, and a bare-chested movie star behind her. She muttered something unintelligible and fled out the other side of the room, which miraculously emptied into a hall leading to the front door.

"Alice, stop," Peter said, but she did not. "Where do you think you're going?"

She retrieved her purse and dug for her keys. "That, actually, is none of your business either!"

His eyes hardened and his jaw stiff, he grabbed the purse from her hands and held it out of her reach. "You are not going anywhere."

"What the hell, Peter? I just want to go home." She covered her eyes with her hand and released an exhausted sigh. *Don't cry. Don't you dare cry.*

"I'll drive you. You've had too much to drink."

"I'm fine."

"You just told me the only reason you couldn't keep your hands off me was because you were drunk!"

"Amazing how anger can be so sobering. Let me have my purse!"

"I said I would drive you."

"You have a house full of guests – you can't leave.

And look at your shirt. Please let me go before someone else sees us and thinks we…"

"I'll drive her," Mr. Peacock said behind them. They both turned to him as he came forward and yanked her purse from Peter's hand. He looked Peter up and down as if he emitted an offensive odor, then with his arm around Alice's waist, he walked her out the front door.

CHAPTER 9

Rich tapped a knuckle on her open door. Alice hadn't bothered to close it, too exhausted even to say come in. She lifted her eyes from her book to him without a word.

"Do you want to go get some lunch?"

"No, thanks. I brought mine." She motioned to the remaining half of her sandwich with the paperback.

"What're you reading?"

"Research…on melodrama."

He walked in and sat on the edge of her desk. "I feel like you're avoiding me. Are you still pissed about the party?"

"I told you when you called Sunday, I think you were right not to come. I'm not avoiding you. I'm just busy."

He held her gaze for a moment, gritting his teeth. "Is it because of Peter?"

She rolled her eyes. "What are you talking about?"

"People saw you, Alice. They saw you kissing him."

Alice dropped her forehead onto her desk and covered her head with her arms, one of which crushed her lunch. "Oh, God. No. No no no no no no…" She banged her head on the desk.

"They saw you go inside with him."

"No no no no no…"

"And then neither of you went back to the party." *Peter didn't go back?* "You slept with him. Didn't you?"

Her head shot up. "No! Absolutely not!"

"Then why is everyone saying –"

"Shit. Everyone? OK, listen. I got drunk and, yes, I kissed him. But that was it! Not even second base." *That's technically true.*

"Did you kiss him like you kissed me?"

Her cheeks heated from the memory of kissing Peter, and an unwelcome tremor rolled through her. "No, it was nothing like when you and I kissed."

"So where did you go?"

She stood up, and her chair rolled back and hit the wall with a thud. "What is this, the Inquisition? I was drunk, Peter and I kissed, we had this huge fight, then Peacock drove me home."

"What did you fight about?"

"You, actually. He warned me not to get involved with you."

Rich dropped from the desk, his face blooming red. "What did he tell you?"

"Nothing, really. Just that I needed to be careful. I don't know what his deal is with you, but I think he just said that to try to get me into bed. Winnie wasn't there, so he probably wanted a one-night stand and assumed a lowly writer would jump at the chance. When he realized there was no way in hell I would ever sleep with him, he probably grabbed the first convenient female that walked by." For some reason, that thought tugged at her heart.

He released the breath he had been holding and smiled. "So you really are not interested in him?"

"I can safely say that Peter Walsingham is the last man in the world I would ever sleep with. He cheated on his wife with Winnie, he would have cheated on Winnie with me, and God knows how many bimbettes he's had in between. He is the last person I would ever listen to for dating advice."

"Relieved to hear it. Most women would love to scratch 'movie star' off their bucket list."

She corrected his agreement error in her head. "I'm not one of them."

"Well, your lunch has had it. Now will you come with me?"

"All of this has really made me lose my appetite. Now not only do I have to write Eileen out, I have to contend with the rumor mill. I need to get this Peter story nipped in the bud."

"Then how 'bout dinner?"

She stepped around and took both of his hands. "I've been thinking – and this has nothing to do with Peter or the party or anything like that – but I think we need to slow things down."

"How slow?" He furrowed his brow.

"Don't do that. You'll get wrinkles." He obeyed immediately. "I mean slow – really slow. So slow that we are moving backwards."

"I don't get it! If this has nothing to do with the other night –"

"The last relationship I had was with an actor on the show, and it did not work out well. It really affected *All My Tomorrows,* and I can't let that happen again."

He squeezed her hands. "How do you know this can't work out with us? I'd like to try."

"I...I would, too, but I have to put everything into the show for the rest of the month to have a cliffhanger for the Olympics."

He nodded, although his expression did not agree. "Then we'll try it during the Olympics."

"No, I can't then." She glanced down at their hands and released them. "I...I'm going on location with Eileen. She asked me to come along."

"For how long?"

"I'm not sure. A few weeks."

"But I want to spend time with you, get to know you better." He reached out and tucked a lock of hair behind her ear and left his hand against her face.

"If you still feel this way in September, we'll see where this goes."

He kissed her tenderly on the lips before walking out.

What is the matter with me? He was sexy, funny, obviously attracted to her, maybe a good kisser – she wasn't sure. *Why have I damned myself to Louisiana in August to avoid him?*

"Alice, we have a problem."

"My five favorite words." She grabbed her iPad and followed the stage manager to the park set where Giselle sat on a bench with Rich and the cameramen and other crew standing around. "So what is it?"

"It's Giselle."

As soon as she reached Giselle, she understood the problem. Giselle's face was red, her nose swollen, and her eyes puffy. She looked like someone who had been crying for hours. Alice sat down beside her and placed a hand on her arm.

"What's wrong? You look like you've been crying for hours."

Giselle sniffed, and more tears began to flow. "It's Jack. I haven't seen him or spoken to him since the morning after the cast party. When he left my place, he said he would call me once he got Peter settled in Toronto, but I never did hear from him. When I tried his cell, it would go straight to voicemail, so I thought maybe he didn't have service out there. He didn't reply to my texts either. This morning I called his office to leave a message with his assistant, and she told me he's been back in L.A. since Friday!"

Alice rubbed her hand up and down Giselle's arm she hoped in a reassuring way, but she couldn't keep thoughts of the storyline out of her head.

"Giselle, he's obviously a dick. He doesn't deserve you. You should just delete his number from your cell."

"I already did."

"I hate to say it, but he might have just wanted to get you into bed. He's had a crush on Sienna for years."

"I know, but it just didn't feel that way."

We need a scene in the can. "If I can put together an emotional scene for you, do you think you can use all of this as Sienna?" Giselle sniffed and nodded, and Alice stood up and glanced at her tablet then around the soundstage.

"Who is still here?"

"Only Rich and Eileen from the cast," the stage manager said.

"Any writers? Go find them and tell Eileen to come here. Where's Peacock?"

"Gone. It was supposed to be a simple three-camera scene, already blocked."

Alice exchanged her iPad for a script, which she pulled apart then rearranged its pages. "OK, Rich, you can go. We'll have to film your romantic scene with Sienna tomorrow. So move the scene with Raife and his priest later, after the scene on the waterfront."

Eileen and the writers appeared. "What's up?"

"Thank God, you're still in make-up. You haven't discussed the whole Tristan/brother bit with Sienna, right?"

"No. Tristan told me, but I haven't had a scene with Sienna since."

"OK, good. She's about to show up at your doorstep in hysterics. Everyone, move over to Clarissa's living room. Eileen, go put on scrubs or something. Writers, come with me."

Romance and soap operas do not mix.

☼

"Cut. Print. That's a rap!" Buzz.

Thank God – it's finally over. The last week on set had been miserable. Eileen had gone to New Orleans the week before, and Alice missed her already. Giselle moped around the set every day, which did not help the on-air chemistry between Sienna and Raife. Although she did miss the attention and the fun of flirting, Alice figured cooling it with Rich made the disappearance of Jack at least a little easier on

Giselle. In fact, off-screen Rich had offered a shoulder for Giselle to cry on much like Raife did for Sienna.

Hmmm. Giselle and Rich walked off the set together, and she definitely smiled up at him. *Perhaps Rich has decided not to wait for me after all. Oh, well.* She could hardly blame him. A beautiful actress and a handsome actor naturally gravitated toward one another – especially when they were playing lovers on screen.

Mr. Peacock broke her from her reverie. "Alice, we need to talk."

Ah, my second favorite five words. "What is it?"

He handed her a thick stack of legal-sized paper. Perusing the top sheet, only the names of the network executives and Peter Walsingham made any sense.

"What is this?" she asked.

"Peter's attorneys have been at it with the execs. Peter is suing us."

"For what?"

"So he doesn't have to come back to *All My Tomorrows.*"

All the blood rushed out of her face, causing a chill and a wave of nausea. "I can't believe it." She handed him back the papers.

"Believe it. At the very least, he will not be back in September. The judge has granted his motion not to return until his court date. The network attorneys said then he could request a continuance, and this could drag out for months and he still wouldn't come back."

Her shock gave way to anger. Her heart raced and her eyes burned. "That son of a bitch."

"I'm sorry, Alice. I must admit, you were right to cut his romance with Sienna."

"That son of a bitch!"

"I know you and your team have mapped out a story arc for him."

"I'll kill him. I swear to God, if I ever lay eyes on Peter Walsingham again, I'm going to kill him! And here he offers to host this congratulatory party for saving the show when he is putting the final nail in its coffin!"

"Well, we don't know when this was decided. He might have thought –"

"Oh, no. I have every reason to believe that, even that night, he had no intention of seeing *any* of us ever again."

She marched into her office and slammed the door but with such force that it bounced back open, giving her the pleasure of slamming it again. And then she roared at the top of her lungs.

Alice had calmed down, for the most part, as she walked through the soundstage for the last time for a month. Rich's presence near the exit startled her.

"What are you still doing here?" she asked.

"Waiting for you."

"I guess you've heard."

"About Peter? Well, I can't say I'm sorry – or even surprised. He thinks he is too good for this."

"This could be the end. It's a good thing we have the Olympics. Our ratings can't decline if we're not on the air."

He smiled then and stepped forward. He lifted his hand to her face and tucked her hair behind her ear. "Alice, I know we said we would wait until September, but have dinner with me tonight, just once before you leave."

His words and his thumb rubbing her cheek confused her. "I thought you and Giselle were getting close."

"No, of course not. We're just friends. She's been so upset over this break-up, I've been like a brother to her."

"But –"

"I've been keeping my distance because you asked me to, but I've hated it. C'mon. Dinner."

Tempting. Very tempting. Now she couldn't even remember why she had decided to go to New Orleans in the first place. She closed her eyes and leaned against his hand. *Oh, this could be very nice.*

"Urrg," she groaned and opened her eyes. "I wish I could. Believe me, I really do. Unfortunately, I have a six a.m. flight tomorrow, which means I have to be at the airport by four, and I haven't even finished packing."

He nodded and moved his hand to the back of her head. "Then a kiss goodbye?"

She dropped her purse and book and wrapped her arms around his neck, stepping into the kiss, willingly opening her mouth to him, welcoming his tongue and pressing her lips tight against his. And it was...nice.

CHAPTER 10

The Edge of Darkness
Chapter 17

I was extremely hesitant to read the reviews the morning after opening night. Actually, because of the cast party the night before, which lasted until dawn, I didn't see the morning paper until two in the afternoon. This was my first review, and, not being one to take criticism well, I was reluctant to read it. I kept telling myself, even the best get bad reviews in the preface of their careers.

The article read, *Last night I was treated – and I use the term loosely – to what might be considered a mixture of vaudeville and war protests.* I put the paper down. I picked it up. Curiosity might have killed the cat, but satisfaction revived him. *This version of Gypsy, as seen through the eyes of producer/director Melvin Patrick, makes one think Nixon wasn't that bad after all...The choreography was so bad, even the strippers were off beat...The lines were delivered with such monotone, it made me wonder if Rose were Camille.* I put the paper down and drown this cat in coffee.

The doorbell rang. Frank Wilson, a farmboy in the cast who had been asking me out since the night of auditions, though I persistently declined, rushed in. "Hey! Congratulations!"

"Have you no respect for the dead? How dare you be so cheerful!"

"Oh, you're just hung-over. Wait 'til you've read the reviews."

"I have. That's why I'm in mourning."

"Mourning? You should be celebrating! This could be the best thing ever to happen in your career."

"Oh, yeah, bad reviews are like having one foot in the door."

"I thought you said you read it." He took the paper and opened it to the column.

"I did. We're worse than Watergate."

"You obviously didn't finish the article." He read, "'The lines were delivered with such monotone, it made me wonder if Rose were Camille.'"

"I've already heard it. Why rub salt into open wounds?"

"'But,'" he continued, "'in spite of Rose's death, *Gypsy* was full of life and spirit.'"

I stood up. "What?"

"'The young actress Alex Hollingsworth made the entire play worthwhile just to see this new talent. And talented she is. Never before have I seen an actress who made me believe she was actually portraying herself. I hope we will see a lot more of Alex in the future, with or without clothes.'" I just stared in disbelief with my mouth hanging open.

Despite my good reviews, the play closed after the second performance drew an exceptionally small audience. So on I pursued my dream of acting, having little experience and one good review. Although I auditioned for Broadway shows, I would only be offered a part in the chorus, and I preferred an actual role on a smaller stage.

I auditioned for *Hair* off Broadway and got the part of Sheila – taking off even more clothes – receiving reviews similar to those of *Gypsy*. This time, however, the play finished its full run.

Next I was cast as Janet in *The Rocky Horror Show*. I had not had that much fun with a cast since I was in high school with *Godspell*. On closing night, as I sang "Touch-a, Touch-a, Touch-a, Touch Me," I spotted the duke in the audience smiling at me. I winked at him without missing a note, then ripped off my bra.

After the curtain call, I went to my dressing room and found it filled with red roses, all from Robert, who was sitting in my room.

"I told you I would be back for you."

"Has it been a year already?" I tried to play Miss Cool – I knew exactly how long it had been – and sat at my dressing table brushing my hair. Then I saw in the mirror I still only had on a corset, and I was completely exposed on top. I went behind the screen and took off the corset and put on a robe.

He walked up to me. "It has been the longest year of my life." He took me in his arms and held me close. "And I still love you."

I tried to resist at first, but then I gave in to my feelings and put my arms around him, too. I wasn't in love with him, but I loved the fact that he was so in love with me.

"Please come back with me."

I stepped back out of the embrace. "I can't. I'm going to be in *Jesus Christ Superstar*. Rehearsals begin next week. I have the role of Mary Magdalene."

"You cannot mean to send me away again."

I looked into his eyes and saw such pain, all the pain I had put there, and remembered seeing that look in Tony's eyes. "No. Never. After this play, I will go back with you. It will only be three short months. I promise."

He ran his hand down my face and neck to the opening of my robe and brought his mouth close to mine. "How long must I wait until I can have you?"

I could feel the blood rushing to my face, and I looked away.

He pulled my robe together and pulled me to him. "Are you still my sweet, innocent Virginia girl?" I nodded. I could understand why he might not believe it, considering how he had seen me on stage. "Then I will wait for you." He kissed me. As aggressive as he acted, I expected him to kiss me hard, but he didn't. Instead the kiss was full of love and longing.

As promised, after the run of the play, I went with Robert to England. I hadn't told Mother of my plans because I was afraid she would try to keep me from going. Perhaps down deep, I still had some hope she would hear from Tony, and if so, I didn't want him thinking I was leaving him to be with another man. If he had come back, I would have broken my promise to Robert in a heartbeat and run back into Tony's arms.

The day we got to London, I called Mother to let her know where I was.

"My children certainly are full of surprises."

"What do you mean?"

"Tony has crawled out of the woodwork. I just found out he is running for state senate."

I fainted. It was that simple. I was standing at the payphone at Heathrow Airport, and when she made this announcement, I passed out in Robert's arms.

The doctor at the hospital said it was jetlag, but I knew the truth, though I couldn't tell anyone. After all this time waiting for any word from him, two years after he disappeared, I leave the country to start a new chapter in my life, and he resurfaces running for public office.

"How are you?" Eileen squealed like a ninth-grader when she opened her hotel door and found Alice on the other side.

"I'm HOT! How do you think I am? I went from the air conditioned airport to the air conditioned cab to the air conditioned hotel, and I am still drenched. I feel like I am swimming here – and look at my hair!"

Alice's hair had curled in the humidity, and Eileen pulled down one ringlet and laughed as it bounced back. "I know women who would kill for those curls. So you've been to your room?"

"Yeah, it's on the next floor up. I like we're so close to Bourbon Street! I hope you have time to hit the bars and don't need me to be running lines with you all the time."

"Hardly! I have several scenes but not many lines. They've changed the role now from 'old hag' to 'voodoo woman.'" They laughed together, but then the smile fell from Eileen's face. "Alice, I need to talk to you about something."

Uh-oh. How many words was that? "That doesn't sound good." They sat down on the bed.

"It's about Peter. He's here."

"What." Definitely a statement of disbelief and not a question.

"He told me not to say anything, but he's the one who helped me get this role."

"What!" Alice jumped off the bed and gaped at Eileen.

"I had been telling him how I wanted to be a character actor, and he got me the audition. I couldn't tell you it was on his film without you figuring it out. I had no idea he was suing the network, and I didn't think he would be here the same time as you. Do you hate me?"

"Hate you? *Au contraire.* This is perfect! I'm going to kill him!"

Eileen stood and took her friend's arm. "No, no. Please don't. At least not until after production. I don't want to lose this part. There's no reason for you even to see each other. He never goes out with us, and he and I only have a few scenes together."

Alice rubbed her eye and temple. "Oh, don't worry. I would never do anything to jeopardize your career. But if I'm still here when the film wraps, you better believe he's going to get it."

Alice's stay in New Orleans fell into an easy routine of eating too much rich food, partying all night with the cast and crew, drinking far too many cocktails, and being too hot and miserable during the day to move any faster than a slug. It was perfection. Plus, all of Eileen's scenes had been filmed in the French Quarter while Peter filmed at a plantation house up river, so she had not even seen him.

She heard about him, though. Eileen had become fast friends with Evan, the flamboyant costume designer on the film, and he loved gossip. His latest scoop was the torrid love affair between Peter and Cleo Crandell, the young lead actress in the film.

"There is no doubt," he told them as he held various dresses up to Eileen with Alice sitting nearby, watching while eating a Lucky Dog. "They are definitely doing the nasty. That's why they never come out of that hotel."

"Maybe they're trying to stay cool," Alice said.

"Uh-uh. Two nights in a row, they have holed up in his suite and had romantic dinners brought in."

"Ha! Poor Winnie."

"I do feel sorry for Winnie," Eileen said. "You know this is going to hit the tabloids. I wonder why she didn't come down with him."

"I think *COD* is back in production. I don't feel sorry for her. She's getting a taste of her own medicine after splitting up Peter's marriage. My mother always said, 'Once a cheater, always a cheater.'"

"You know that's right," Evan said.

"Well, we have our first scene together tomorrow," Eileen said. "What're you going to do? Would you rather he not know you're here?"

"Who? Peter?" asked Evan. "He already knows Alice is here."

"What?" Eileen and Alice asked together.

"Mmm-hmm. The others were talking about how you have been going out every night, and he asked if they were talking about Alice McGillicutty."

Alice rolled her eyes. "Great. I can only imagine what he had to say about me."

"Actually, the only thing I heard him say was that he hoped you were being careful. Waaait...Did you two...?"

"What? No. Oh no. Ours was a professional relationship that did not end well."

"Well, he doesn't seem to have held a grudge."

"He has no reason to! He is the offending party here."

"So what about it?" Eileen asked. "Are you coming on the set with me tomorrow or not?"

"I have no reason to avoid him. If he feels uncomfortable having me there with this lawsuit hanging over our heads, it serves him right."

Alice stood back at a discrete distance as the actors rehearsed the scene. She couldn't help but laugh to herself at the travesty of a production. The leading lady's inability to act did nothing to aid the preposterous dialog. *And he had the audacity to ridicule our scripts!* From Peter's weary face and defeated posture, she suspected he held the same opinion. *Or maybe he's just hot.*

Peter, Cleo, and the director were discussing the blocking when Peter said, "What if, right after that, she turns around with her back to me so we are both on camera. Then my reaction to her lines will be more ominous as I come up behind her."

Alice burst out laughing and, even covering her mouth with her hands, could not control herself. Peter straightened and faced her, his intense stare squelching her laughter. He said something to the director, prompting the latter to call for lunch, and then strode directly toward her as her eyes widened at his approach.

"You find something amusing, Miss McGillicutty?"

"That's soap opera blocking!" she said with an incredulous grin.

"I don't know what you're talking about."

"What you just suggested to the director – you got that from us!"

He didn't refute it. "How...how have you been?"

The memory of their last meeting rushed through her, her face enflamed from the awareness of that encounter.

"I heard you were here," he said when she didn't answer.

"I thought you were filming in Toronto."

"We did for a month, then production moved here."

"If I had known you were here..."

He finished her thought. "You wouldn't have come."

His eyes held her in place with the force of gravity, and a curious lump formed in her throat. For a moment, one brief moment, she forgot why she hated him – his arrogance, his vanity, his concupiscence – but then Cleo's voice rang out calling his name and popped the bubble that had surrounded them.

"Just a minute," Peter called out.

Alice shook her head to clear the dizziness. "Peter, this movie."

"I know."

"The dialog."

"I know."

"And vampires in Louisiana? How original."

"I signed on when, well, things were different. More as a favor for a friend."

A vaguely familiar actor whom Alice had seen in several scenes but didn't know by name walked up to them. "Hey, Pete, who's your friend."

Peter cringed and sighed. "Alice, this is Dirk – Dirk Schoenstein – he plays Portia's nephew. Dirk, Alice is the head writer for *All My Tomorrows.*"

"You're kidding!" Dirk said as he shook her hand. "I was on that soap for two years."

Peter scowled at this information. "You never mentioned that."

"Oh, yeah! As Sienna's love interest of the moment. She gave up the Church for me."

Alice chuckled. "Oh, so you're the one! That was before my time."

Dirk's eyes were smiling and friendly. "I'm sorry I missed you. Or maybe I just don't remember because of my amnesia." He and Alice laughed.

Peter said, "Seems like everyone on the show has slept with Sienna except me."

"Oh, yeah," Dirk said. "I heard about the 'shocking revelation.' So how is Giselle? I haven't seen her in a dog's age."

"To be honest, she's having a rough time right now," Alice said then turned to Peter. "You know, your friend is a real ass."

"Why? What happened?" Dirk asked.

"Giselle and this guy were dating, pretty seriously she thought. Then once his pal Peter was off the show, he disappeared and she never heard from him again. Bitch-buttoned her calls, wouldn't reply to her texts. No fight, no break-up email, nothing."

"He sounds like a douche."

"That's what I told her, that anyone who would do something like that didn't deserve her; but she's still really broken up about it." She glanced at Peter for his response, but he just scowled at her through narrowed eyes. "You're not going to defend him, are you?"

"Peter!" Cleo's voice pierced through the thick air from the other side of the set.

"You better go," Alice said. "If she screams again, I might have to strangle her."

He smiled and walked away.

CHAPTER 11

Alice, Eileen, Evan, and Dirk made up an odd foursome at a corner bar with an eighties cover band, but of the Def Leppard/Bon Jovi variety. No fear of hearing "Careless Whisper" there. Alice had volunteered to get their third round of drinks but had waited so long holding up a twenty trying to get the bartenders' attention – the bevy of girls with breasts as fake as their IDs having rendered her invisible – finally she inhaled fully and exhaled a lengthy, aggravated breath and lay her head on the bar, the strains of "You Could Be Mine" mocking her as if the band spoke of her longing for the sour mash just ten feet away.

"Get me a Jack Daniels and ginger ale and a double Jack on the rocks."

The voice. She heard it just as his presence compressed the humid air against her back, its timbre as sultry as the Louisiana heat. *Stop that!*

Without lifting her head from the bar, Alice turned her neck to see Peter, his eyes and mouth smiling at her. Arrogance, no doubt, as the bartender set two plastic cups in front of him within seconds.

"I guess it pays to be a movie star when you want a drink," she said. "I've been trying to get his attention for twenty minutes."

"I'm sure it's just because I'm taller than you. Stand up, Alice."

Alice stood, and he plucked the twenty from her hand, replacing it with a plastic cup—half ice, a quarter Jack, and a quarter ginger ale. For a second, she thought he intended to keep the bill, but he slipped it into the pocket of the sundress she wore with a disconcerting familiarity while she was distracted by finally taking a sip of the long-sought yet disappointing cocktail. Although he had once been far more familiar with her still, their chests pressed against one another.

No! Mustn't think of that! He had vanished the next day, taking with him the man who had broken his sister's—well, his *fake* sister's—heart.

She started to protest but could tell from the glint in his eyes that he expected her to do just that, and so she chose to disappoint his expectations instead. He drank as well, his gaze never leaving her face, although her eyes wandered back to her table of friends—now joined by Cleo.

At that moment, a stool adjacent from where they stood became available, and Peter pulled it around and nodded for her to sit. Which aggravatingly enough she did.

"I thought I might find you here," he said, the song having dipped to a volume over which he could speak.

"How come?"

"I just followed the eighties music."

Tilting her head to her shoulder, she said, "Ha. Ha. What are you *really* doing here?"

"Dirk told me he was meeting you here...you and Eileen."

They both glanced back at the table where Cleo had taken *her* stool. *Too bad you can't get skinny off a seat like herpes. But it would probably come with that duck face.*

"And you and Cleo decided to join us? *Slumming* it, I see."

"Not at all. I just thought, well, earlier we didn't have much of a chance to catch up."

She raised her eyebrows, a wrinkle forming above her nose. "Catch up?"

Catch up. About what? The lawsuit that could destroy the show or almost coaxing her into his bed the last time they were together. Although, to be fair, not that it would have taken much coaxing until she had come to her senses.

Alice chomped on ice as she looked back at the high table they had claimed near the back of the club, longing to return to it. Her best friend stared her down, shaking her head with eyes bulging, which might have been intended as a telepathic signal for Alice to keep her mouth shut had it not been so blatant. Alice rolled her eyes and offered a single nod of acknowledgment, prompting Peter to look over his shoulder at the table before returning his focus to her.

"Something I should know?"

"No, just something between Eileen and me."

He leaned against the bar near her as the band segued into "Wanted, Dead or Alive," and Alice scoured her brain for any safe topic of conversation.

She couldn't slam him about his hypocrisy regarding the lawsuit, which essentially meant the soap, *er*, daytime drama was off-limits as well. His agent and her friend were on opposite sides of a lovers' spat, so they certainly couldn't gossip about them. And one thing for certain, they definitely could never, ever, ever, *ever* discuss the night of the cast party.

His impassive face gave every indication that he could be content with no conversation at all, which only compelled Alice into wanting to force him to talk. She finished off the small amount of liquor in the ice-filled cup, soothing her throat and heartening her confidence.

"Thanks for the drink," she yelled over the band, and he glimpsed up at the bartender with a nod and two fingers raised before returning his attention to her. "How'd you know I liked Jack and ginger?"

He blinked and his brows drew together in puzzlement, as if surprised she had to ask. "From eighties night, at that club."

Oh, thank God! A safe topic of conversation.

"I gotta admit, you impressed me with your knowledge of George Clinton."

Their drinks arrived, and he handed her a full cup. "George Clinton?"

"Taking Eileen to task—" *Yeah, well, she deserved it at this point...* "about the Parliament song."

He grinned down at his shoes then back at her. "I'm surprised you didn't think I was an arrogant prick for contradicting her like that."

She smirked back at him because she had. "I like George Clinton. His other band Funkadelic recorded one of my all-time favorite songs. Amazing guitar line." She closed her eyes and shook the song playing beside her out of her head to pull the chords of Funkadelic into her head. "Definitely in my top ten guitar players. I mean, not George Clinton, but—"

When she opened her eyes, his features had softened; but as he drank again from his cup, she realized it must be the Jack Daniels relaxing him, as he leaned closer toward her on the bar. He had to, regardless, to speak in her ear so she could hear his words over the band.

"You have a top ten list of guitar players?"

She grinned and squinted playfully. Yeah, the JD had definitely affected her as well. "Of course! Doesn't everyone?"

"Maybe *Rolling Stone* magazine. So let's hear it."

"Hear what?"

"Your top ten."

"Oh! Well, number one has to be—"

"—Eric Clapton," they said together.

She laughed and he smiled, his eyes roaming over her in an unsettling way that caused her chest to tighten. She ignored it and said, "Well, he *is* god."

"True enough. And who's next on your list?"

"David Gilmour. George Harrison."

"And here I thought you only liked music from the eighties."

"Well, Prince is in my top ten, too."

"Prince?"

"Have you heard his rendition of 'While My Guitar Gently Weeps'?"

"Ah, that's Harrison again."

"Prince was amazing." She counted off on her fingers. "Carlos Santana. Joe Walsh. And I think Lindsay Buckingham is highly underrated." She drew her brows together. "Is that an oxymoron?"

"At least we have progressed to the seventies."

Peter looked even more handsome when he smiled, his teasing tone translating onto his lips. Alice hadn't seen him smile often, not even on screen since he usually took dramatic roles. His smile—magnetic and contagious—sent a ripple of remembrance through her, of his hands on her skin, of the kiss they had shared , along with a consciousness of the minute distance between them, and she leaned away from him.

Right then Dirk popped up on her other side, and she smiled as she expelled a breath of relief.

"I thought you might need a hand," he said, his eyes darting from her to Peter then back again. "You left a lot of thirsty people over there."

She grimaced. "I—uh—I'm sorry. I had a hell of a time getting the bartender's attention. Then Peter showed up in all this state to intimidate me with his celebrity."

"Is that true, Pete?"

Peter sniffed, still smiling at Alice. "I have no reason to deny it because you and I have been acquainted long enough for me to know you are not impressed or intimidated by celebrities."

To Dirk, she said, "I am when it can get me a drink."

"I don't think my face is famous enough to pull that act," Dirk said, then managed to wave down the bartender. "Two Turbodogs and a cosmopolitan," he called out.

"Peter," she said with a smile and widening her eyes in challenge, "don't deny that you expect special treatment because you're a movie star. The first time I saw you on the set of *All My Tomorrows*, you..." She broke off when she spotted Eileen from over Peter's shoulder, slashing her finger across her throat while staring arrows at Alice. She wanted to tell Dirk everything, about what a pompous prick Peter had been from day one. How even now he had a pending lawsuit to keep him off a show he found so beneath him. Instead she stared down into her plastic cup.

"C'mon, let's hear it," Dirk prodded. "I'd like to hear how Pete behaves around mere mortals."

"Go ahead, Alice," Peter said, bringing her attention back to his smiling face. "I'm not afraid of you."

"He, uh." She spoke to Dirk, but Peter's eyes held her trapped. "He tried to refuse the role of Tristan. He thought it was beneath him to take another actor's part, like he was an understudy."

"That was only at first. I had never been in a soap, *er*, daytime drama before, so I didn't understand that—in that context—such a thing would not be considered unusual, let alone implausible. But it was your writing, Alice. Your writing has helped me make the role my own."

She frowned and opened her mouth to speak, but confusion had rendered her mute.

"*Peter!*" Cleo's childish whine preceded her as she filled the narrow gap between them with her back to Alice. "*Where's my Chardonnay?*"

With lips together in a tight line, he lifted his eyes to the ceiling as if he might find a bottle of white wine above them. He said something to Cleo, which Alice couldn't hear over "Pour Some Sugar on Me," but Cleo walked back toward the table. The bartender returned and set two bottles of beer and what might have been a cosmo in front of them, and Alice pulled the twenty from her pocket and handed it to him, asking for another Jack and ginger.

As Peter ordered a Chardonnay, which the bartender said they did not have, and Peter told him something to the effect of *just give him any white wine—she won't know the difference anyway*—Dirk grabbed the cosmo and one Turbodog, leaving the other on the bar as he said, "I'll be right back," then stepped away to deliver the drinks to Evan and Eileen.

"Now where were we?" Peter asked as he stepped closer to her barstool.

Alice blinked rapidly, shaking her head. "Huh?"

"Your top ten list. Guitarists. I believe we left off with Lindsay Buckingham."

"Oh, right."

"What about Stevie Ray Vaughan?"

"Yeah, he makes the list because I appreciate his talent. It almost seems unfair because it was so effortless for him, like seeing him play 'Voodoo Child,' as if the guitar is an extension of his body. Overall, though, I just don't really like his musical selection."

He leaned against the bar, turned so they were face to face. "You don't like the blues?"

"Oh, no, I do. It's just a geography thing."

He raised his eyebrows. "Geography?"

"Yeah, I have to be there. Just like big band music. I love to hear it performed live, but it's nothing I would have on my playlist."

He finished off his drink then spoke not loud but deep enough for her to hear despite the band. "If you like to hear blues guitar played live, we're in the right city—especially for Delta Blues. I know of several clubs near hear, one even on Bourbon."

"Oh. Um. I think, uh, everyone is pretty comfortable here."

He responded with a barely perceptible motion of his head in the negative. "I just meant the two of us. You and me."

Confused, embarrassed, mortified, she knew the dim lighting and fog of tobacco smoke would have hidden the warmth that rose in her face, but not her expression or the way she dropped her gaze.

Dirk and the bartender arrived at the same time, and Peter straightened up from the bar. The barstool next to Alice's was then vacated, so Dirk sat down and took a swig from his bottle of beer while the bartender apologized to Peter for the pink wine in the plastic cup.

"Sorry, man, that's the best I could do. White Zinfandel."

Peter smiled with that ironic sniff of his and handed the man a hundred then walked off to bring Cleo her "Chardonnay."

"So how do you like New Orleans?" Dirk asked. "Is this your first time here?"

She turned her full attention to Dirk and her back on the others at the table. "No, I've actually been here a few times. In general, I love it; but the heat is killing me. And look what the humidity has done to my hair." Smiling, she pulled at a ringlet and let it spring back into place.

He laughed as his eyes traveled around her head then back to hers. "That's from the humidity? Well, I think it's very pretty." His eyes focused past her a moment. "So what were you and Pete talking about so seriously over here? You had Eileen in a panic."

"Well, she shouldn't have worried." *Actually, she was probably right to worry. If I'd had Peter alone...* "We were just talking about music."

"Music?"

And from there they proceeded to talk of music and movies, places they'd been, people they knew in common. Dirk didn't have the charming good looks of Rich, and he wasn't drop-dead-gorgeous like Peter; but he had an open and fun personality that reflected in his face. The more they talked, the more they flirted; and the more they flirted, the more Alice liked him.

Then the opening strains of "Sweet Home Alabama" set everyone in the bar screaming; and a few seconds later, Eileen had pulled her off the barstool and onto the crowded dance floor, with Evan and Dirk right behind them. Alice caught a glimpse of the table where Peter sat simmering and Cleo sulked, but the energy ran through the place like an epidemic, and the swarm overtook her.

She laughed when she and the others joined in the cry of *ooh, ooh, ooh* then shouted at Eileen, "WHY DO WE LIKE THIS SONG?"

"BECAUSE IT'S FUN!" Eileen screamed back.

Alice and Dirk had ceded their barstools when they got up to dance, and they followed Eileen and Evan back to their table where Peter and Cleo now occupied two of the four stools. Peter stood to offer his seat, but Alice waved as she walked past them.

"I have to go powder my nose."

Even in the poor lighting of the claustrophobic two-stall ladies room, she could still see her sweaty, blurry face in the mirror. She splashed water on her face, on her neck, chest, and under her arms and patted dry with paper towels. She shook her head at her reflection, thinking of flirting so flagrantly with Dirk and wondering what the hell was going on with Peter. *Did he actually plan to leave Cleo and go to a blues club? With me?* "That's it," she said aloud to herself. "No more cocktails...tonight."

When she returned, the others had managed to scrounge up two more stools and crowd them around the tall table, the only one not occupied between Dirk and Evan. Peter and Cleo caught her attention as soon as she sat down. Cleo blew cigarette smoke away from the table, swinging one leg crossed over the other and paying no attention to the others. Thin, pale, almost sickly, as befitting her role as a vampire, contrasted with the tall, strong, masculinity of Peter, Alice could not see them as a couple; and Peter certainly did not attend to her as a lover. *Maybe he's just using her for on-set sex and Winnie has nothing to worry about after all.*

Peter caught her staring and met her eyes with a slight grin. "So, Alice, who's next on your list?"

"What list?" Dirk asked.

"She's been telling me her top ten favorite guitarists."

"You have a top ten list of guitarists?"

She shrugged. "I do love a good guitar line."

Peter raised his eyebrows. "I'm waiting."

"Eddie Hazel."

He frowned and shook his head. "I don't think I know him."

Oh, this is too good. She ran her tongue across her teeth with a sly grin. "You should. He played lead guitar for Parliament. You know. 'Give Up the Funk.' So he also was with Funkadelic. I guess you don't know George Clinton as well as I thought."

Peter nodded. "I concede defeat. That's the band that recorded your favorite song."

"What is it?" asked Dirk, giving her an excuse to tear away from Peter's penetrating stare.

"It's only one of my favorites, but I'd rather not say."

"Miss McGillicutty," Peter said, capturing her attention again. "You mustn't leave us in suspense."

"The only reason you could possibly want to know is so you can make fun of my taste in music some more, so I suppose you will just have to get used to disappointment."

"No one who has ever heard you talk about music could ever doubt your taste."

Her eyes downcast, she knew she could not attribute the flush heating her neck and face to alcohol. She could feel him watching her as Evan and Dirk wheedled her in stereo to give it up.

She held up her palms to quiet them. "All right, all right. I'll tell you. But after all this build-up, you're going to be disappointed." She tried to catch Eileen's eye, but peering straight ahead, Eileen finished off her beer as though she wanted no part of the conversation, leaving Alice no choice but to face Peter. "It's 'Maggot Brain.'"

Peter winced and looked at her with the condescension she had expected.

"'Maggot Brain,'" Evan repeated.

"You know how they say not to judge a book by its cover? Well, you shouldn't judge it until you've heard it."

"I doubt I'll ever have the opportunity to listen to a song called 'Maggot Brain,'" Peter said.

"You can listen to it anytime you're willing," Alice said. "I have it on my phone."

"All right, then. Let me hear it now."

"There's no way you could hear it over the band."

"Maybe we could request that they play it."

"No way! Even if they know it, which I seriously doubt, they couldn't do it justice."

Peter stood up from his barstool, prompting a glance from Cleo and causing confusion among the others. "Then let's step outside. Bring your phone and let me hear it. As you said, how else can I judge?"

Without thinking, she said, "Eileen, hand me my bag." Eileen pulled Alice's small purse out of her larger one and handed it to her. Alice set her phone on the table then continued to fish through her bag. "You'll be able to hear it better with earbuds."

"You keep earpods in your purse?"

She slipped them out then slid off her stool. "Yeah, well, I'm always pretending to myself that I'm actually going to get some exercise." She located the song on the phone as she stepped over to Peter then held it out for him. "Here you go."

He flinched back. "Oh, no. If I'm going to listen to something about *maggots*, you're going to listen with me." Then he walked away, the obvious implication being that he expected she would follow.

She sighed and turned to go, but Eileen stopped her with a hand on her arm. "Alice, just the song. OK?" She pleaded with her eyes.

"I know, I know."

"What's going on?" Dirk asked.

Evan leaned toward Dirk and spoke in a conspiratorial tone. "Alice and Peter have some big feud going on."

Puzzlement creased Dirk's features. "Really."

Before skulking away, Alice said, "If I'm not back in ten minutes, come rescue me."

When she met Peter at the side exit, he motioned for her to pass. "After you, Miss McGillicutty."

They walked only a few yards away from the bar before Alice stopped, unwilling to go farther with him even though the music had followed them.

"Shouldn't we move down more?"

"No, this will be fine." She plugged the earpods into her phone. "Just stick your finger in your other ear."

Peter leaned against the brick wall with a scowl and a huff as she ascertained the left from the right earpiece. Handing him the right and pushing the other into her left ear, she glanced up as he inspected it. "Now, you have to understand it's not going to sound as good if you don't use both of them. Are you sure you don't want to use both earbuds? You know, I have heard it before."

"No, no." He shook his head, and the frown fell away as he placed the bud in one ear and his finger in the other. "Whenever you're ready, Miss McGillicutty."

The short length of the cord forced her closer to him, and she pressed play.

During the opening arpeggio, his straight mouth and eyes rolled up to the sky told her he expected to be unimpressed. Then on that first dramatic intense riff of the lead, his fathomless eyes fell upon her, the serious line of his lips denoting something far different from ennui. The song had always affected her, but now the strings of the guitar reached deep beneath her sternum and tightened around her heart.

Halfway through, the song drew quiet, and she didn't think she could bear another five minutes in such close proximity with her head swimming in whisky and his heat causing her a chill.

"After that, it's just pretty much more of the same."

She reached to take the earbud from him, but he clasped her hand near her cheek. "No. I want to hear the rest."

When the screaming guitar line began again, their eyes met, and she lost her breath and pulled her hand away. Her breasts felt heavy, and her nipples tightened as if a cool breeze had fluttered between them, but the night air was as hot, dense, and still as ever.

She squeezed her eyes closed both to block out the man sharing this moment and to revel in its succulence.

Once it ended, they pulled the buds from their ears and he locked her in his gaze. "That is the sexiest song I have ever heard, and *you* are the sexi—"

"Peter!" Cleo, who, like an apparition, appeared out of thin air beside Peter—to Alice, both her greatest annoyance and her avenging angel. Ignoring Alice, she whined, "What are you doing out here?"

His eyes closed and his hardened jaw thrust forward as he gnashed his top teeth against the bottom, he took in a full breath through his flared nostrils. Then opening his eyes, he spoke on the exhalation. "We were discussing music."

"Music? Well, good. Can't we go someplace where they play *real* music?"

Peter half-turned in her direction. "Real music? Like a blues club?"

"What? No. I'm tired of listening to all these oldies. There's a club down closer to Canal Street with a DJ playing music, like, you know, from *this century*. Someplace we can really dance."

Backing away and twisting the cord around her trembling fingers, Alice said, "You should take her, Peter. You might even get to do the Cupid Shuffle."

She hustled away from them as the Cleo squeal continued behind her and rushed straight to the bar. The bartender met her in an instant. "Double Jack on the rocks with a splash of ginger ale."

She lifted the cup with a shaky hand and drank it all down before returning to her friends, grateful that Peter did not follow her in, and loving Cleo more than she ever thought possible.

CHAPTER 12

The group of cast and crew were virtually the only inhabitants of the courtyard at McMurry's; and Alice sat with Eileen, Evan, and Dirk at a table near the flaming fountain.

Dirk said, "I'm surprised there aren't more tourists."

"Well, it is a Monday night," said Eileen. "They are probably going home or still recovering from the weekend."

"Or maybe they are just hot," Alice said, eliciting groans from Evan and Eileen.

"How long are you going to bitch about the heat?"

"I guess until I cool off."

Then *the voice.* "Try this. Maybe it will cool you off."

Alice spun her head around and reflexively accepted the glass Peter extended to her.

"A mint julep," he said. "May I join you?"

Well, who is going to tell Peter Walsingham no? Alice didn't budge but sipped her drink as the others rearranged chairs to accommodate the new arrival.

"It's delicious," she said to Peter once he had settled beside her. And it was. "Thank you." He nodded in reply.

"What brings you out again, Pete?" Dirk asked with a concerned glance at Alice. "You aren't afraid that the film will suffer if you aren't holed away rehearsing?"

"I don't think the film could suffer any more than it does already," Peter said.

"And where is your lovely co-star?" Alice asked.

"Cleo? I sent her to bed with warm milk and the script."

"Here I thought she was known for her extraordinary talents and miraculous virtues."

"Is she? I'd like to see that side of her."

"Perhaps she could put the script under her pillow and learn her lines by osmosis."

He smiled at her. "Nothing else has worked."

*He smiled at me...*He often smiled at her. In fact, that was the only time she saw him—

"Thank you for sharing your song with me," he said low, close to her neck. "It truly is amazing. I doubt I ever would have heard it if you hadn't played it for me."

She nodded and turned away to hide the blush burning her cheeks. *Her* song. She doubted she could ever listen to it again, not without thinking of *him*.

The song she had loved so long and so deeply had betrayed her, coerced her body's traitorous reactions, gripping her by the ankles and transmitting a sensation through her calves, between her thighs, and into her womb. It had wound its way through her stomach and between her breasts, forming a lump in her throat before squirming into her head.

Like maggots.

Eating away all sense in her brain.

She swallowed and cleared her throat. "Did, uh, did you take Cleo to that dance club?"

"I did, under your recommendation, but I think you might have been having a little fun at my expense. In any case, we didn't stay long because once we were recognized, the paparazzi descended on us like a plague of locusts."

"So you didn't get to do the Cupid Shuffle? I would have paid to see that."

"I'm afraid the opportunity did not present itself. What is it, anyway?"

"It's just a fun little dance. Cupid actually is from here in Louisiana."

"Cupid in Louisiana? Perhaps the gods are in my favor after all." He took another sip of his drink without his eyes ever leaving her.

Nothing felt right. Nothing felt real. Conversations continued around her, but she heard all of the voices as if she were underwater. Her skin waged a shoving-match with the atmosphere, the heavy, floral-scented night air covering her like a warm, damp blanket. She had already had three cocktails. She must be drunk from the alcohol and the humidity. She drank the mint julep then fished two ice cubes from the glass and put them on the nape of her neck. She closed her eyes as the ice melted into a cool rivulet down her back.

"Are you OK?" Peter asked, and she opened her eyes.

"Yes, I really am just hot and tired and – oh, my God." At the sight of the scurrying creature on the wall, she spoke low but wanted to scream.

"What is it?"

"What was in this drink? Please tell me I'm hallucinating." He followed her line of vision. "On the wall. Right there. Running on the wall. Is that a…a rat?"

"Do you mean with the white fur?"

"Well, yes!"

He turned back to her. "No, I don't see anything. I think you *are* hallucinating." He stuck two fingers into her glass and retrieved more ice. leaning toward her, he ran his hand beneath her hair and held the ice against her skin.

The nearness of his mouth made her dizzy and her heart race, and his holding the ice against her somehow made her warmer. "Then how did you know it was white?"

"Oh, the *white* fur. No, that's not a rat. That was a cat."

She narrowed her eyes at him. "I don't think I believe you. Eileen?" But by the time she got Eileen's attention, the ivy-covered walls were critter-free.

"Do you want another drink?" Peter asked.

"Are you trying to get me drunk?"

The ice had melted, but he still held his hand against her damp neck, his fingers gently massaging the base of her skull. "I think I'm too late for that."

He's trying to seduce me. He's trying to seduce me, and it's working.

Eileen called out, "Alice, are you ready to go?"

Alice nodded, and Peter stood with his hand still on her neck and offered to walk them.

"No, we'll be OK," Eileen said. "It's just a few blocks."

"I'm worried about her."

Once Alice realized Peter meant her, she forced herself to her feet.

Dirk stood as well, his iron chair scraping against the concrete. "Alice? Is something wrong?"

"No, I'm fine. You stay here and enjoy your juleps."

Peter reached for her hand, but Alice turned and walked across the courtyard and through the hall out to the Quarter before he could say anything.

Eileen ran up behind her. "Alice, what is going on with you and Peter?"

She shook her head. "Nothing. I'm like the Matterhorn to him."

"The Matterhorn?"

"Just another conquest he has yet to make. He wants to plant his flag in me."

CHAPTER 13

"Why are you crying?" Alice asked Eileen when she found her sitting alone in the courtyard behind the bar.

"I don't know." Eileen sniffed and wiped at her eyes with a cocktail napkin. "I'm happy; I'm sad. I can't believe it's over. My first film!"

Evan walked over from the bar and set down three cocktails. "She's just sorry our little family is breaking up," he said as he sat down.

"Don't make fun, Evan. I am going to miss everyone. I wish I were going to Toronto with you."

"We only have to reshoot a few scenes, just a few days. I will call you as soon as I get back to L.A. Now stop all that crying and let's have a good time tonight. A toast." They lifted their plastic cups. "May all the bridges we burn light our way."

After one recklessly large sip, Alice contorted her face and stuck out her tongue. "Blech! What is that?"

"Red Bull and vodka. Keep drinking – you'll get used to it. I want you girls to have plenty of energy tonight for *singing!*" He sang the final word.

"Oh, yeah – no one told me this was a karaoke bar. Eileen knows I hate karaoke."

"Come on," Eileen said. "It'll be fun. It's our last night. You have a wonderful singing voice."

"Uh-uh. No way. Since it's the last night and won't become a regular thing, I'll stay and laugh at all of you, but I am not getting on that stage. There's a reason I work behind the scenes."

"What reason is that?" Peter's voice asked behind her.

Alice twisted her neck to face him. "I do not perform for strangers."

The corners of his mouth turned up a fraction of an inch. "May we join you?"

"Where is Cleo?"

He blinked and said, "How should I know?"

Dirk had walked out with Peter and maneuvered another chair next to Alice and sat down. "How are you, pretty girl?"

After the night of what Alice referred to as the "Rat McFurry's Incident," the cast and some of the crew had continued to patronize the French Quarter's drinking establishments. Peter would appear wherever they were, sometimes with Cleo. In general, Alice had managed to keep her distance since Dirk monopolized her attention while Peter hovered nearby. Occasionally the paparazzi would arrive, snapping photos of the film's two stars, prompting Peter to leave. For the most part, in a city known for leaving celebrities alone, no one approached him, although there were plenty of gawkers and phones taking pictures.

Peter pulled a buzzing cellphone from his pocket

and, after checking the screen, excused himself to take the call.

"Why did you bring him here?" Alice asked Dirk the moment Peter walked away.

"He didn't give me much of a choice. I think he was waiting for me, then he asked if he could join us. What was I supposed to say? It's Peter Walsingham, for Christ's sake."

Alice took another sip and her lips squinched involuntarily. "Karaoke and now Peter. Can't I at least get a decent cocktail?"

"I could take you someplace else."

Eileen glared at him. "Don't you dare!"

"No, it's OK," Alice said. "I can tolerate him for one last night. And now that you're done, I can confront him about the lawsuit."

"Please, Alice, not tonight. Can't you just let it go for one more night?"

Alice blew out a deep breath and nodded. "The things I do for you."

"I gotta say, this is really refreshing," Dirk said. "Most women – especially from L.A. – are constantly throwing themselves at Peter hoping he will get them into movies."

"Maybe they just want to screw a good-looking movie star," Alice said.

"Hmm…maybe, but some people will do anything to be 'discovered.' When we were up in Toronto, Peter told me he found out this woman had been sleeping with his agent to help her film career."

Alice stopped breathing. "What?"

"Yeah, she was probably using him to get to Peter. Jack looked really bummed about it when he found out."

Alice's face went numb, and once she realized she still hadn't taken a breath, she gasped for air.

"Are you OK?"

Before she could answer Dirk, Peter returned and took the seat across from Alice. "Sorry about that. I'm trying to straighten some things out for tomorrow."

Alice told Dirk, "I'm going to need more alcohol. Can I get a real drink?" He signaled for one of the waitresses who had been loitering nearby. *Hoping for the opportunity to serve Peter, no doubt.* "I'd like a whole lot of vodka and a splash of cranberry."

After one of those, Alice's mood had improved substantially, and she laughed with the others as they recounted anecdotes from the film as if reminiscing about things that had happened years ago instead of just the week before. A waitress approached Peter with a rack of bright-colored test tubes.

"So what do you have here?"

The waitress pointed them out. "Grape crush, sex on the beach, lemondrop..."

"I like sex on the beach." Then he looked straight at Alice. "How 'bout you?"

"How about a body shot?" the waitress asked as she pulled out the test tube.

"How would that work?"

"Well, I could put it here," she said pointing to her cleavage, "or you could drink it from my mouth or...wherever."

The others at the table called out their encouragement, but Peter shook his head and took the test tube and drank it back. The others groaned and Dirk called him a chicken.

"That's exactly the thing that would wind up on

the front page of the tabloids," Peter said.

"I'll do it," Alice said and stood up.

Peter raised his eyebrows to her then looked again at the tubes. "All right, Miss McGillicutty, I will pick one out for you. What is this one?"

"Love potion number two," the shot girl said.

"Perfect." He pulled out the tube and handed it to Alice.

"How do you want it?" the waitress asked her.

"Mouth is fine."

The girl took the shot and placed it in her mouth, she and Alice locked lips, and with a quick twist they separated, with Alice holding the empty test tube in her teeth. She shrugged at the cheers of Eileen, Evan, and Dirk. Then she tossed the tube to Peter, who sat silently smiling.

"Any more?" asked the girl.

"No more of those," Peter said. "I think we need real shots. What kind of tequila do you have?"

After the first round of salt/shot/lime, they pulled Alice inside where the strains of karaoke music echoed throughout the crowded bar. A table had been held for them, and their appearance provoked points and stares, which Peter ignored. Somehow Alice ended up between Peter and Dirk, but after the next round of salt/shot/lime, she didn't care.

Then the moment she had dreaded arrived – karaoke. Eileen and Evan begged and cajoled, but she wouldn't budge. They were the first of them to go on stage with a ridiculous rendition of "I Got You, Babe" that had the audience howling.

Later, as Eileen and Dirk launched into "Summer Nights," Peter said something to Alice, but she couldn't hear.

"WHAT?"

"I ASKED IF YOU FINISHED YOUR BOOK," he said over the noise.

"HOW DID YOU KNOW I WAS WRITING A BOOK?"

"YOU'RE WRITING A BOOK?"

"ISN'T EVERYONE?"

"WHAT'S IT ABOUT?"

"I'M NOT GOING TO SCREAM OUT THE PLOT LIKE THIS."

"I ACTUALLY MEANT THE BOOK YOU WERE READING. THE EDGE OF DARKNESS."

"OH. ALMOST. I'VE BEEN READING IT MAINLY FOR WORK, FOR INSPIRATION."

Eileen and Dirk finished their song to raucous applause.

"ARE YOU READY FOR ANOTHER ROUND?" Peter asked Alice.

"YOU'RE DOING IT AGAIN."

"WHAT?"

"TRYING TO GET ME DRUNK. IT WON'T WORK."

He shook his head. "NO. NOT YOU. IT'S FOR ME."

The noise abated somewhat while the emcee chatted with potential performers from the audience.

"Why do you want to get drunk?"

"Not drunk. Just courage." He reached out and wrapped one of her curls around his finger, watching as he played with her hair before bringing his gaze to her eyes.

"Why do you need courage?"

He leaned over and put his mouth to her ear. "I need to talk to you about something, Alice." His lips grazed her ear as he spoke and made her shiver. "Just talk. I want to ask you something. Will you let me? Can I talk to you tonight?" He sat back, staring at her awaiting an answer.

Eileen appeared before them, grabbed Alice's hand, and pulled her up. "No more excuses. You are going to sing with me – now!" Alice followed her to the stage as if sleepwalking. *Just talk. What does he want to talk to me about? It must be the lawsuit!*

After Alice, Eileen, and Evan belted out "When Will I Be Loved," Evan forced Alice into "Don't Go Breaking My Heart" even though she had always hated that song. Evan's boisterous imitation of Elton John had everyone laughing.

"That was...interesting," Peter said when she returned.

"I don't see you up there," Alice said standing over him. "When are you going to enthrall us all with your song?" The others joined her in the peer pressure.

"I'm not sure I want to see that on the tabloids either," he said, but they wouldn't let up. Finally he stood and the others applauded. "OK, I will under one condition." With his eyes on Alice, he said, "If you sing with me."

"Oh, no! I don't want to be part of your tabloid shame."

"C'mon, you sang with them. You can sing with me."

Dirk said, "Pete, if she doesn't want to, leave her alone."

"Just one song."

"And after hearing me, you still want me to sing with you?"

"You have an incredible voice. That's why I need you."

Does he always have to look at me with those eyes? She relented. "One song – but it depends on what you pick. None of those sappy singers. Or Parliament!"

Peter ran over and checked with the stage for a few minutes then returned. "How about Ozzy Osborne?"

She chuckled. "Seriously? Black Sabbath Ozzy? That's what you want to sing."

"I will if you will."

"I can probably sing metal." *What Ozzy song would they have for karaoke? Maybe "No More Tears"?*

He took her hand and pulled her toward the stage as the gathered crowd parted like the Red Sea. He signaled to the emcee who introduced him and incited screams and applause from the audience. Their hands parted as he mounted the stage. He took a microphone then held his hand out for her again, but she hesitated. Almost everyone in the bar had his cellphone ready to record. *Am I really going to get on stage and sing Sabbath in front of all these people?*

Then the music began, and it was no Sabbath song she knew. The opening guitar was slow and melodious. Then he sang the first verse as he stared down at her, and she knew she'd been had. "Close My Eyes Forever." She was about to be publicly serenaded.

"You promised," he said at a pause, and she took his hand and joined him.

For some reason, people clapped when she got on stage, even though she knew they had no idea who she was or why Peter Walsingham would be singing to her; but the thing was, as he held onto her hand and gazed into her eyes, she could almost believe he meant the words he sang. Then she reminded herself. *Actor.*

Somehow a microphone materialized in her hand, but – too stunned to move – she couldn't bring it to her mouth. After singing the refrain, he began the second verse, and she forgot he was acting. She might have stood there transfixed if he hadn't squeezed her hand to remind her to sing. When she began, the audience cheered, perhaps vicariously joining her on stage; but then they all disappeared. She couldn't see anyone, she couldn't hear anyone except Peter. He pulled her closer to him, and it pulled at her heart as well. He kissed her hand, closing his eyes and letting his lips linger until he sang again. They switched some of the parts, not singing the lyrics as assigned for the duet but instinctively knowing which words belonged to whom.

And then it was over. The music ended, and they stood staring at each other until the applause returned them to the stage. As the audience cheers rose, Peter dragged Alice off the stage and out onto Bourbon Street. She had no idea where he was taking her at this frantic pace, navigating through the crowds on the street and sidewalk, and everything happened too quickly for her to wonder or protest. Then he led her into an empty alley, but halfway down, he stopped and turned around. They were both breathing heavily from the exertion, and a sheen of sweat glistened on his forehead.

"I'm sorry," he said. "I can't take it anymore."

He wrapped his arms around her, brought her tight against his body, and covered her mouth with his. A sensation she could only identify as relief flooded through her, relief in finally getting something she didn't even know she had been needing. Her arms crawled up around his neck, and he walked her back against a brick wall, providing him leverage to deepen the kiss even more. His hands roamed over her body then made their way up her shirt, flesh to flesh, as their tongues continued to tangle.

The kiss continued on and on, for minutes, maybe hours. She didn't know or care or want it to end, but end it did. He pulled his hands out from beneath her shirt to hold her head between them, and he broke the kiss to regain his breath.

As he laid kisses on her forehead, eyes, cheeks, nose, he whispered, "Thank God, thank God, thank God," again and again. Then his mouth returned to cover hers, and she could have cried out a prayer of thanks that their lips and tongues were back where they belonged. He claimed her. In that moment, he owned her and could lead her wherever he wanted and she would follow.

"It's him." The words broke the spell, then the camera flash reminded them where they were.

After a glance in the direction of the disturbance, he brought his lips to hers in a gentle kiss. "Where's your hotel?" he asked but kissed her before she answered.

"Paparazzi?" she asked between slow, lingering kisses, which continued as they spoke.

"Tourists…"

"My hotel…this next street…up a few blocks…"

"I'm at the Ritz…"

"Naturally…"

"Shall we go there…"

"No...too far..."

He lifted his face from hers. "My thoughts exactly."

They walked the few blocks with arms around waists without saying anything more, and he occasionally dropped a kiss on the top of her head. They stopped for a moment before entering the hotel, their mouths demanding a reunion after a separation of several blocks. Inside, he had her in his arms again before the elevator doors had closed; and as she fumbled with the key card, he moved her hair aside and kissed the nape of her neck.

The door opened, and they fell into the room as he turned her around and pulled her mouth to his again. They stopped only long enough for him to slide her shirt over her head and then for him to discard his own. The bed took up most of the room, so he didn't have to go far to pull the covers back in one swift movement. He laid her down against the cool sheet and then lay over her. The light spilling in from the bathroom illuminated his face as he gazed down at her and caressed her temples and cheeks with his thumbs.

"Tell me this is real," he said. "Tell me I'm not dreaming."

"Shouldn't I be saying that?" The frenzied, ravenous kisses from the alley had transitioned into gentle lips upon lips, which somehow were more intimate.

"After the party, I thought I'd never see you again. I hated how we left things."

As his kisses deepened, he unhooked her bra and slid the straps from her shoulders, then he caressed from her neck down to her elbow.

"I couldn't believe it when I heard you were here. I wish I didn't have to go to Toronto tomorrow."

Wait. What? When he tried to kiss her, she didn't kiss back, and she turned her face away. "Oh, no."

"What is it?"

"The Matterhorn."

"What?"

"You want to stick your flag in me!"

"Well, I've never heard it called *that* before."

She shoved his chest but didn't even manage to move him a millimeter. *God, his chest feels good.* "This is a one-night stand. I'm one of your bimbettes."

"What? How can you even think this is a one-night stand? And why are you always talking about my 'bimbettes'? I don't even know what the hell that means."

She shoved him again. *Ugh. Better stop that.* "True. I guess I am too old to be a bimbette. Just like last time, you try to get me in bed when you are leaving the next day and, coincidentally enough, both times to Toronto."

"For work – not to leave you. That's who I was on the phone with earlier, trying to arrange so I could wait a few days. I wanted to go back to L.A. with you."

"Why would you want to do that?"

"Why do you think? I'm in love with you, Alice."

Oh, brother. She rolled her eyes. "Would you get off of me, please?"

"Not exactly the response I had hoped for."

"You are not in love with me."

"Then why would I say it?"

"To get me in bed."

"I *am* in bed with you!"

"Because I'm trying to get you out of it!"

He pushed himself up and off the bed and turned his back on her, and she sat up, covering herself with the sheet.

"Do you really think I would say that just to get you to have sex with me?"

"Men do it all the time."

"I don't."

"Why won't you look at me?"

He shrugged. "I thought you'd want to get dressed. I was giving you privacy."

"Oh. Well, would you throw me my shirt?"

He picked up the shirt and, handing it to her, sat on the bed. Leaning over, he cupped her face in his hand and rubbed her cheek with his thumb. "I love you. You have to know it. Videos of us together will be on the web by – well, they are probably already up now. Do you think I would have done that if I weren't in love with you?"

She shook her head. "Wait. What do you mean? You wouldn't have done what?"

"Been videoed together."

"Why not?"

"Because, you know, because you're not…"

"What? Pretty enough for you?"

"Of course you are!"

"Good enough for you?"

"No!"

"Famous enough?"

"Well…"

"Get up!" He stood and turned away, then she pulled on her shirt without bothering with a bra and hopped off the bed. "I cannot believe you did not want to be seen with me because I am not another Winnie or Cleo."

"That's what I'm trying to say! I love you, so that doesn't matter! I don't care what anyone else thinks."

"Well, for not caring, it seems like you've given it quite a bit of thought! You're acting as if you were singing with Osama Bin Laden!"

He closed his eyes and squeezed the bridge of his nose. "No, I'm not."

"How is it different?"

"For one thing, he's a terrorist, and for another, he's dead! You just don't understand."

"Then why don't you explain it to me?"

"My image is everything. It's my career. They would misinterpret why I am with you. People don't expect someone like me to…"

"Oh, I see. Someone like you would never be involved with an Alice McGillicutty!"

"That's just how it is. They won't understand. They will think –"

"What difference does it make what 'they' think?"

"That's what I'm trying to tell you – I don't care anymore!"

"What do you mean, 'anymore'?"

"Well, of course I hesitated at first. Why wouldn't I? You're just…It's not…"

"I'm just a lowly writer, and you're a big movie star?"

"I wouldn't exactly put it like that, but none of that matters anymore. I tried to stay away from you, but I couldn't do it."

He reached out to touch her, but she swatted his hand away. "You have to be the most vain, most arrogant human being I have ever met. And the sad thing is, you don't even realize how arrogant you are. I guess you just *assumed* I would be waiting in the wings ready to be swept into your arms with your professions of undying love."

"Well, you certainly have not seemed indifferent."

"That's right; I'm not. Almost from the moment we met, I have hated you!"

He started at this and stepped back as if he had been stung.

"From the moment you showed up at *All My Tomorrows,* you made it clear that you were too good to be there, far better than the rest of us. But then you spent time with us and seemed to find some value in what we did, and I thought you were coming around – becoming human. Then you SUE so you don't have to come back! After having everyone at your home! That's not just arrogant – that's two-faced."

"Are you finished?"

"Oh, not by a long shot! What did you say to Jack about Giselle?"

"What?"

"What did you tell him about Giselle that made him completely bail on her? Did you tell him she was just sleeping with him to get into movies?"

He didn't answer.

"I'll take that as a yes. Why would you say such a thing? She has been devastated, and according to Dirk, Jack was hurt by it, too."

"The night of the party, I heard Mrs. Jellyby saying that once Giselle was a star, it would save –"

"You're going to listen to her? She's an idiot! She entertains all kinds of pipe dreams she hopes will save the show. Giselle has never wanted to do anything besides what she is doing right now – except maybe be with Jack. She has never wanted the pressure of a film career. Not everyone wants to be a big movie star like the Great Peter Walsingham!"

"Well, you certainly became defensive at the pool when Winnie said Giselle would never get out of soaps!"

"That had nothing to do with what Giselle wants and everything to do with both Winnie and you – because you were right there in league with her – both of you believing that you are better than other people just because of the size of the screen or the time of the show."

"We were just stating facts."

"They wouldn't be 'facts' if people like you did not keep reinforcing these stereotypes. You know, when soaps got started, it was actors from Broadway who performed on them."

"We don't make the rules."

"Yes, you do! You are exactly the ones who make the rules of this exclusive club so you can pretend superiority while you teeter on the precipice of fame. You've become so imbued with 'the rules,' you believe your own press. You think it's within your purview to control the lives of people like pieces on a chessboard – whether it's Jack and Giselle or me or Rich –"

"What about Rich?"

"He told me what you did."

"And what is that?"

"That you got him thrown off your last movie. Do you deny it?"

"No, I don't deny it. Did he tell you why?"

"He said he had started dating Winnie and you didn't like it. Next thing he knew, he was off the set and couldn't even get an audition in primetime."

"Why would I care who Winnie dates?"

"Obviously, because you intended to have her for yourself. I bet the only reason you even looked at me twice was because you knew Rich and I were dating. The competition – the conquest. But then someone else would come along who presents a challenge, and you would just throw me to the side like Winnie and Cleo and your wife."

"I think I've heard enough. This is how you really feel about me?"

"How could I possibly feel anything else for someone who leaves so much destruction in his wake?"

He picked up his shirt and started for the door, but then he turned and stepped over to her with only a few inches between them. "You despise me this much, yet you kissed me with so much passion, and you were going to let me make love to you. Would you really sleep with a man you hate?"

"Huh. How 'bout that. You're the only man I hate, so I guess I would. Until this moment, I never knew myself."

He said nothing more, only turned and walked quietly out of her life.

CHAPTER 14

Peter closed her door just before two, and Alice stood staring at it for several minutes after. Once able to shake off the shock of everything that had happened in the last hour, she took a shower and cried. Not gentle tears but full-blown sobs, which depleted her such that she braced her arms and head against the shower wall. And yet, she had no idea why she was crying.

Once she had run out of tears, she got out of the shower and put on a thin robe. A storm had come in, and rain pelted against the balcony like rocks. She opened the French door and realized it *was* rocks – or hail, rather – and wondered if he had made it back to his hotel before the storm hit. *If he went to his room. Maybe he went back to the bar. He had been pretty wound up – he still has time to get laid.* She slammed the door.

She curled up on the bed, staring at the wall, considering Xanax and sleep, wondering what would have happened if she hadn't kicked him out of bed.

No. That would have been a tragedy. Damn tequila. I hate him. He is the last man in the world I would want to sleep with.

But could he really be in love with me?

The thought of a major motion picture star falling in love with her defied even her imagination. Although he did appear in public with her, even though she is so beneath him.

Oh no. Forget what people are going to say about him when that video got out. What would they say about her? *I still have to face everyone back at the show! Well, maybe none of them will see it...*

She continued ruminating over various scenarios, all equally mortifying, until light drifted through from the balcony and she gave up on sleep. The rain had somehow rendered the city less humid, and after a few minutes sitting on the balcony in just her robe, she caught a chill and went in and got dressed. She pulled a sweater around her and sat on the balcony as the sunrise changed the light-play on the buildings around her.

The eerie silence of the Quarter piqued her curiosity and coaxed her outside where the smell of wet concrete overwhelmed all others. Bourbon Street had been transformed into a bacchanal ghost town, dampened debris the only evidence of the previous night's festivities. When she came to the karaoke bar – neon sign dark, doors closed – the night before seemed like a dream. Except she still hadn't slept.

She turned the opposite way of "the alley" and meandered toward Jackson Square as she reflected on every look, every touch through the filter of his confession. The aromas of powdered sugar and beignets boiling in oil aroused her senses, but she couldn't eat. She considered getting a café au lait, but she didn't want to speak to anyone – even to order a coffee. She walked up the levee to the Moon Walk and wiped the rain off a bench before sitting down and pulling her sweater tight around her as if it were autumn and not late August.

She had no idea how long she had been there when his voice made her jump.

"I've been walking around trying to find you. I'd almost given up."

Her heart began to race, she told herself because he surprised her, and she would not face him. "How did you know I was out?"

"I went to your hotel. Not your room – I was going to call you from the lobby, but the front deskman had seen you leave.

"Don't worry – I didn't follow you here to throw myself at your feet." He spoke with a firm voice, enunciating each consonant, leaving no doubt that his anger had not waned. "I will not embarrass either of us like that ever again, but I have to discuss something with you. It is very serious, and I couldn't let anger and hurt feelings stop me."

She wanted to tell him to go to hell, but her curiosity got the better of her. She scooted to the far side of the bench to make room for him, and they both peered off out at the river.

"Did you make it back to the Ritz before the storm?" she asked, maintaining a tone as curt as his. "Or you probably didn't go straight there."

"Of course I did. Where else would I go?"

"So what is so important that you had to tell me face-to-face?"

"I would have emailed you, but what I have to say

must stay between you and me. I couldn't risk having it intercepted. Not that I do not trust you – I don't trust technology."

"Even a phone?"

"If I had called, would you have answered?"

She responded with a shrug and swallowed. *Probably not.*

He glanced at his watch. "But I'll get to that in a minute. First, I need to clear up a few things. You had a lot to say last night, and I hope you've gotten it all off your chest, so I would appreciate it if you not interrupt me."

After a moment's thought, she nodded.

"Look, I can't change how things are in the industry and the public eye, that actors are expected to marry other actors like they are their own species. They would assume, as you apparently do, that I was just using you for sex. I wish it weren't like that. I wish I didn't have a publicist and an image consultant trying to control my every move. And you're right – it is an exclusive club – but the truth is a lot of people will do anything to get in. I'm sorry I misjudged Giselle, and even though he may hate me for it, I will tell Jack that I made a mistake."

She found this admission so shocking, she wanted to say something but couldn't think of what it should be. Perhaps it was better she had agreed to remain silent.

"Now about the lawsuit. My attorneys put that in motion the day they sent me to *All My Tomorrows*. I had no idea when anything was filed or that you and everyone with the show didn't know about it. I had every intention of coming back to the show next month, and I was as surprised as you to hear about the injunction. I think you will agree, though, with everything…it is better that I not return.

"Now I have to tell you something, and you must swear not to tell anyone. I'm not trying to protect myself, but this would hurt someone else if it got out, and I can't be responsible for ruining her reputation."

She nodded.

"Rich was right – I did get him fired, but he didn't tell you why. He didn't even tell you the events in order. I thought Rich was all right when he came on location, and I even ran lines with him like I did with Dirk, and we'd go out sometimes after filming. One night we're at a club, and he offers me some Special K – ketamine. I considered it, but I pulled up the effects on my phone and decided against it. I didn't think anything of it, figured he had just come across some and decided to try it. But pretty soon it seemed like everyone on the set was using it, at least half the cast and crew; and people were showing up late and exhausted, and it was affecting production. I found out Rich was the supplier. First I confronted him and told him if he would stop, I wouldn't report him. He said I had gone from being Hollywood's bad boy to being a choirboy or something since I hadn't tried it when he offered. When he refused to stop selling it, I told the producers, and they told him if he would go quietly and not reveal who he had sold to, they wouldn't press charges.

"Before all this happened, like I said, Rich and I would hang out; and we talked about a lot of things. I told him how much I hated going out on location because it was hurting my marriage, and I didn't get to spend any time with my daughter. I didn't tell him this, but I will tell you. It finally came to a head when

I was working on location filming *Cause of Death*. My wife...she...she had an affair. After my initial anger, I didn't blame her – I blamed myself for never being around. So when they offered me *COD*, I jumped at the chance of a regular series, hoping I could put my marriage back together."

When he admitted to his wife's affair, Alice's head jerked around to face him. He still kept his eyes on the river, but the pain in his face led her to believe him, and she turned back away.

"You might have noticed that Winnie has not even come up yet. That's because she had nothing to do with him getting fired but everything to do with him getting revenge. While we were working together on *COD* last year, unbeknownst to me, she and Rich began dating. When she started behaving erratically on the set, I didn't know what to think – until I saw them together. First I tried to warn her about him and the drugs, but she said I was jealous. She had made it clear to me that she would like our relationship to be more than professional, but...that would never happen in a million years. One night Jack calls me, frantic. He's at Winnie's – he's her agent too – and she's all messed up. I went over there, and she was out of her mind. She didn't know who she was, where she was, even what she was! My wife wasn't home when I left, and I sent her a cryptic text about needing to help a friend. I thought I'd be right back. Then Rich showed up and told me to stop interfering, and we really had it out. Jack and I knew we had to get her out of town to keep her away from Rich and the media away from her before they saw her having what amounted to a psychotic episode. I kept trying to call my wife but it went straight to voicemail, and I didn't say much when I left a message or texted her – just that a friend was in trouble and I'd be gone longer than expected.

"We took Winnie to my place in Park City, and you know most of the rest. Rich figured out where we were and called the paparazzi, so when we came out, our picture ended up everywhere. Jack had left earlier that day, so it looked like...what it looked like. That was the final straw for my marriage. I tried to explain, but she wouldn't listen. The worst, though, was what it has done to my daughter. She doesn't really understand, only that Daddy was with a woman other than her mother, and that's why we got a divorce. On top of that, I still don't get to spend much time with her. I won't say he destroyed my family because I now know that nothing would have saved my marriage, but it shouldn't have happened like this."

She stole a glance at him again, his chin firm and his teeth clenched. He hadn't shaved.

"When Rich showed up at *All My Tomorrows,* Jack and I confronted him. He said he had cleaned up and wanted another chance. I didn't say anything just to keep his mouth shut about Winnie. You can see why I must have your discretion, but I couldn't leave you without warning you about him, to be careful and watch him. I hope I'm wrong, but I don't trust him. You could ask Jack about him, too, if you don't believe me. He can tell you what happened with Winnie and how he more than I took care of her in Utah."

He looked at his watch again. "I want to tell you one more thing, and then I have to go or I'll miss my flight. I've heard you talk about my 'bimbettes,'" he spit out, "and harem, but I never thought you were serious – at least until the cast party. When I was younger and getting my first taste of fame, I admit I was pretty wild, and most of what you saw in the tabloids back then actually was true. Now you know nothing ever happened between Winnie and me. She was hanging out at the set because she's Jack's client – not at my invitation. The only reason I spent so many evenings with Cleo was because she is a terrible actress. And I guess that gave me an excuse to avoid you. Then when you came to the set that day and laughed at me, I couldn't... I would never have embarrassed myself or humiliated you by publicizing a one-night stand." Although his speech had begun with anger, he had gradually calmed down and spoken for some time in a normal, if emotional, voice. But he added volume and an edge to the end of his soliloquy. "The point I am trying to make is, in the last ten years, I have only slept with one woman – my wife! And I have only wanted to sleep with one other!"

He stood with such force it shook the bench, and her widened eyes went straight to his face, hard as stone.

"I have to go. I'll miss my flight." He started walking away.

"Wait!" Alice's voice halted him, but he kept his back to her. "Last night you said you needed to ask me something, discuss something with me. Was it about Rich?"

He froze for a moment then took a full, rattling breath and released it. He turned just enough to meet her eyes. "No."

Then he stepped back over to the bench and, crouching before her, placed his hand against her cheek and kissed her forehead. The dark circles under his red-rimmed eyes attested he had not had much sleep either. "Take care of yourself, Alice."

He walked away before she could think of any way to stop him or even if she should.

Eileen was waiting in the hotel lobby when Alice returned.

"Where have you been?"

"Walking."

"When you weren't in your room, I thought you were probably with Peter, but then they told me here that Peter had come looking for you, and you had already left. And where is your phone?"

Alice couldn't remember the last time she had gone anywhere without her cell phone. She had walked out of her room with only her key card in her back pocket.

Eileen followed her to the elevator. "Dirk was here looking for you, too."

"Oh, no." Alice rubbed her temples as the elevator doors closed.

"He was really upset last night. I think he was in a state of shock when you and Peter were singing to each other – we all were – and then you both just took off. He said he should have expected it but that he thought you were different." They stopped on Alice's floor, and Eileen got out with her.

"Are you following me?"

"I already checked out. We have to hurry if we're going to make our flight."

"Oh, shit. I didn't realize I had been gone that long. I'm not even packed."

"I'll help you."

They got to the room and began flinging suitcases and clothes.

"So...Are you going to tell me what happened?" Eileen asked.

"Nothing."

"Between you and Peter."

"Nothing happened between Peter and me. We didn't sleep together."

"Dirk will be relieved to hear that."

"No, Dirk deserves someone better than me. To just walk out on all of you like that." She was too tired even to bother correcting her own split infinitive.

"Well, where did you go? What did you do?"

"We came here, and I did exactly what I told you I was going to do. I confronted him."

"About the lawsuit?"

"About everything." Alice stopped packing and sat on the bed with her hand over her eyes and forehead. "I made a mistake."

"What are you talking about?"

"Well, he really is an arrogant ass, and he really does think he is better than everyone else, but he really had no idea what was happening with the lawsuit."

"So what happened when you found out?"

"He didn't tell me until today, and then he went to catch his plane. Last night we just had this huge fight."

Eileen sat on the bed and put her arm around Alice's shoulder. "So you think it was a mistake to confront him about it?"

"Well, that was only part of it, but it's for the best. If we hadn't fought, I would have slept with him, and then I'd feel like shit today. Well, even more like shit."

"Why? We all got the impression that you two –"

"Eileen, I've never even liked him. The minute he walked onto the set, he made it clear he was above all of us. He will always think he is too good for me."

"That's not how it looked to me." Eileen pulled out her phone.

"Oh, no. Tell me it's not already up."

Eileen started the video of Peter and Alice singing and turned the phone to show Alice.

"I really cannot watch that right now."

Eileen paused it, the screen stopped on Peter kissing Alice's hand. "That does *not* look like he thinks he's too good for you to me. And you sure don't look like you dislike him."

"Tequila," Alice said on a sigh and flopped back upon the bed.

"Maybe when he gets back to L.A. you can talk."

Alice shook her head. "Uh-uh. I mean it – I really don't like him. Yes, I am obviously wildly attracted to him, but that's it – physical attraction! And I made it quite clear how I felt about him last night. What is it Evan said? 'May the bridges that we burn light our way'? Not only did I burn that bridge, that video will just add kindling to the fire."

Alice tried to sleep on the flight to L.A. and pretended anyway to prevent any conversation. She kept going over everything Peter had said that morning – she didn't even want to think about the night before – trying to remember every word he had said and commit it to memory.

Then her eyes flew open. *He said "marry."*

CHAPTER 15

PETER WALSINGHAM SERENADES
WOMAN IN NOLA

"I guess there's something to be said for being insignificant after all," Alice said, reading the title of the video on Mr. Peacock's phone.

"Have you seen it?"

She handed him the phone and groaned. "I don't have to see it. I lived it."

"I don't think any of them had your name."

She groaned again. "How many are there?"

"A dozen, I think."

"I suppose everyone has seen it."

"I haven't spoken with any of the cast since they're not due in until next week, but the writers and crew…"

"And what are they saying?"

His lips disappeared into his mouth, and he stood mute.

"That bad? C'mon, give it to me."

"That you had a fling in New Orleans, and then he…"

"Dumped me."

He responded with something between a shrug and a nod.

"Well, they can think what they want, but neither is true."

"So you didn't have a fling? I have to admit, I was surprised when I saw the video the first time."

"How many times have you watched it?"

"Especially with the lawsuit and how you left Peter's house the night of the party, but then I started thinking about how you two were at the party."

"I have got to stop socializing with my co-workers."

"Do you want me to say anything to them?"

"No, let them believe it – especially the writers. Maybe it will help them write melodrama." *Plus, if they think I'm heartbroken, maybe they won't make me watch it.*

Mr. Peacock started out of her office but then turned back. "Alice, do not ever believe you are insignificant."

For a week, writers reworked the scripts to erase every scene with Tristan, but they squirmed and averted their eyes when Alice joined them, as if cutting Peter out of the show sliced pieces out of her heart. At one point, when she had had enough of the sympathetic head-tilts, she tried to tell them nothing had happened, but her denial only fueled their speculations.

The day the cast returned, Giselle and Rich arrived together, exchanging glowing smiles. They made goo-goo eyes at each other throughout rehearsal, and

Alice noticed him tucking Giselle's hair behind her ear. *At least no one took any pictures of me kissing Rich. Then I'd be a double-dumpee.* Then her face grew hot as she imagined Peter seeing a photo of her kissing Rich. *God, I hope he doesn't think I slept with Rich.*

Alice meandered back to her office to have her lunch at her desk with her book, but moments after she sat down, Rich appeared in her doorway and said her name. She had taken to leaving her office door open so they wouldn't think she spent her time crying over Peter, but she would rather not deal with Rich at the moment either.

"Hi, Rich. Is there something I can do for you?"

"I haven't seen you in over a month. Thought we'd catch up. That's what friends do, right?"

He started around her desk to sit on the edge as he had in the past, but she cut him off at the pass. "Have a seat." She motioned to the chair across from her desk. He hesitated a moment before sitting down. "I would say you and Giselle have become quite friendly."

"Giselle...she's something special."

"But not quite like a sister after all, I take it."

He grinned and cast his gaze down.

"I suppose a month was too long to wait."

He lifted his eyes to her, and she wondered how she had ever thought him attractive. "Alice, I know the night before you left I said I would, and I meant it. But after we saw the videos of you and Walsingham, it looked like you weren't waiting for me."

"Convenient that Giselle happened to be there."

"You know how it started. I was just being supportive after that toad Jack ran over her."

"And now it has blossomed into something more," she said with a lilt and a wave of her hand.

"Yes, it has. I mean, what am I supposed to think when one minute you hate Peter and the next you're singing love songs together?"

"Well, I wouldn't exactly call it a love song. It's Ozzy –"

"I didn't know he would break up with you like that."

She rolled her eyes. "He did not break up with me. There was nothing to break up – we were never together."

His eyes shifted back and forth as he furrowed his brow but then, perhaps in anticipation of her admonishing him, relaxed and rubbed out the crease, but she had no intention of reminding him.

"What you saw on the video was too many shots of tequila."

"I figured he would have turned you against me."

"Really? And how on earth would he have done that?"

"By telling you things."

"What kinds of things, Rich? What would he have told me that would have you so concerned?" She did not mean for the sweetness of her tone to comfort him, and she thought she must have succeeded judging from the blood coming into his cheeks and those telltale beads of sweat she had noticed form on his lip before.

"Well, he has his own version of events, and I have mine."

"Then perhaps it is better for you both to keep them to yourselves."

He gasped out half a laugh. "Yes, well. I'm sorry it

didn't work out between us. I hope you won't hold a grudge."

She stood, prompting him to do the same. "Of course not. If you and Giselle are happy together, it can only be good for the show." He nodded and turned to walk out, and then she added, "But if anything happens to her, remember – it is within my power to kill you."

A few weeks into production, Alice walked into a quiet studio. Too quiet. She found Mr. Peacock flipping through a magazine in the breakroom.

"What's going on? Why aren't you taping?"

"Still waiting on Giselle. She was supposed to be here over an hour ago."

She pulled out her cell and called Giselle's number. "Where is Rich?"

"He's not due here until nine."

Voicemail. "Giselle, it's Alice. You had a seven o'clock call. Where are you?" *Who am I kidding?* She ended the call and sent Giselle a text.

The stage manager popped his head in. "They're here."

Mr. Peacock and Alice walked out together and found Giselle leaning on Rich, both pale and puffy and smelling like they had been out all night.

Alice marched up to them and, ignoring Rich, tried to make eye contact with Giselle. "Can you work, or do we need to write around you?"

Giselle smiled and rolled her head on Rich's arm. "Why wouldn't I be able to work?"

"Are you drunk?"

She giggled. "No, of course I'm not drunk!"

Then Alice turned her attention to Rich. "Do you want to tell me what's going on?"

"I don't know what you mean, Alice. I'm not late."

She sighed and rubbed at the imminent headache on her forehead. "Just get her to make-up."

As Alice walked backed to her office, her phone began to vibrate. *Jack?* She closed the door and took the call.

"Hello?"

"Hi, Alice. It's Jack."

She hoped the connection caused that ringing tension in his voice. "Hi, Jack. I haven't heard from you in a long time. Not since July."

"I know. I'm sorry. Listen. I've been trying to get ahold of Giselle for a few weeks now. I know I deserve this, after the way I treated her. I just...I just want to tell her I'm sorry and explain."

"Explain what exactly? How you trusted some unsubstantiated gossip instead of believing she cared about you? Why you didn't even bother to give her an explanation?"

Silence.

"Hello?"

"Yeah, I'm here. I know, you're right. I should have trusted my own feelings instead of listening to..."

"Peter?"

"Yeah. You probably won't believe it, but it...it wasn't easy on me either."

She remembered Dirk's words. "I believe you."

"So could you just give her the message for me? Tell her I was wrong, and I'm sorry. I just wish she would talk to me."

"Funny, I think she said the same thing about you. I don't know if it will make a difference, but I'll tell her."

"Thanks, Alice. How's everything going?"

"Well, so far the ratings have only slipped a bit, but it's kind of soon to tell."

"No, I meant how's everything with you."

"Oh, I can't complain. Or I guess I could, but I won't bother you with mundanities."

"Any fallout from the karaoke?"

She closed her eyes and brought her hand to her warming cheek. *I knew I hated karaoke!* "Uhhh... around here, there was some speculation, but I'm just 'a woman in New Orleans.' How did he handle it? He must have been mortified the next day."

"No, not at all. But he hasn't been around town much. Since Toronto, he's been keeping to himself or spending time with his daughter. He said he needed to take a break, at least until the lawsuit is settled. He seemed more upset about the photos."

Photos? "What photos?"

"The ones printed in *The Intruder* yesterday. He was really worried about how you were taking it."

Shit. She opened her office door and held the cell against her shoulder while she yelled. "Somebody get me a copy of *The Intruder*!" She brought the phone back to her ear. "Jack, I'm sorry. I don't typically read the tabloids. So what kind of pictures are they, and why did he think I'd be upset?"

Silence.

"Hello?"

"They're pictures of you together. And an article."

She held the phone down. "Somebody bring me the Goddamned *Intruder*! Don't try to tell me not a single person on a soap set has a copy!" Her heart pounded in her chest, which rose and fell with quick shallow breaths.

"Alice, are you there?"

"Yes, Jack. I'm trying to find a copy. So was he embarrassed to be photographed with me?"

"He sounded more concerned that *you* would be embarrassed. He made me go down to *The Intruder* to buy the originals."

"To stop them from being printed?"

"No, this was after it had already come out. He didn't know about them before then."

"Then why would he want to buy them? That doesn't make sense."

A cameraman walked up and handed her the paper. "I'm sorry, Alice."

"Jack, I'll call you back."

She closed the door and walked around to sit at her desk, focusing on a black and white image of Peter standing over her on the Moon Walk under the headline "Peter's Mystery Woman Revealed." Her hands were shaking as she flipped the pages to the story. The photo essay began with a few stills of them on the stage at the karaoke bar, followed by the picture taken of them when they were kissing in the alley. *That tourist must have sold it to them.* Clearly not a professional shot, she and Peter were hardly recognizable, but there was no denying the heat between them, smoking on the page.

The rest of the photographs revealed a completely different story. Definitely professional, most likely through a telephoto lens, they painted an intimate portrait of that morning when they parted. The first must have been when he first walked up behind her.

The only picture of them on the bench together showed her staring at him with round, tired eyes – eyes that looked like they had cried as much as they truly had. The other four in the series had been shot right before he left. His hand cupping her cheek. His lips on her forehead with her eyes closed. Him peering at her as he told her to take care of herself, though only she knew what he said. Then a final shot of him walking away.

She knew why he wanted them. She hated to admit it, since they were shot by a paparazzo, but they were...stunning. Even the poor quality of the newsprint did not diminish their breathtaking beauty – artistic yet natural, with the morning light through the misty haze casting an ethereal quality to the scene. No trace of Hollywood glamour marred a single image. She wore an old sweater and no make-up, and she had done nothing but comb her fingers through her hair, which hung in loose, damp curls off her face. He wore jeans, an open Oxford shirt over a t-shirt, and pure raw emotion on his face as they said their parting words.

And no one who saw these pictures would ever believe she was not in love with him.

The accompanying article, though short, told the story with uncanny accuracy. They had her name, even spelled correctly. They had met on *All My Tomorrows*, where she is head writer. They were seen together frequently while he filmed in New Orleans (the implication being she had no reason to be on location there except to be with him). Then the last night, after their song, they were heard arguing in her hotel room, and he ran out without a shirt on. They met on the Moon Walk the next morning and mutually agreed to part ways. *At least in this version he didn't dump me.*

She needed Eileen. She called her number and it rolled to voicemail just as someone knocked.

"Alice, it's me," Mr. Peacock said through the door.

She closed her eyes and took a deep, steadying breath. "Come on in."

Closing the door behind him, he walked around the desk and placed a hand on her shoulder. "Are you OK?"

"Sure. Why wouldn't I be? All things considered, I think I look pretty good. There must have been a lot of photosho –"

"You know what I'm talking about. You have not been completely frank, and that's not like you. Do you care about Peter?"

She leaned over her desk – over the photographs – and dropped her head into her hands, covering her eyes. "I don't know. I'm so confused. I never entertained the possibility that he actually cared for me; and I spent so much time disliking him, I never considered that I even *could* care about him."

"Have you spoken to him?"

"Not since…these were taken."

"Call him."

"No. He wouldn't want to speak to me. I outlined for him precisely every quality of his that I despise – and they are all still true. He will always think he is better than me or you or anyone outside the upper echelons of the Hollywood elite. There isn't room for both me and his ego. I'll be fine. I just hate having all this aired in public. I'm surprised the tabloids haven't hunted me down for an exclusive."

"Well, they've actually tried to reach you, but Mrs. Jellyby and I have been fielding the calls."

"You're kidding."

"She was hoping you would do it, thinking it would help ratings, but I told her in no uncertain terms the answer is no. You are not in front of the camera. You are entitled to your privacy."

"Too bad *The Intruder* doesn't think so."

"You know, we can keep the photographers off the lot, but eventually they will find out where you live."

"I'm sure this will die down before then. Besides, I'll be leaving for Napa soon, although I was thinking of cancelling because of the way Giselle has been lately. I'm worried about her."

"Oh, Giselle will be fine."

"Well, keep an eye on Rich. I don't think he's good for her."

"Everyone will be fine. You need a few days away from here, out of L.A. When you get back, no one will even remember any of this thing with Peter."

The Edge of Darkness
Chapter 18

Robert had a castle. If I had known that sooner, I might have gone with him more eagerly. It was as if it had been taken out of an encyclopedia. He spent a lot of time explaining about being in the House of Lords and how he came to be a duke, how the castle had been passed down through the generations. He was a Knight of the Red Garter and several other orders passed to him from his father and his father's father and so on. It was all impressive, but it didn't make me love him.

I tried to reach Tony, but he wouldn't take my calls. I wrote the first of what would be hundreds of letters to him. If Robert had known I thought of Tony as something other than a brother, it would have devastated him.

Mother told me Tony would not take her calls either. He would only speak to Annette. He wanted nothing to do with his mother after finding out his parentage.

"Annette won't tell him the truth, that you aren't related," Mother said. "When she found out about the two of you…I think it made her resent you because you had gotten closer to Tony than she ever had. She is angry and bitter and full of hate for both you and me."

With twenty bedrooms, sleeping arrangements were not a problem, until the second night. I knew what Robert expected from me, and I had made him wait over a year and across an ocean. I had no reason to save myself for Tony anymore.

The servants had been dismissed early so we could have a romantic evening alone. After dinner, we sat on a sofa in the parlor drinking cognac. When we set our glasses down, we moved closer together, put our arms around each other, and started kissing. As Robert kissed and fondled my breasts, I recalled those nights in the back of Ben's car. Then my memory traced to that night when Ben had come to my bedroom, and Tony had burst in on us.

I could feel the beginnings of tears in my eyes. To block out the past, I started kissing Robert's neck. I took his face in my hands and looked into his eyes and said softly, "Love me."

He gently took my hands from his face and held them. "Come with me." He stood and pulled me up.

Robert led me to double doors, which he opened to reveal an enormous bedroom – larger than Mother's party room – and a bed to match. The room and the furniture were amazing, and he saw me caught up in their opulence.

"Every time a ruling body got new furniture, we got the old." He smiled and proceeded to the bed as I remained in the doorway.

"This was a baron's room a few hundred years ago." He lay across the bed horizontally, his feet still on the floor, and looked up at the painted ceiling and then at me. "This is the most fantastic bedroom in the entire house, and never once have I slept here. I have never so much as sat on this bed before."

He sat up and extended his arm out to me. I walked over and got up on the bed beside him, pulling my feet under me.

"They say that he was a very good baron but a very poor gentleman." I lay back with my arms over my head, and he reclined on his side, head on his hand, looking down at me. "According to the legend, he courted a beautiful contessa in hopes of winning her legacy, but she hated him with a passion because she could see right through him." He took my hand and rubbed it against his cheeks and lips. "But to resume friendly relations between their two families, she accepted his invitations to dinner." He started kissing my hand and fingers between words. "On one such occasion he drugged her wine and then led me to this bed and made love to her so she would be forced to marry him, which she did; but she refused to lie with him ever again, so he never had a legitimate heir. His plan backfired, for he fell in love with another woman but couldn't have her because of his wife. He had sacrificed the chance of love for wealth before he realized the great price he was paying."

We were silent a moment, both reflecting on the tale. "How sad," I said.

Robert reached behind him and turned off a lamp, leaving only the light from candles burning all around the room. He had planned this, I thought, but I was glad he had.

"And you've never made love before?" I shook my head. "Then let me make love to you."

He kissed me, his body to the side but his lips over mine. Then he pulled me up and slowly undressed me as we continued to kiss. I reclined vertically, naked before him, and he gently moved his fingers from the hollow at the base of my neck to my navel and then back again, and he traced that same path with tender kisses. He unbuttoned and removed his shirt, and he finished undressing as I got between the sheets. I closed my eyes until I felt his warm body beside me.

He squeezed me in his arms then loosened his grip enough to kiss me ardently. I held onto him as we kissed and arched my neck as he nibbled at it, savoring the pleasure. He stopped a moment, and I realized he was sheathing himself. When he turned back to me, slowly his hand traced my frame then grasped behind my knee as he moved on top of me. Without a word, he plunged inside of me.

With the pressure came pain, seeping into the walls of my inner self. The pressure continued to build as he moved until I reached the point where I thought I would burst. With this came the pang of memories, and I began to cry from the deep hurt of both.

Finally he stopped, but I still clung to him. "It's all right now, darling, it's over now."

No, it's not, I screamed in my head. It would never end. My love for Tony would always rule me. I knew he should have been my first. He should have been my only.

I regained my composure and looked into Robert's frantic face. "I'm all right now," I lied, echoing his words.

Relief replaced the worry on his countenance. "Thank God. I've never been with a virgin before. I promise, next time it will be better for you."

We snuggled together, and I rested my head on his chest as he ran his hand down my hair. He told me again and again how much he loved me, how happy he was that he finally had me with him. I began stroking his chest and running my fingers over each contour of his body. I kissed his chest and neck and whispered, "Make love to me again." He looked at me confused. "You said it would be better next time."

He smiled, then he chuckled and rolled on top of me. I could never be with my true love, but this was the closest I had ever felt to anyone.

Alice knocked on Giselle's dressing room door. "It's Alice. Can I come in?" After a lengthy pause, Giselle granted her permission to enter, and Alice closed the door behind her. Giselle sat at a dressing table facing the mirror, and Alice tried to catch her eye in the reflection.

"I feel like you've been avoiding me."

"Don't be ridiculous," Giselle said with a world-weariness Alice never would have expected from her.

"We haven't done anything together since the Olympics. Why don't you have dinner with Eileen and me tonight?"

"I already have plans with Rich."

"Of course. Rich."

Giselle finally lifted her face and met Alice's eyes in the mirror. "Yes, Rich. He and I are together now, and you need to get used to it."

"I just don't think he's good for you. You've been late for tapings several times now, you're having trouble with your lines, you've lost weight, and those dark circles under your eyes say you haven't been getting much sleep."

"OK, yes, we've been going out to clubs a lot, but I have been 'little miss responsible good girl' all my life. I'm just blowing off some steam. I'll try not to be late anymore."

"And what have you been doing to blow off steam?"

"What do you mean? Going out dancing."

"So Rich hasn't...you haven't been doing any drugs?"

Giselle's pale face blossomed with rosy cheeks, and she averted her eyes. "Yes, a little coke – but just a little. And X or molly a couple of times."

"Did Rich give it to you?"

Giselle's head jerked around, and she glared at Alice. "No, and why would you think such a thing?"

"Because you weren't using it before you and he got together."

"That's not altogether true. You know at the

Christmas party, we –"

"You know what I mean. Regularly – like a habit."

"It's not a habit. Rich didn't give me anything. He doesn't even use coke. A friend of his from Malibu gets it."

Malibu? "Well, will you lay off the party favors?"

Giselle sniffed and nodded.

"There's something else I needed to talk to you about. Jack called me a few days ago."

Giselle started but then turned back to the mirror. "Why would he be calling you?"

"Because he can't reach you. He says he's been calling and texting you for weeks."

"Why should I take his calls when he wouldn't take mine?"

"I know, but he wants to apologize and explain what happened. I think you should at least listen to him."

"Why? Nothing he could say would make a difference. I'm with Rich now."

"Well, you need to be careful with Rich. You don't know everything about him."

"And you do?"

"I know that he could hurt you."

"Not as badly as Jack did." Giselle pushed herself up from the dressing table and whirled around on Alice. "Look, I know you liked Rich, and maybe something could have gotten started; but you went off with Peter, and Jack went off with whoever, and Rich and I were there for each other. I'm sorry things didn't work out with you and Peter, but you had your chance with Rich and you didn't want him. You blew it. So get over it!"

"That's not –"

"I think you should go."

With an exasperated sigh, Alice turned and walked out but didn't make it twelve feet before she ran into Rich.

"And what have you been telling my lady love?" he asked, stepping close to her.

"I told her she needs to cut back on the partying because it is affecting production."

"And you think I'm responsible?"

"Do you deny it?"

"Just helping her mend her broken heart."

"Well, do your mending early enough so she's ready to tape."

She tried to pass, but he blocked her path in the narrow hallway. "I saw those pictures, Alice." He reached up and tucked her hair behind her ear and rubbed her cheek with his fist. "You try to pretend you aren't hurt, but I could see it in your eyes. He did break your heart. I can help you, too."

"What about Giselle?" As he ran his hand behind her neck, she was filled with disgust – not just with him but with herself for not being able to see through his slick shtick.

"I'll work it out with Giselle. She likes you. Once I've explained everything, she'll play along. I'm good with easing women's pain – especially pain caused by Walsingham."

She winced at the name and twisted out from his hand. "Can I get back to you on that?"

She pushed past him and walked straight to the writers' room. They had a storyline to revise.

CHAPTER 16

Eileen insisted they splurge and rent a convertible for their wine tasting tour of Napa Valley. Alice relented but had to wrap a scarf around her head to keep her hair out of her mouth.

"I think you look very French," Eileen said. "Very *je ne sais quoi*."

"Or very *Thelma and Louise*. And how can something be VERY *je ne sais quoi*?"

"I don't know, Alice. We're on vacation! Don't be copy-editing me – even in your head."

Alice had to admit the open-air enhanced the experience of driving along the Silverado Trail viewing the spectacular landscapes of row after row of grapevines with hills and mountains in the distance. After L.A., Napa seemed like another planet – or at least another continent. They stopped at the wineries they had mapped out on the route, and that evening she arrived at their resort deliciously tipsy.

Alice checked in with Peacock, and he assured her the only drama had occurred on set.

"So I take it Rich doesn't know yet," she said.

"No, we are going to wait until the last possible moment when he absolutely must see the script."

"I don't blame you there. Good luck! I'm almost sorry to miss it!"

Day two proceeded much as day one but on a different highway and with different wineries, except Alice detected a subtle change in Eileen. Whereas they had planned it as a wine *tasting* trip, Eileen actually developed an interest in the production. After she had tasted all the samples, Alice would wander outside to inhale the beauty of the vineyard while Eileen talked yeast and bottling.

The third winery on the third day offered some of the best wines they had had on the trip, as well as a host more than willing to provide a few extra samples. As he and Eileen launched into a discussion of varietals, Alice said she would be outside.

"The house on the property is incredible," she said. "Would they mind if I got a closer look." He offered no objection, so out she went.

She wound along the paths in the direction of the villa – no other word would do it justice – which turned out to be much farther than she had thought. Since Eileen clearly would not want to leave anytime soon, Alice pressed onward. She hadn't made it quite two-thirds of the way when she came upon the last thing she expected to find in a vineyard – a little girl sitting alone under a large fig tree. The child watched her approach, so Alice had no choice but to acknowledge her.

"Hello," Alice said and kept walking.

"What's your name?"

Damn. So close. She turned to the girl. "Alice."

"Like *Alice in Wonderland*?"

"That's right. What's your name?"

"Britney. How old are you?"

"How old are you?"

"Seven."

"Then you are old enough to learn not to ask a lady her age," Alice said smiling, and the little girl grinned back. "Seven is a scary number."

"Why?"

"Because seven ate nine." The little girl giggled. "What are you doing sitting under this tree?"

"Waiting."

"This is a good place for that – nice shade. Waiting for what?"

"My parents to find me. They're talking."

"Where are your parents?"

Britney pointed at the main house.

"You live there?" The little girl nodded. *Holy crap!* "Then perhaps you won't mind if I ate one of your figs." Britney shook her head, and Alice reached up and plucked two ripe figs nestled together. "Do you want one?"

"They haven't been washed."

Alice examined the figs. "Well, they look clean enough to me." She grabbed a few more then sat down next to the girl.

"Alice in Wonderland sat under a tree, too," her new friend said.

"And this fig says, 'Eat me.'" After Alice took a bite and did not drop dead, Britney accepted one and bit into it. "That's a beautiful house. You must love living there."

She shrugged. "Not really."

"I would love to live in a house like that."

"I want to live in Hollywood and be a movie star!"

Naturally. Alice finished one fig, and – sleepy from the walk and the wine – leaned against the tree and bit into a second. "Do your parents know you're out here?"

"No."

"Then how do you know they will find you?"

"My daddy will find me. He says he loves *Alice in Wonderland*, so he will know to look for me under a tree."

"Don't you think you should have told them you were leaving?"

"I don't like it when they talk about the divorce."

Just as Alice thought she was getting the picture, someone came out from behind the tree, and the little girl jumped up.

"Daddy!"

"Peter." Alice couldn't be sure if she had actually spoken aloud since her heart had lodged in her throat the moment she saw his face.

"Daddy! Her name is Alice, just like in Wonderland – and she's sitting under a tree!"

Her appearance had stunned him as well, and he only managed to say, "Yes."

Britney continued to jump around and say words that Alice could not hear through the fog of shock as she and Peter stared at each other. She felt so exposed under his scrutiny, she wanted to grab some of the fig leaves to cover herself.

"What are you doing here?" he asked, but not in the accusatory tone she would have expected – just gentle curiosity.

"I've come to kidnap your daughter and hold her ransom for wine and figs."

Britney tugged on his arm. "Daddy, Alice gave me figs and didn't wash them, and we ate them."

"Oh, really?" he asked, glancing from daughter to former-almost lover.

"I like to live on the edge. Sorry to have been a bad influence on your daughter."

"I doubt that's possible."

She wiped the fig juice off on the skirt of her light dress and started to push herself up from the ground when he offered his hand. She took it, and he pulled her to her feet.

"So you won't tell me why you're here?" he asked with his eyes fixed on hers.

"Eileen and I are taking a little vacation, touring vineyards. She's still in there talking grapes. I should get back to her." Only then did he release her hand.

"Yes, I should take Britney back to her mother."

"I won't keep you. Britney, it was very nice meeting you."

"Bye." The little girl waved, and Alice turned and walked away as fast as she dared.

Oh, God. Oh, God. Oh, God. She could not believe what had just happened. *Of all the vineyards in the world, and he had to walk into – Oh, God! This must be* his *vineyard!* She had no idea who owned the winery – his name wasn't on the label – but he would never believe that. He would think she'd tracked him down deliberately. *For what? To try to get him back? Shit, he really might think I planned to kidnap his daughter.*

She had walked quickly and with her head down and arms across her chest and hadn't paid attention to the paths until she realized she had gone the wrong way. She stumbled around some more until she decided she would never find the right path and would just have to march through the grapevines or die in the middle of Peter's vineyard. *They'll find my body and say I just couldn't live without him.*

"Alice." His voice filled her with trepidation and relief, since at least he would know how to get her the hell out of there. "Where are you going?"

She fixed a smile upon her face before turning around. "I was about to sacrifice myself to Bacchus. I seem to have gotten hopelessly lost. Could you tell me which path to take?"

After all the publicity and the photos of them in the tabloids, Alice thought he would want to get her off his property as soon as possible, but he said, "How 'bout I walk with you?"

As they began to walk, she searched the catalog of her brain for any topic they could discuss that would not be attached to a painful memory.

"So this is your vineyard?"

He laughed. "No, not hardly. It's beautiful, though. I wouldn't mind living out here. It belongs to my wife's…my *ex*-wife's boyfriend. She and my daughter have been living here since we split."

She wondered if it was the man from his wife's affair. "Your daughter is charming."

"She thought the same about you."

"I…you know I had no idea she was your daughter. I wasn't trying –"

"No, I know. It's just a coincidence, a happy one. I hope it is for you as well."

She felt a flutter in her heart or her stomach or both. Here she had believed she would be the last person he would want to see, and he called their chance meeting a "happy coincidence."

"Where are you staying?" he asked.

"The Veritas. You?" *No! Why did I ask him that? He'll think I want know.*

"I've actually rented a small house not far from here."

"To spend time with your daughter?"

"That's right. How long have you and Eileen been here?"

"Since day before yesterday."

"What do you think of the area?"

"I love it. It's so beautiful – so different from Southern California. Reminds me of Tuscany."

"You've been to Italy?"

"Yes, a few times with my mother. She loved it. This is like my Tuscany away from home. Except Tuscany is really Tuscany away from home. I don't know what the reverse of that would be. I'm sorry, I'm not making much sense. That's the problem with tasting really good wine – I don't want to spit."

He laughed softly. "No, I think you make perfect sense. Like a little piece of Tuscany here at home. I agree. I am seriously considering finding a place out here."

"What about your house in the Hollywood Hills? Or would you keep it as well?"

"No, you've seen that house. It's too big for one man. I think I'm ready to get away from L.A."

"Really? You'll start a vineyard, open a winery?"

"Oh, no, none of that. Just the house. Although I might try to find one with a fig tree."

They had arrived at the winery, and Eileen's expression as she watched them emerge made it seem as though zombies had walked out of the vineyard.

Peter offered her an abbreviated hug and a kiss on

the cheek. "Good to see you, Eileen."

"What…what…what?"

"We just ran into each other," Alice said. "I couldn't figure out how to get back here, so Peter showed me the way out. Are you finished with your wine lesson?"

Eileen had not yet recovered and only nodded as she continued to gape at them.

Alice turned to Peter, thought of offering her hand to shake but decided that would feel too awkward. "Good seeing you again, Peter. Thanks for showing me the way. Maybe I'll see you again some time with another happy coincidence."

They were almost to the car when Peter walked up behind them and said, "Wait," and Alice turned to face him. "It doesn't have to be a happy coincidence. I mean, we don't necessarily have to wait for the next coincidence. Jack is coming in town this evening. Would you consider dinner? The four of us?"

Alice couldn't move or speak, paralyzed by the invitation. Eileen stepped in. "Yes, I would love to see Jack again, and you and I could catch up. Why don't you tell me when and where, and we'll meet you there."

"Would you like to go to Alsace Aquitaine?"

Alice shook herself out of her stupor. "You have reservations there tonight?"

"Not yet."

"I thought you had to make reservations two months in advance."

"Is that a yes?" She nodded. "I'll see you at eight?"

They agreed by silent assent and climbed in the car.

All the way to the resort, Eileen interrogated Alice and demanded to know every detail about what had occurred at the vineyard, and Alice did her best to satisfy her.

"Do you want to know the variety of fig? I think they were mission but I'm not sure."

"I know it must have been so uncomfortable for both of you."

"Yes. Especially at first."

"If you would rather not go tonight, I'll call and cancel. I completely understand."

"What? And miss out on probably our only chance to eat at Alsace Aquitaine?"

"I'm serious, Alice."

She said nothing a moment, silently recounting each glance and every emotion elicited. "No. I want to go."

"Are you sure? Do you really want to go?"

"Yes, I really do."

Alice and Eileen arrived at the restaurant and were led outside to the courtyard. Peter had arranged for a table for four to be set up for their own private dining. Both men greeted Eileen with a kiss on the cheek, but only Jack offered one to Alice, which made her wonder if Peter held a grudge after all, despite the invitation and his behavior at the vineyard.

Jack wanted to know everything going on with *All My Tomorrows,* but Alice hesitated because of the pending lawsuit as well as everything she had said the night she and Peter fought. Eileen jumped in with all the latest news and gossip about the cast and crew, since Alice had kept her up to speed on all the events since she left the show, but they all avoided any mention of Giselle.

"And how is Mrs. Jellyby?" Jack asked. "Are the ratings going her way?"

"No," Alice answered. "They've been on a steady decline since we returned from the Olympics, but we're optimistic about a new storyline we are introducing."

"What do you have up your sleeve?"

"You know I can't reveal the storyline of a soap opera!" They all groaned and prodded until she relented. "As long as you promise it won't leave this table. We have decided Brother Raife is not a good match for Sienna after all."

"Do you mean you're writing Rich out of the show?" Eileen asked.

"For the most part, yes." Alice glanced at Peter, who stared silently at her from under a raised brow.

"So are you killing him off?" Jack asked.

"No. He's being ordained." All four of them burst out laughing. "Would you believe that son-of-a-bitch had it in his contract that his character could not be killed off for three years? So he will be taking his final vows. I think the ordination will make for riveting television – and all the turmoil he has gone through before choosing God over Sienna."

"And how did he take the news?"

"I have no idea. They weren't telling him until today." They laughed and congratulated her for wisely being out of town.

"Of course," Peter said, "it's not quite as bad as being her brother."

"I hope you aren't still holding a grudge about that," Alice said.

He peered into her eyes until she thought her heart

had stopped beating. "No. You were right. It was an inspired twist – no one saw it coming. I don't hold any grudges...about anything."

Alice couldn't be sure what happened in the moments she and Peter sat staring at each other, but she imagined some sort of sign language passed between Eileen and Jack since they were simultaneously overcome by exhaustion.

"I am really wiped out after the flight up here," Jack said with a dramatic yawn. *An hour flight?*

"Yeah, going to all these wineries has worn me out. I think I'm going to have to call it a night."

Clearly alarmed, Peter looked back and forth from Eileen to Alice. "But you can't go yet. We just opened this bottle of wine!"

Alice sat frozen with her mouth slightly open, not comprehending the conversation around her.

"No, I'm sorry, Peter, I'm just beat," Jack said standing up from the table, "but I don't want to spoil the evening for everyone. You stay and enjoy the wine."

Then Eileen pushed her chair back. "Jack, I can give you a ride. Peter, you don't mind bringing Alice back to her cottage. Do you?"

He had barely shaken his head before the pair disappeared into the night, leaving Alice still unsure of what had just happened.

"For being so exhausted," she said, "they sure ran out of here."

"Do...do you want me to take you to your room? If you're uncomfortable..."

"Are you kidding? We have a bottle of Bordeaux to drink." She smiled, but he did not smile back. "Unless you feel uncomfortable."

"Alice, I can honestly say there is no place in the world I would rather be right at this moment."

She wasn't sure if she was about to implode or melt or both. His words gripped her chest so tightly she lost her breath.

The wait staff ran out and efficiently transformed the setting to a table for two then disappeared, with a word from Peter that he would call them if they needed anything, leaving them as the only two people in the candlelit courtyard under the glittering night sky.

He poured the wine himself and handed her a glass. "I want you to know, I did not arrange this. I mean, for you and me to be left alone together."

"I know you didn't."

"But I can't say I'm sorry."

She stalled for time by drinking her wine. "I have to admit, I am rather surprised by that. After the way we left things in New Orleans."

"Let's just leave all that in New Orleans. We're here now."

"I do thank you for arranging this amazing dinner under the stars."

"I know how you enjoy courtyards."

"How do you know that?"

"Because even though you were so miserable from the heat and humidity, you always wanted to sit out on the courtyard. Here you have it with no heat and no humidity."

"And no paparazzi."

He squeezed his eyes shut before returning them to her. "Alice, I am so, so sorry about the photos in *The Intruder*."

"It wasn't your fault. I'm the one who elected to

sit in a public place."

"But you didn't know I would follow you there."

"Hey, I thought we were going to forget about New Orleans. It's so beautiful here."

"Do you really think so?"

"Of course. Who wouldn't?"

"But you would never want to leave L.A. Would you?"

"Are you kidding? In a New York minute. I'm a writer – I could certainly do that better someplace like this. I'm only in L.A. because of a job writing, even if it is for a soap. I'm not like you, Peter. I'm not part of that Hollywood culture and the Southern California lifestyle."

"I don't think I'm like me either." He took a sip of his wine while Alice puzzled over his cryptic remark, but before she could ask him to explain, he said, "Alice, there's something I need to talk to you about."

"Is it what you needed to talk to me about in New Orleans?"

"No, forget all about that. Remember – no more New Orleans. I've already told Jack this, but I wanted to be sure it wouldn't upset you."

"Oh, for the love of God! Just say it! The build-up is killing me!"

"You don't think we should cut for a commercial break?" He grinned. "Tag you in a close-up?" She playfully punched him in the arm then realized it was their first physical contact since he had helped her up at the vineyard. That light punch must have broken down some barrier because he took her hand in both of his. "Alice, I'm going to tell my lawyer to drop the lawsuit. I want to come back to *All My Tomorrows* and finish out my contract. I'll stay for a full story arc if you let me. But I don't want to do anything that will cause you any kind of discomfort or embarrassment."

If she had devoted every cell in her brain to predicting what he would say, she would not have come to that conclusion. "Peter, do you mean it? Are you sure? You'll stay through sweeps? That could save the show!" A smile broke across her face.

"So you're OK with it?"

"Of course! Why wouldn't I be?"

"I didn't know how you would feel working with me again after…all that has happened. Plus, with the paparazzi, you know there will be speculation. People might think that you and I…"

"I can think of worse fates than being mistaken for a movie star's girlfriend." She pulled her hand free from his and wrapped her arms around his neck without even thinking. "Thank you. I would put up with all manner of mortification to save those jobs."

Resting his hands on her upper arms, he did not hug her back. After too many seconds, humiliated by her impetuous reaction, she released him, sat back, and drank her wine. He wiped his brow and took a sip from his glass, too, and the silence fell over them like a hot New Orleans night. *No! No more New Orleans!*

"I'm sorry, Peter. Now I've made *you* uncomfortable. I'm just so happy and so grateful, you have no idea. In fact, for a split second I thought you were telling me that so I'd sleep with you."

"Would it have worked?" he asked quickly.

"I guess we'll never know."

He smiled and shook his head. "No, I wouldn't want you that way. I wouldn't want you to sleep with me out of gratitude or pity."

She barked out a laugh that startled him. "I'm sorry, but the very idea that someone would sleep with Peter Walsingham out of *pity* is an inherently ridiculous proposition."

They eased back into the relaxed banter of earlier that evening and spoke of his daughter and traded anecdotes from their own childhoods. They discussed their mutual fondness for French literature and how she had managed to get a degree in it and still couldn't communicate with a Parisian cab driver. They talked until the bottle had been depleted and they had no excuse to stay. The quick car trip required minimal conversation and nothing to strain their imaginations. Then he pulled the car into the gravel drive way and put it in park, and they were silent.

"Would you like to come in for a nightcap?" she asked, then realized she had nothing to drink in her room.

He kept his hands on the steering wheel and his eyes straight ahead. "I can't."

Oh. "All right then." She unbuckled her seatbelt.

"Eileen said you are in a cottage?"

"Yes, just around the main building."

He turned off the engine. "I'll see you to your door."

Neither spoke as they walked on the narrow path to her cottage or when she unlocked the door. She turned back to face him, unsure what to do or say.

"Thank you for a magical evening," she said.

"But magic isn't real. Is it? It's all an illusion."

She couldn't tell if she detected bitterness in his tone or defeat, but either way it squeezed her heart and made her eyes burn.

"Good night." She moved to embrace him, a kiss on the cheek; but he grasped her arms and held her back, and she didn't know how long she could stave off the tears. "I suppose a part of you must hate me."

He shook his head gently without taking his eyes from hers. His grip tightened on one arm as he raised his other hand to the side of her face and swept his thumb from her temple, down her cheek, to her lips. As he rubbed his thumb on her lower lip, her heartbeats and breaths quickened, and her eyes slid shut. He rolled his thumb all around her lips, inside and out, sending a current of desire through her core until she thought she might burst if he didn't kiss her.

His thumb still against her lip, he leaned his forehead against hers and spoke with a low ragged breath. "Alice, I can't. I can't kiss you."

Why not? She thought the words but could not speak, too wrapped up in the sensations he aroused in her.

"If I kiss you, I won't be able to stop. I won't stop kissing you. And I won't stop with just kissing you. I will have to make love to you, and you won't be able to stop me. Not again. Do you understand what I am saying, Alice? If I kiss you, I will not be able to stop until I have had you, completely, and nothing you say or do will do any good. If I kiss you, I *will* make love to you. Do you understand?"

She nodded as much as their position allowed. Then his thumb stopped its ministrations and he held his hand on her cheek, and she said, "Kiss me."

And he did. He pulled her body hard against his and stabbed his fingers into her hair as his mouth covered hers, plunging his tongue in with the first savage embrace. She tried to kiss him back, but he controlled it, his hunger overwhelming them both, and she surrendered fully.

He pushed her back through the open door and reached behind him to close it. In that moment, she dropped her purse and curled her arm around his neck to pull him closer, bring him deeper, as their mouths melded into one. He snaked his arm around her back, tightening his hold as if she might float away, which she thought she very well may. Then with a quick twist and a move she thought he must have used in a movie, he had her off her feet and in his arms. Without breaking the kiss, he hesitated in his steps before carrying her into the bedroom, dark except for the light from the moon and an outside lamp streaming in through the French doors. He laid her on the bed, and only then did he pull his mouth from hers.

Without taking his eyes off her, he kicked off his shoes and unbuttoned his shirt. She sat up as he did so, and once he had divested himself of his shirt, he leaned around and pulled the zipper down her back. He took her hand just long enough to bring her to her feet, then he pushed her dress off her shoulders and arms, and it fell into a puddle on the floor. As he reached over to turn down the bed, she stepped out of her dress and shoes and stood only in her lingerie. He turned and took her into his arms again then fell with her upon the bed, crushing their bodies together and his mouth upon hers.

She touched him, wherever she could, running her fingers through his hair and her hands down his neck and back, as their mouths moved together. When he rolled over, he brought her with him, their lips still sealed, and she ran her hands over his chest as he unfastened her bra. They worked together to free her arms of its straps, and he tossed it away. Then they lay on their sides, chest to chest, their hands roaming as they continued to kiss. His fingers traced a path from her neck to her breast and lingered there, making her cognizant that he had never actually touched her breast before, which thrilled her that much more.

After an excruciatingly light pass over her nipple, his hand continued its journey and touched her over the thin silk between her legs, rippling shockwaves out like from the epicenter of an earthquake. He worked his fingers under the waistband, and she trembled when he fondled her feminine flesh and whimpered into his mouth as he rhythmically touched her inside and out. Tension coiled in her womb until he stopped and pulled his mouth and hand away from her. His breathing heavy, he gazed at her as he eased her back against the mattress and held himself over her. Working his way down her body, he kissed her forehead, the hollow of her throat, and between her breasts. He placed a kiss on her navel and then just above the lace waistband before inching the silk and lace over her hips and down her legs, exposing her shadowed form to him completely. He rolled off the bed and stood devouring her with his eyes in the dimly lit room as he unbuckled his belt and removed his slacks.

He climbed back into bed and took her face in his hands, allowing no escape as he joined their lips and teeth and tongues in another deep embrace. When he ended the kiss, he lifted his head and traced her features with his eyes as he caressed her cheeks with his thumbs.

"I think you *are* in love with me, Alice. You're just afraid to admit it."

Without waiting for a reply or admission, he brought his lips to hers in gentle, lingering kisses. He maneuvered between her legs, kissed her once more, then held her eyes with his as he pushed inside of her. She gasped and her eyes closed with the welcome intrusion. He didn't move at first; he held steady there, being one with her, still watching her when her eyes opened, and nothing had ever felt so perfect, so complete. In that moment, she knew he was right. She was in love with him. Desperately. Madly. Violently.

He moved within her in a slow, languid tempo, punctuating each stroke with a soft kiss as if intending to tattoo the moment on her memory. He had not lied. He had said he would make love to her, and this could be called nothing less – not sleeping together or having sex or intercourse or screwing. With each thrust, he pushed her deeper and deeper, with the well of emotion overflowing until a tear trickled from her eye. He didn't ask why, only wiped it away with his thumb and kissed her lips again.

A force more powerful than gravity held her against the bed, but her skin tingled and her limbs felt light enough to fly, like a lead zeppelin. With such a relaxed pace, she didn't think she could ever come – not that she cared – but even in this he knew her better than she knew herself. The sudden spark ignited a fuse wielding through her and took her by surprise, and with little warning she exploded and cried out. When she did, he claimed her mouth with the deep, probing kisses that drove her insane; and as her tremors subsided, he convulsed within her.

He rolled to his side, taking his weight off her, and

they lay in silence caressing each other with their fingers, lips, and eyes. They made love twice more through the night; bathed each other in the garden tub; with wonderment, explored the other's body with hands, lips, teeth, and tongue. They said very little, no words of endearment of declarations of love, perhaps both afraid they might say something to break the spell woven around them. Instead, their bodies spoke for them, giving voice to every ineffable emotion.

CHAPTER 17

Although they had fallen asleep entangled with one another the night before – or, more accurately, earlier that morning – Alice awoke in her typical sleep position, curled on her side, with her back to Peter. She rolled over and found him sleeping flat on his back. The sight of him in the daylight, so peaceful and beautiful, sent a tremor of memories of their lovemaking from her core through to her face, enflaming her cheeks. She was smitten.

Should I wake him? She considered cuddling up against his chest, or maybe waking him with a kiss. She ultimately decided to tend to practicalities and then wake him up. That might also allow her to determine when and how to tell him. *Maybe I should wait until next time he says it.* But he hadn't said it again, not since "that night." The way he said she was afraid to admit it implied he expected her to tell him when she could.

She continued to ponder as she padded into the kitchenette in her thin robe to wrangle with the pitiful excuse for a coffee pot and to figure out how to get a decent cup using the premeasured filter disks. Glancing at the clock, she wondered why she hadn't heard from Eileen to begin their next tour since it was nearly noon but then realized she had dropped her purse by the door with her phone in it. She had low expectations for the coffee as she pushed the button, but she could always order room service. *Perhaps that's part of their devious scheme to get us to pay fourteen dollars for a pot of coffee.*

She retrieved her phone. *Thirty-seven missed calls!* Twenty were from Mr. Peacock, and most of the others were numbers she didn't recognize. *Oh, no. This is not good.* Her heart rate accelerated and nausea clogged her throat. Fourteen voicemails, but she didn't have the patience for that. She hoped someone from the show had texted her, as Mr. Peacock assuredly would not.

Last text received a few minutes before from Eileen.

> Still in bed? Wanted to see if you two wanted to break for lunch maybe dinner ;)

Eileen had texted earlier as well, asking Alice to call when she woke up but not to rush.

Skimming over the other forty messages, she noted one pervading theme. They couldn't find Giselle. *Have you talked to Giselle? Walked off the set yesterday. Never showed up today.* She scrolled down to see if she had any texts from Giselle – none. She pulled up her email – nothing there either. She called Mr. Peacock.

"Oh, thank God. Why haven't you been answering your phone?"

"I was sleeping. It was in my purse. Have you heard from her?"

"Didn't you listen to my voicemail?"

"Of course I did not listen to your voicemail! No one listens to voicemails! Just tell me!"

"Rich was not happy to read about Raife's ordination."

"No surprise there."

"First he demanded to know where you are."

"I hope you didn't tell him."

"Of course not!"

"What happened with Giselle?"

"Rich walked off the set, and Giselle went with him."

Before Alice could scream as she would have liked, Peter walked in with a towel wrapped around his waist and curious concern pouring from his face. "I'm sorry," she said to him. "Did I wake you?"

"Who are you talking to?" Mr. Peacock asked.

She ignored the question. "When did this happen?"

"Yesterday morning."

"Did Giselle have any scenes to tape?"

"Yes, but they were with Rich, so we didn't think much of it. Today, though, she had an early call and never showed up, and no one can find her."

"She has been staying out late a lot recently; maybe she's still in bed."

"Alice, I drove out there. She's not at home. Her door was unlocked, and it looked like she had left in a hurry. And…there was a mirror on the table. Looked like cocaine. We can't find her or Rich."

Shitshitshitshitshit. She covered half her face with her hand. "OK, it's noon now. See if they can get me on a flight to L.A. around four."

She ended the call and tore past Peter back into the bedroom, yanking out her suitcase. "I'm sorry. I have to go. Giselle is missing."

"Missing? What's going on?"

"Lemme call Eileen."

Eileen answered with, "Well, hello, sleepyhead!"

"I have to go back to L.A. this afternoon. Giselle is missing. I hate to cut into your vacation. You don't have to come, but –"

"Of course I'm going with you!"

"OK, good. I was hoping you'd say that."

"I'm having lunch with Jack, but we'll leave right now."

Crap! Crap! Crap! "Don't tell Jack what's going on. Giselle would kill me if he knew. Why don't you call Peacock – he can get you on my flight."

When she hung up, Peter had pulled on his pants and was putting on his shirt. "What happened?"

She ran around the room like a madwoman throwing clothes onto her suitcase and scrambling for her toiletries. "This is all my fault. I never should have left. I knew he wouldn't take it well but –"

"Who are you talking about?"

"Rich! When Jack dumped Giselle, Rich was right there to swallow her up. I tried to warn her about him, but she wouldn't listen – thought I was jealous! And I couldn't tell her the truth!"

"So Giselle is with Rich?"

"As soon as he found out about the change for his character – also my fault – he stormed off the set and Giselle went with him. No one has heard from her since." She had nearly finished packing then glanced down at her robe and began digging through the suitcase for something to wear on the plane. "Peter, if someone finds out she's using drugs, her image as Sienna is ruined, and so is *All My Tomorrows.* She couldn't be the girl-next-door if she's powdering her nose."

"You know she's using drugs?"

"She said just a little coke, and she swore she didn't get it from Rich and he wouldn't even touch the stuff, but Peacock found a mirror with it in her house."

"It could have been ketamine. It looks like coke."

"Ugh! I should have tried harder to convince her he would drag her down, but I couldn't tell her about Winnie; and I was afraid if I pushed too hard, she would tell him and he would go to the press. I should have written him out of the show as soon as I found out. I knew he wouldn't take the script changes well, but I had no idea...But after what he said to me, I knew I had to do something!"

Now completely dressed, Peter stood in the doorway watching her fly around the room like a Dervish. "What did he say to you?"

"He said he was mending Giselle's broken heart, and he could mend mine, too."

"Why would he think you had a broken heart?"

She stopped and faced him. "The pictures, Peter! The pictures in *The Intruder!*"

He flinched and squeezed his eyes shut a moment, then he stepped forward and grasped her shoulders. "I know you need to get back to L.A., and I'm doing nothing here but distracting you while you try to pack. I'll go and let you finish." He placed a kiss on her forehead. "Goodbye, Alice."

As she stood stunned, glued in place, he walked out without another sound except the door closing behind him. Comprehension dawning, she ran out of the cottage barefoot and in her robe, but she only made it to the parking lot in time to see him driving away. She slumped back to her room to find she had locked herself out.

The Edge of Darkness
Chapter 20

Robert continued to ask me to marry him and I continued to say no. I told him I couldn't give up my dream of acting, which I would certainly have to do as his duchess. Although in my mind I told myself that Tony and I would never be together, my heart still held out hope that one day he would respond to one of my letters.

Robert moved us to London so I could pursue my stage career. I wondered if he thought I would fail in the West End and then agree to marry him, but I didn't. In the two-hundred year-old tradition, I became an actress and mistress to a wealthy benefactor. After performing in a few plays and a variety show at the Theatre Royal, I was cast in the lead in a small British film. This then led to another film role in France, and Robert followed me to Paris.

Then I got my first part in an American film, *Tainted*. I was going back to the US for the first time in almost five years. At first, Robert was upset and tried to talk me out of it, but then he agreed to go on location with me in New York.

Near the end of the shoot, Mother joined us in New York and came to our hotel suite to meet the duke for the first time. After the introductions and her word to call him Robert and not Your Grace, I asked what I most wanted to know.

"Have you talked to Tony?"

"No, only your sister has, and she won't tell him anything. Oh, Lexie, she is sick in the head. She needs help."

"I need to make a few overseas calls," Robert said, "if you'll excuse me."

"Thank you," I said as he went to the bedroom, since I knew he only wanted to allow us privacy to discuss "family matters."

I sat close to her on the couch. "What's wrong with Annette?"

"I don't know. I feel like I have failed as a mother. Tony wants nothing to do with his whore of a mother, and Annette is a pathological liar. I am so glad I have you. At least I know you are doing well, even though I never see you."

"Tell me more about Annette."

"She hates you and me so much, it is incomprehensible. She hates me for cheating on her father and for adopting you. She says Tony is her brother, and she will not share him with you. She has told him wicked things about you."

"Could you elaborate?"

"She told him you have been sleeping with men to further your career, that you are with the duke for his money and connections. She told him...she told him that you knew that you and he are brother and sister even before you slept together. That you only did it because of his inheritance since Molly had not adopted you."

"Tony would never believe that."

"I have no idea which of her lies he believes."

"I know he would never believe that. Besides, we never slept together."

"But I saw you!"

"Shhh...Robert can never know any of this. You interrupted us."

"Well, Tony believes enough of her lies not to want to have any contact with you. I am glad you are moving on with Robert. You have no future with Tony."

I don't know why I didn't cry. Perhaps I had shed all my tears, but my heart ached. "Has he? Has Tony moved on?"

"I've occasionally seen him photographed with women. I've never heard of an engagement, but that doesn't necessarily mean...He's running for the Senate now, so in that way he has moved on."

That night, when Robert asked me to marry him after we made love, as he often did, I said yes. I had given up my dream of being with Tony, and I was ready to give up my dream of being an actress. Two days later, he held a small reception in the hotel to formally announce our engagement. There he presented me with an engagement ring with the biggest diamond I had ever seen. I acted thrilled. I acted happy. Then I realized that I would probably be acting for the rest of my life after all.

On our last day in the US, I caught the news on the telly and saw Tony's face for the first time in seven years. I went completely numb. The reporters screamed questions at him, asking him about his senatorial campaign.

"Mr. Hollingsworth, how do you feel about the upcoming election?"

"I am cautiously optimistic. I think the people of my state know that I want to carry out my father's legacy."

"Mr. Hollingsworth, do you think your sister

renouncing her citizenship will hurt your campaign?"

He looked confused. "What? Annette renounced her citizenship?"

"No, Alexandra Hollingsworth."

He looked like he fell into the same trance that had captured me. "Lexie," he said quietly, more to himself than the reporters.

"You haven't heard that she's marrying an English duke?"

He said nothing as camera flashes bounced off his face.

"Mr. Hollingsworth, do you think this will hurt you in any way?"

"No comment," he said and walked away.

Robert and I were married the next spring. At my insistence, we had a small, private ceremony at his castle. I did not want Tony to be besieged with questions about why he hadn't attended the "royal wedding" or open the newspaper to a full photo spread.

Then in August, everything changed.

Robert found me in the library. "Darling, I have just had the most interesting call from my secretary." He sat beside me and took my hand, and I wondered what kind of news his secretary would report that he would worry about telling me. "She said she was contacted by Senator Hollingsworth's office, your brother Tony."

I held my breath. "Is something wrong?"

"No, darling, I should have said at the first, everyone is fine. It seems he is coming to London, some sort of official junket, and he would like to see you."

I felt so dizzy, I thought I would faint. "What? Why? Why now after all these years?"

"Alexandra, I know you have never wanted to tell me why you and your mother are estranged from your brother, so I didn't know how you would feel about him coming here."

"Here?"

"Yes, they would like to keep the visit private. It sounds like perhaps your brother has never spoken of your estrangement in public, and they thought it might look peculiar if he were to come to England and not see his sister."

"I…see."

"What shall I tell them? Shall we invite him?"

I only thought for a moment. "Yes."

Another day passed with still no word from Giselle – or Peter. Alice stared at her phone and willed it to vibrate, but she couldn't decide whom she wanted to hear from more. *No, of course Giselle!* The show, her career, her life were all in jeopardy. *But why won't Peter call?*

Come to think of it, he's never called or texted me. Maybe he didn't have her number. Of course, if anyone could get her number, he could. She played with her phone and toyed with the idea of calling him herself, but she couldn't understand what had happened to make him leave so abruptly that morning. He wasn't distracting her that much from packing. After this incredible night of lovemaking, for him to walk out like that made no sense. She could not have misinterpreted what had happened between them that badly. *Could I?*

The way he touched her and talked to her – *had it*

all been an act? She would have to go back and watch all of his movies to be sure. Had it all been some elaborate scheme to get her into bed? *But why me? I'm nobody. He could have beautiful women lined up for him. He certainly went to an awful lot of effort. Jack would have had to be in on it, too.* She rolled her eyes at herself. *Yes, it's this great conspiracy to bed you, Alice! He probably followed you to Napa and hired an actress to play his daughter. The Illuminati is probably involved as well!*

No, something had happened that morning to make him walk out. *Was he afraid he would be caught up in this All My Tomorrows drug scandal? Does he think I am a terrible person for letting this happen? Does he...does he think I slept with Rich?*

She couldn't think about any of that right now. She had a script to rewrite. She stuffed her traitorous cell phone in her pocket and strolled out of her office to where the others were sitting Shiva for the show.

"I don't suppose anyone has heard anything." The glum faces rendered her statement redundant. "OK, enough moping. Let's get busy! I think this murder mystery is a great idea! We haven't had a good murder on the show in a couple of years."

"What are the other characters going to say about Sienna?"

"That will be part of the mystery! Everyone will ask if anyone has seen Sienna, dramatic music, viewers are hooked!" She exaggerated her enthusiasm and optimism in hopes of energizing the crew, but their expressions reflected her true feelings. If something didn't happen soon, they were going to start jumping ship, saving themselves before they were drowned like rats in a sea of unemployment.

"What if Giselle never comes back?"

"Then during sweeps, they will find a decomposed body. Everyone will be glued to their TVs while waiting for the dental records."

"And if she does come back?"

"Sienna's been through a lot – she needed time to think. She went on a religious retreat. She was going to be a nun, after all." They remained unconvinced. "Come on. This is not over! It's not over until we say it's over! Was it over when the German's bombed Pearl Harbor?" No response. "Really? None of you has seen *Animal House*?" They gawked at her as if she were covered in purple spots. "I give up."

Alice marched on toward the writers' room when she spotted Mrs. Jellyby in her path. She almost turned around to avoid her but then thought better of it.

"Hi, Mrs. Jellyby. How's everything going?"

Mrs. Jellyby shook her head and quivered, and her eyes threatened an onslaught of tears. "Oh, Alice. I just don't know. I don't know. I was just talking to the writers. Do you really think this serial killer will work?"

"Well, if I didn't think it would work, I wouldn't have thought of it. Would I?" Before Mrs. Jellyby could consider the logic of that statement, Alice asked, "Have you heard anything more about Peter Walsingham's lawsuit?"

"No, dear. Not since the injunction."

"So you haven't heard anything about it being withdrawn?"

"Withdrawn? No. Why would…oh, you poor dear. Yes, I saw the videos and *The Intruder*. I'm afraid you are going to have to let that go. He's not coming back. In time, you'll be able to move on."

Mrs. Jellyby squeezed Alice's arm with a sympathetic frown before walking away. A week before, Alice would have corrected Mrs. Jellyby's assumption about the pictures and laughed at the notion she hoped Peter would come back to the show for her. Only now, it was true.

The Edge of Darkness
Chapter 21

When Tony's eyes met mine, neither of us could control our tears or resist pulling each other into a tight hug as Robert stood back, blending into the background.

"God, I've missed you, Lexie," Tony said against my ear.

"Why wouldn't you answer my letters?"

"I couldn't. Annette said...oh, forget what Annette said."

"Whatever she said, it wasn't true."

"I know. I know now."

"But now it's too late." I pulled away from him and stepped back for Robert to join us. "Robert, this is my brother Tony. Tony, this is Robert. My husband."

"Senator."

"Your grace." They shook hands. "I hope you're good to her. She is the most important thing in the world to me."

Knowing we had not spoken in eight years, Robert was clearly confused by this. "You needn't worry. She is to me as well."

After he and his two assistants were shown to

their rooms, they were to join us in the parlor in the east wing. Tony arrived early and found me alone, and I began to think our warm reunion had been an act on his part for the benefit of the others.

"You have done well for yourself," he said tersely as I handed him a glass of cognac. "Duchess. I suppose not everything Annette told me was a lie."

"What is that supposed to mean?"

"This marriage! To a Duke! He's old enough to be your father."

"Age is not important."

"Especially with enough funds to offset it." I could not believe his harsh words and was too shocked to reply. He grabbed my wrist tightly and pulled me closer and snarled in my face. "Is that why you did it? Was it for his money? Or was it to rub my face in it?"

I gathered all my reserves not to burst into tears. "I didn't think you cared."

Then we heard footsteps, and he released my wrist just as his assistants joined us. I turned around and took a large sip of my cognac in hopes of making my hands stop shaking.

Tony's assistants chose not to dine with us, although I was certain that Tony had helped them in that decision. I felt strange at dinner, being married to one man when I was in love with the one a few feet away from him. The feeling was pain, and I reacted to it by inflicting pain on the origin of mine.

"Why haven't you gotten married, brother dear?"

He looked at his plate but paused in his eating. "I have only been in love once, but I lost her."

"Oh, really?" I asked in the most innocent voice I could. "Please tell us what happened to her," then added with my teeth clenched, "brother dear."

He looked at me with cold eyes. "I think she died."

"Really? And how do you think she died?"

"I killed her."

Robert choked a little on his dinner and drank down the rest of his wine.

"I use the term figuratively, of course," Tony told him. "Actually, I killed the part of her I loved, and she went on to marry someone else. But it's just as well." He looked at me. "I am not sure she ever loved me. She never told me she did."

He was right. I never had told him, but I had felt it. My eyes were stinging, but I held back the tears. "I'm sure she loved you," I said, my voice no longer tinged by anger. "Do you still love her?"

"I will always love her."

"If she weren't married, would you let her go again?"

"It's complicated. We were too much alike, had *too* much in common. We could never be together."

Perhaps Robert felt left out. After a moment of Tony and me returning our attention to our plates, Robert said, "When I first fell in love with your sister, she made me leave for a year to be sure I really loved her because someone had abandoned her and broken her heart."

"Oh, really?" Tony sounded almost happy, pleased with himself for causing my pain.

I spoke up. "But it was a good idea, because now we are very happy and we are both very much in love." It wasn't really a lie. I just wasn't in love with my husband.

The rest of the dinner and a nightcap passed politely and awkwardly, and I think we were all glad to end the evening early.

Later in our room as we got ready for bed, Robert said, "Darling, I thought you were rather cruel to your brother the way you talked to him about his former lover."

I was sitting at the vanity brushing out my hair. "They never became lovers." Then I added quickly, "Tony told me all about it a long time ago."

I looked into the mirror and reflected on my past. "At first, they did not get along well at all. But then both of them lost someone very close to them. That was the summer that our brother and his father died. They held onto each other at first to relieve their grief and sorrow, but then their feelings grew into something so much more. They were so in love, and he had even proposed to her. Then a lie came between them. Tony believed the lie and abandoned her."

"How sad."

After a long moment of silently staring at my reflection, I stood up and put on my robe. "You're right. I should go apologize to him." I left the room before he could say anything.

I walked through the long corridors to the guest wing and knocked on Tony's door, but before he answered, I walked in and closed it behind me. He dropped the book he had been reading and got out of bed. I took a step closer, but he put up his hand.

"Please stop."

"Why did you come here?"

"I…I had to see you again. When I found out

you were getting married it was a stab in the heart. I have never stopped loving you, Lexie. I even deluded myself that we could be together anyway. I didn't know if you'd be willing to move to Sweden, but I couldn't do that to you. I thought maybe now that you are married, I could move on, accept that you and I could only be brother and sister. It hasn't worked. I need you to go."

I gasped. "Oh, God. You still don't know."

"Don't know what?"

"I cannot believe she still hasn't told you. I was adopted by the Haywards."

The significance seemed lost on him. "Oh, really. I didn't know that."

I said it again. "Tony, I was adopted."

He started to shake his head, but then, as understanding dawned, his face changed, displaying a rapid sequence of emotions. "You mean you and I aren't...Oh, dear God. Jesus fucking shit. Why didn't you tell me before?"

I turned away to conceal my tears, but I couldn't stop them from coming out in my voice. "I did, hundreds of times. Why wouldn't you read my letters?"

"Jesus Christ." He started walking towards me.

"No, stop. I can't. I'm married now. I can't betray him."

But he hadn't stopped and now grasped my arms and pulled me to force me to face him. "You came to me. You left your husband's bed in the middle of the night to come to my room. Why are you here?"

I shook my head. "I don't know. We were both so angry at dinner, I didn't want to go to sleep with that between us."

"Is that the truth, Lexie? Then let me kiss you one time. Just once and I'll let you go back to your husband."

He brushed my hair from my face and held the back of my head. And then we kissed. His breath within me made me tingle all over and sent a surge of excitement through my body, and I knew I couldn't stop with one kiss.

But that first kiss took us all the way to the bed, where we kissed and discovered each other's bodies as we never had before. He kissed and touched all over my body, and then, at last, he and I became one. One solitary being merged by love. Making love had never felt like this with Robert. I guess for it to be like this, you have to love your lover. I wanted him to stay inside me forever, to sleep inside me. I had to be content to sleep with his body wrapped around me.

The next morning, I told Robert we had stayed up all night talking, working out our problems.

As Tony was leaving, we were left alone to say goodbye, but he did not want to leave it at that. "Lexie, come with me. I'll go now, but you can meet me in London and we'll go back to the States together."

"What are you saying?"

"Come be with me. You cannot tell me, after last night, that you love him. We belong together."

"You want me to leave my husband?"

"Divorce him and marry me."

"It's not that simple. I…I am a duchess now, and this could destroy your political career."

He pulled me close to him. "I don't give a damn about being reelected. I just want you."

Then he kissed me until I was breathless. "I'll be in London all week. I fly out on Friday. Be on that plane with me."

When Tony left, I stared after him. What was I going to do? I felt like the baron who was married to someone but loved another. What could I do? I had to stay with Robert. He was my husband, and I had vowed to stay with him until death. But I felt such guilt for being dishonest by pretending to love him when I loved Tony. How could I go on pretending not to love Tony? I knew we could never have a platonic relationship, but I couldn't bear to have him out of my life again. Isn't divorce better than adultery? What was I going to do?

☼

Giselle stepped into the writers' room a week later as if nothing had happened.

"Hi, everyone. Mr. Peacock said I should tell you all I am back so…here I am." She smiled, as lovely as ever.

Alice gaped at her in silence as the others welcomed her back with a startling lack of curiosity. When Giselle walked out, Alice jump up and ran after her.

"Giselle. Giselle!"

Giselle stopped and turned around. "Hi, Alice."

"Where the hell have you been?"

She donned Sienna's complacent smile. "It's not important. I'm here now."

"You're just going to waltz in here as if nothing has happened with no explanation?"

"There's nothing to explain. I'm sorry I caused

245

you all so much extra work."

"Forget that! Well, no, don't forget that because that wasn't good either, but I was worried sick about you!"

Although Giselle fought it, eventually her face cracked and tears welled in her eyes. "I'm sorry, Alice. I'm so sorry. I should have listened to you. I've been an idiot."

"Well, where's Rich?"

"I don't know. Frankly, I don't care. I want you to know how sorry I am that I didn't trust you. I don't know what I was thinking. I *wasn't* thinking."

With beautiful, sweet Giselle crying before her, Alice couldn't bring herself to press for more information. Instead, she pulled her into her arms and hugged her close. "If you ever do want to talk about it, I am here for you."

"Yes, I know. You always have been. That's what I told him. You are the most forgiving person I know."

Giselle had already walked away when Alice realized she wasn't exactly sure whom she meant by "him."

CHAPTER 18

The Edge of Darkness
Chapter 24

Almost three months had passed since I had walked out on Tony in his London hotel room after making love and arguing, when I left him to break both our hearts. The next time I saw him, once again he filled my television screen.

"Eight years ago," he said from behind the podium, "my father, Senator Molly Hollingsworth, brought this bill before Congress. It is my intention this time to see it become law." And then two shots rang out.

Many Americans had seen it live, but I didn't see it until I woke up the next morning. The caption at the bottom of the screen did not prepare me, and at the echoing shots, I started screaming.

It took us forever to get to Washington. No amount of wealth makes the ocean smaller. We arrived the following day, and I realized it was the twentieth anniversary of the fire. We were met at the airport by hoards of reporters taking pictures and yelling questions, but I just kept crying and walking with Robert holding on to me.

We went straight to the hospital. Tony was unconscious and looked like death in the hospital bed with tubes and monitors around him. They had operated, but the doctor told us his chances of surviving were low. "I'm surprised he's held on this long," he said.

As I sat next to his bed, I recalled waking up the morning after my brother's death to find him sitting there. I remembered tasting his sweat on my lips and being jealous that he had been loving another woman. That night when we were dancing in the rain, holding hands, being glad to be alive. Now I wasn't. As long as Tony was alive somewhere in the world, even though I couldn't have him, it gave me a reason to live, remembering him telling me how precious life is. Now I knew if he died, that part of me would die with him.

Then I remembered our bitter parting words when I refused to go to America.

"When you are in bed with the duke, are you thinking of me when you fuck him?"

"You should be asking if I think of Robert when I fuck you!"

They made me cry even harder. Those couldn't be the last words I ever said to him.

Tony's eyes fluttered and opened, and I flew to his side. "Oh, God. Tony! My Tony."

"Lexie, don't cry," he said, his voice weak and just above a whisper. "Life is too short and precious to waste grieving."

I brushed my hands over his hair. "Hold on. Don't give up. It will only conquer us if you let it."

"Did…did they catch him?"

I nodded. "Over that same damn bill."

"Lexie, will you ever forgive me for leaving you that day without saying goodbye, never reading your letters?"

"I did a long time ago."

"Lexie, that night we were together, that was the most amazing…"

"I know. I will always remember it. There is something I never told you but I always felt. I love you. I love you more than life itself, and nothing will stop me from loving you – even death."

"I love you, Lexie. After I left you, I never loved anyone again." Then his eyes closed, and the monitor screeched.

"Tony," I cried, and then I screamed. "Tony!"

As the hospital staff surrounded us, I kissed his face and lips, still warm, and my tears fell on his cheeks. He looked so peaceful, and I thought, he's only sleeping, but the doctor only shook his head as the screeching stopped.

I turned around and faced Robert standing near the corner. His face looked as devastated as I felt. I clung to him in my agony. "He's gone, Robert. Tony is gone." My voice was trembling, and so was I.

"I know," he said levelly, then he led me into the corridor.

I looked up at him, and he looked so sad, on the verge of tears. I remembered seeing that pain in someone else's eyes. "Tony, Tony, it will be all right."

"I'm not Tony, Goddammit! I'm your husband! Remember me?" He shook me as his own tears began to fall. "It was you! You are the one Tony spoke of as his only love! It is he who had broken your heart!"

He continued to shake me and scream at me, but I couldn't hear any more through my own hysterics.

I screamed back, "Don't you know he's dead? I will never have him again! The only man I ever –"

"The only man you ever loved? That's it, isn't it?" He was enraged and shook me again. "Isn't it? Answer me!"

I jerked away and took my pain out on him. "Yes! Yes, it's true. I never loved you. I only used you to help me forget Tony. I didn't know what I was sacrificing! And you know what else? I conceived his child, but I had an abortion to save your feelings! I will never forgive myself for killing his baby and for not going with him when I had the chance."

Then he slapped me across the face. "You may as well have gone with him because you have lost us both now." He stormed off as I held my cheek and fell to the floor, weak and dizzy.

Mother appeared and cradled my head in her hands. "Lexie, my sweet Lexie."

"Tad is dead," I cried. "They killed Tad. My brother is dead."

"Dear, Tad has been dead for a long time."

"No. They came yesterday. Tony's taking care of me."

"No, baby, Tony's been shot. Tony's dead."

Then I pulled away from her and, kneeling on the hospital floor, began screaming. "Mommy!

Mommy! Tad, get Mommy! Tad, go get Mommy!"

I knew the press must have been having a field day with this, especially in Britain. "Duchess Freaks at Senator/Brother's Deathbed."

After a few days of denying the deaths of Tad and Tony, I started making "progress." Soon I was allowed visitors, although that was more punishment than privilege.

Mother came. "They say you could be out in a week or two. Yesterday was Tony's funeral..."

Of all people, after all these years, Annette showed up. "I just want you to know that I do not regret anything, and if I had it to do again, I would."

"Even knowing all the pain you caused?"

"As long as I caused it for you, and look where you are now."

"Annette, why do you hate me so much?"

"I was Mother's favorite until you came. And then she started loving you more than she did me. You even got my brother to love you. He betrayed me because of you."

"If you had just told him the truth, he could have had some happiness these last years."

"I don't care, if he would have had it with you."

Robert came, too. "Hello, darling." He kissed me on the forehead and handed me a bouquet of flowers.

"Th-they're beautiful." I looked into his smiling face. "Then you've forgiven me?"

"Of course, darling. I want you to concentrate on getting better. Because the sooner you get well, the sooner I can have my divorce."

My God, my God, what have I done? Twenty-six, and I had nothing left to live for. I had destroyed my marriage to a man who loved me. I had lost all the men I cared about – Daddy, Tad, Tony. I lay in my starched white bed and wished I were that little girl listening to the raindrops on the awning of my home and smelling Mommy's homemade bread. How complicated life becomes. I used to make up stories to make my life more interesting, but now I realized truth is stranger than fiction.

But now I am safe, at least for the moment, tucked away from the world. No worries, no responsibilities, no heart wrenching decisions. The world didn't stop just because I wasn't helping it spin. Now I could rest and remember the lizard that used to live outside my window. Now, for the first time in twenty years, I could listen to the rain.

Alice turned the page, but the next one was blank, only to be followed by information on other books from that publisher. *This can't be the end. Where's the happily ever after?* She checked the binding to see if any pages had been ripped out. *That's the end? No deus ex machina?*

"Where's my happily ever after?" She threw the book against the wall.

"Alice," Mr. Peacock said from her doorway just as the book hit the floor, his tone of voice far too grim for first thing in the morning and only half a cup of coffee. "Are you all right?"

"You can tell Winnie Johnson, that is most decidedly *not* a romance novel!"

Mr. Peacock wrinkled his brow at her in confusion, but his curiosity did not rise to the level of requiring an explanation. "Jack Hartz is here. He is asking to see you."

The blood drained from Alice's face and left it tingling. "Oh...OK. Did he say why?"

"Will you see him?"

She nodded and Mr. Peacock stepped back to allow Jack to come through. Jack closed the door and sat down.

"How've you been, Alice?" He spoke like a mortician.

"You're kind of freaking me out, Jack. Could we save the pleasantries for later and get to the point?"

He held up a folded newspaper and slid it across the desk to her. "He...we wanted you to see this before everyone else."

She unfolded *The Intruder* to the front page emblazoned with the headline "Peter Walsingham Engaged!" over a fuzzy picture of Peter smiling, his eyes closed as he embraced a woman with her back to the camera.

"Oh, God." She checked for her trashcan to be sure it was near in case she had to throw up.

"There are more inside."

"I don't think I want to see anymore."

"I'm sorry, Alice. He was right. He said you'd be upset. I didn't realize it would bother you so much."

She rubbed her eyes and repeated the mantra to herself, *I will not cry. I will not cry.* "Oh, he *knew* this would upset me!" She had to know. "Who is she?"

After several seconds of silence, she began to think he wouldn't answer, but he responded with another question. "Who is who?"

"The woman. His fiancée – the woman in the picture."

He said nothing until she looked up at his puzzled eyes. "Alice, it's you."

The shock hit her like a bucket of cold water. "Me?"

"Yes – it's the two of you at Alsace Aquitaine."

She yanked the blurry image up to her face then turned the pages to the story, and there they were. Peter holding her hands as they gazed into each other's eye. Her face then lit up with surprise and excitement. Finally, her grinning from ear to ear with her arms around his neck.

Alice perused the photos and the short article describing an intimate dinner for two during which Peter popped the question.

Then she burst out laughing. She threw her head back and guffawed as Jack sat with his eyes wide and his mouth hanging open.

"So you...you aren't upset?"

"With a story this ridiculous? I can't believe even *The Intruder* could get something this wrong. I bet Peter is livid."

"So he didn't ask you to marry him that night?"

"Of course not. Why? Didn't he tell you it wasn't true?"

"He didn't tell me what was happening in the photos, but he never said they weren't true, so I thought..."

"He probably thought it was too ludicrous for him even to deny!"

"Then what did he tell you that night?"

"That he…oh, it's not important anymore. Tell him I am very sorry he has the discomfort of having to refute being engaged to someone as insignificant as Alice McGillicutty. Does he wish me to issue a statement?"

"No. In fact, he told his publicist not to respond at all."

"That's probably wise. It'll die down much faster if he doesn't issue a denial, which would just incite more questions and keep it in the tabloids that much longer. What I don't understand is why now. This was almost three weeks ago. I thought this rag was all about being first with the 'big story.'"

"I have no idea why they came out now. I think a waiter took them."

She scanned the photos a moment longer until a bittersweet ache just below her sternum compelled her to close the paper. "How is he?"

"Still keeping to himself. Still won't look at any scripts I bring him."

"Did he…" Should she? *Oh, to hell with it.* "Did he have a message for me or ask about me?"

"When he called me, he thought you would be really angry about this engagement story. When I said I'd come see you, he said, 'Find out how she's doing. I hope she's all right.'"

She wrinkled her brow and thought aloud, "How odd." With too much she wanted to ask, she instead said nothing more.

"Is Giselle around? Do you think she'd talk to

me?"

"Well, there's only one way to find out. She should be in make-up or her dressing room."

He grinned and started to go. "Thanks, Alice."

"Do you mind if I keep this?" she asked with a finger on *The Intruder*. "Not every day I get to pretend I'm engaged to a movie star."

A few days later, Alice came out of her office just as Jack and Giselle returned from lunch, smiling and holding hands and even kissing goodbye. As Jack left, Alice hopped to catch up with Giselle.

"Looks like you and Jack have picked up without skipping a beat. I take it you've forgiven him."

"Well, how could I not after Peter explained it all to me and said everything was his fault and how miserable –"

"Peter?" Alice came to an abrupt halt and put her hand on Giselle's arm to stop her as well. "When did you talk to Peter?"

Giselle turned three kinds of red before speaking. "I…He asked me not to say anything."

"Who? Peter?"

Giselle wrung her hands together and glanced around as if she were revealing state secrets. "I'm not supposed to say anything, but when I was gone that few days? Peter found me and brought me back."

"Found you? Where?"

"I had no idea where I was at the time, but I suppose Rich had driven us to Mexico."

"Peter found you in Mexico?" Alice could not suppress the shock resonating in her volume.

"After Rich found out about what you had done to

his role, he wanted to walk out. He told me to come with him, and I wasn't going to be taping anyway, so I went. That night we were going to a club, and he said he had some coke if I wanted to do a line before we went out. I don't know what it was, but it wasn't coke. Once I started, I didn't stop. After that, the only thing I remember is waking up at Peter's house."

"So you were at Peter's house the whole time?"

"No, only a couple of days. He told me about Winnie and how much he had done to protect her career, but he said it wasn't worth letting Rich get away scot free to do it again. He told me he was the reason Jack had stopped taking my calls. He was very kind but crazy worried. He was so afraid someone would see us together, and he was especially concerned that you would get the wrong idea. He said he didn't think you would ever forgive him, but I told him you are the most forgiving person I know."

"Forgive him?" Alice had trouble absorbing all Giselle had told her. Nothing made any sense. Each time her head had come to accept it had only been a one-night stand, something would happen to wrench at her heart. Giselle and Jack spoke as though Peter really cared about her, but he had gone almost a month without a word.

Alice's phone started buzzing in her pocket.

Giselle squeezed Alice's hand. "I have to get to wardrobe. We'll talk more later," she said before walking away.

Alice pulled out her phone. Peacock. "What's up?"

"Alice, could you come to Mrs. Jellyby's office?"

"Uhhh…sure."

Alice wracked her brain trying to remember the

last time she had been called to Mrs. Jellyby's office. In fact, she tried to avoid the production offices as much as possible. *This cannot be good.*

Even before she walked into the outer office, she could hear a man's voice yelling behind Mrs. Jellyby's door. *What now?*

"They said you could go right in," Mrs. Jellyby's secretary told her.

"I'm not sure if I want to." She bit the bullet, tapped on the door, and walked in.

Mrs. Jellyby sat behind her desk with Mr. Peacock standing beside her and a middle-aged, heavyset angry man staring daggers at them both.

"You wanted to see me?" Alice asked.

"Are you the head writer?" asked the angry man. "*I* wanted to see you."

"This is Mr. Burke," Peacock said, "one of Peter Walsingham's attorneys."

"What's going on?"

"He seems to think we've brainwashed Peter."

"I'll tell you what's going on!" the angry lawyer said. "You are all attempting to destroy my client's career! I don't know what you've done to him, but you have got to cut him off of this albatross."

Alice resisted the temptation to inform Mr. Burke that an albatross would actually *be* cut off. "I don't understand. What's going on?"

Mr. Peacock managed to cut in before Mr. Burke could speak. "The network has worked out an out-of-court settlement with Peter."

Her heart flipped in her chest. "Oh." Her voice sounded small and distant even to herself.

"In layman's terms, he would be buying out the

rest of his contract. In exchange for monetary compensation, the network would not force him to return."

Now somehow her heart had crawled up and lodged in her throat. "So he is going to pay, I'd presume, a considerable amount of money *not* to come back." Her legs began to shake with the strain on her weakening knees. *That's it. It's over. It was a one-night stand.* "I think I better sit down." She took a chair in front of the desk, but now Mr. Burke hovered over her. "So why am I here?"

"Because he won't accept it!" She flinched as Mr. Burke's voice rang in her ear. "Mr. Walsingham says he will not accept it unless the producer, the director, and the head writer sign off on it."

"Wait. What?"

"Do you understand how completely preposterous that is?"

"Did he say why?"

"He said his dispute is with the network, not us," said Mrs. Jellyby, "and he did not want to risk anyone's job unless we did not want him back."

"What did you decide?" Alice asked Mrs. Jellyby and Peacock.

Mr. Burke answered. "They have both signed. We now await your signature." He handed her the papers and stuck a pen out toward her.

"You both signed? You don't want him back?"

"We wanted the ultimate decision to be up to you," Mr. Peacock said. "Whatever you choose, we will stand beside you, but it's up to you to say if you want him back."

Alice glanced from paper to face to pen to face and

back to paper again.

"What are you waiting for?" Mr. Burke stuck the pen an inch from her nose. "Sign it."

She perused the papers without reading then handed them back to Mr. Burke. "No, I don't believe I will."

"What do you mean you won't sign it?"

"I am not going to sign something stating that he is not wanted here, and bullying me will not change my mind!"

"Are you determined to ruin his career? Do you know he will not even look at scripts until this matter is settled?"

"I don't see how this prevents him from reading scripts. And I don't see how working on a soap for a few more weeks will be detrimental to his career. He is in the best position to define his career. Having our acceptance was *his* stipulation – not ours. If he wants to leave the show without my consent, he is free to do so."

He took a step back and flapped the papers at her as his eyes bulged out of his head. "Oh-HO! I know you. You're the one from *The Intruder*. Did you arrange those pictures to be taken of his alleged proposal to blackmail him into staying on the show?"

"If I did do something like that, I would certainly be the last to admit it." She stood up and walked to the door.

"And that is your final word on the matter?"

As she started to turn the knob, she stopped to offer one parting remark. "No. You tell Peter there is still a role for him in *All My Tomorrows.*"

☼

"So who do we kill next?" Alice asked her staff of writers.

The first victim in their murder mystery had been simple, since Rich's defection had broken his contract. Poor Brother Raife – brutally murdered before he had even taken his final vows. After all the build-up and excitement of introducing Raife and implying the possibility that he would be Giselle's next love interest, this new twist had stunned the viewers. That along with converting Peter Walsingham's character from her lover to her brother had the critics calling *All My Tomorrows* "unpredictable" – "What will they do next?" – which had unintentionally given the soap a bump in ratings.

Now the writers had to determine how unpredictable they wanted to be in killing off the cast.

"Does anyone want to leave the show?"

"I don't think so," Alice said. "Not since Eileen." *And Peter.*

"Hey, do you think Eileen would come back for a guest stint just so we could kill her off?"

"I don't think so. And plus, I don't want to take away her option of ever coming back. We're just going to have to kill off a few extras. I mean, the killer can't just focus on the five core families on the show."

"And who's the killer? Won't he be off the show too?"

"I think a prison set would be easy, or add a psych wing to the hospital. And why does it have to be a 'he'?"

"Yeah, maybe it's Sienna!"

As they all laughed, Giselle herself walked in. "Alice? Jack's here."

"Oh. OK." Jack had frequently been to the set over the last week, so Alice didn't know why Giselle made a point of telling her then.

"Peter's with him." *Oh...That's why.* "He says he's coming back to *All My Tomorrows.*"

The other writers did not react with surprise or excitement or joy to the news. Instead, all eyes rounded on Alice, and they battered her with questions on how to adapt the storyline. Alice sat there mute, frozen, flushed, deaf to all the words floating around her. She pushed herself up away from the table and followed Giselle out of the room.

Pull it together, Alice. Don't let him see you're affected. If he hasn't called in almost a month, clearly his infatuation is over. But when she and Giselle reached them and Peter turned around, the change in his expression upon seeing her nearly melted away all of her defenses. Nearly.

"Hi, Jack." She spoke in her most professional tone with her posture rigid. "Peter."

"Miss McGillicutty."

"It's been a while – close to a month, I believe. I had come to think we would never hear from you again."

"I know. I thought I might not be welcome."

"Hmm. Peculiar. And how long will you be gracing us with your presence?"

"I think that will depend on where I fit in your story." He glanced at Jack and Giselle then said, "Perhaps we could discuss my role in your office."

The way his stare shot through her compelled her to hold her breath, so she couldn't speak and only nodded and led the way at a quick pace. Once there, she stepped around and sat down, keeping at least a desk-width's distance between them. He closed the door and locked it then took a seat.

"Why did you lock it?"

"I didn't want anyone barging in like they often do."

"It's my door."

"Do you want me to unlock it?"

She didn't answer, and they said nothing for several moments.

"So," she said, her voice not as steady as she had expected. "How is Britney?"

"She's well, thank you. She's asked about you several times."

"Me?"

"Yes, she asks if I've seen my *Alice in Wonderland*."

"Hers?"

"What?"

"*Her* Alice? Does she say 'my' or does she say 'your'?"

He leaned forward in his chair. "She didn't say either. I said 'my,' but I suppose that's up to you."

As she brought her hand up to her face, its shakiness changed her mind, and she hid both hands on her lap. "What are you trying to do? Is this some sort of game to you?"

"I've never played games with you, Alice. Never once."

"What do you call disappearing for a month after

the night…the night we had together?"

"I thought you must hate me. I thought even if that night had meant anything to you, I must have destroyed it."

"You might not play games, but you sure as hell talk in riddles. What the hell are you talking about?"

"Giselle."

Waiting. "You gotta give me a little more than that to work with, Peter. This is not a script I'm writing."

He stood and turned, facing the wall, hands on hips. "I thought, that night, perhaps your feelings toward me had changed, that you could… But then the next morning I woke up in bed alone, and it was as though the night before hadn't even happened. When you found out about Giselle, you were so angry, running around, screaming like a madwoman!"

"I would have said banshee, but go on."

"I knew I had ruined it – with my arrogance and superiority."

Frustration had now calmed her nerves, and she dropped her face into her hands. "*Ugh!* Peter! How had you ruined what?"

"Us. What we had that night. What we *could* have. Giselle was in serious trouble because of me."

"You?"

"Yes. It was all my fault."

"Oh? And how is the great and powerful Walsingham responsible for an actress in L.A. going off on a drug binge?"

He turned to her then, his face so stricken she wished he would turn back around. "I caused all of it. I didn't stop Rich when I had the chance because I was more concerned about the reputations of the other actors. When Rich got here, I didn't expose him just to save Winnie some embarrassment. If I hadn't made you promise not to say anything, you could have told Giselle the truth. I am the one who told Jack to leave Giselle, or she wouldn't have run into Rich's waiting arms in the first place!"

"Oh." He did have a point. "Well, if you put it like that, I guess it is your fault."

"You were so angry and upset, I knew you must blame me and hate me."

"Damnit, Peter, are you so egotistical you think if someone is angry they must be angry with you?"

"Weren't you? The only other time I ever saw you that angry was with me!"

"I was just angry, and frantic, and worried, and upset! It had nothing to do with you! I was mainly angry with myself for leaving and not doing more to stop Rich or warn Giselle. I am as much to blame as you are. But you and I ultimately cannot control the behavior of others. Jack didn't have to listen to you; he should have had more faith in Giselle! Giselle knew she shouldn't be using drugs, and she chose not to listen to me. And Rich! Well, no one is responsible for the way he is except maybe his parents."

"You aren't mad at me?

"Mad? I'm grateful! You went out on your own and found Giselle and got her away from that creep. You probably saved her life."

He averted his eyes and shook his head. "No, I don't want your gratitude. I wish Giselle hadn't told you I found her."

"You can't blame Giselle. She inadvertently said something about 'him' but without an antecedent, so you know I couldn't let it rest until I knew who 'he'—"

With a suppressed chuckle throbbing in his chest, Peter smiled and held up his hand to halt her. "All right, I get it. I know how you despise ambiguous pronouns."

"You do?"

"So you really weren't angry with me that morning?"

"Why did you walk out on me like that?"

"I thought you would want me to leave, like the night in New Orleans when you said you hated me."

"Oh, don't remind me of what I said that night; it makes me ashamed. I didn't want you to leave. I wanted you to stay. I had something to tell you."

He walked the few steps to stand beside her chair. "What was it? What did you want to say?"

"If you thought I hated you, why did you come back?"

"Giselle said you would forgive me, but you are so passionate in everything, everything you do, everything you feel – whether it's saving the soap or defending your friends or hating the heat or loving guitars or the way that you sing or the way you kiss me – I didn't believe it. Then Jack told me how you reacted to that engagement story when you thought I was marrying someone else. So I told my attorneys that you had to agree to the settlement. When you didn't, when you said there was a place for me in 'All *Your* Tomorrows,' I began to hope."

He extended his hand and she took it and let him bring her to her feet before him. "But you'll do the show?"

"You said something to me that night that made me ashamed. You didn't just talk about saving the show – you talked about saving jobs. I had not ever even considered it – all the people depending on this soap for their livelihood. How self-centered is that? I'll stay through sweeps or a full story arc or whatever you need to save it." Taking her other hand, he pulled her closer. "What did you want to say to me?"

He touched her face, and every place his flesh met hers sparked with electricity.

"Would you...would you rather be murdered or be a serial killer?" she asked.

"I don't care. Tell me. What were you going to say?"

"What about your film career?"

"I'm cutting back. Alice, I put my house on the market. I want to find a place up in Napa like we talked about. I want to get away from Hollywood and all the people here. You were right about everything you said – ever since I made it, I have been so arrogant and conceited and superior, and I've been surrounded by people who feel the same way. I want to move somewhere where I can become the person I want to be, for you. I want to be able to see my daughter and never neglect her like I did before. And I want us to go together, once you can give up the soap. You can write your novel or just drink wine and eat figs or whatever you want to do."

He pushed his fingers into her hair and held her head in his hands so she couldn't look away. "What did you want to say to me that you didn't because of my stupidity?"

She couldn't look away, so she closed her eyes,

and he brought his face close to hers, his breath against her lips. She hadn't thought she could say it, after these long, torturous weeks, but he had always known how to seduce her. With her heart pounding and as she struggled to catch her breath, she couldn't *not* say it.

"I love you."

She spoke so softly, releasing the words on an exhalation, she thought he couldn't possibly have heard; but he must have because then he was kissing her, his lips moving against hers with gentle passion, which she returned. He stopped a moment and said, "I love you, Alice," then kissed her again and again. "When did you know?"

"That night in Napa, the moment you…" His lips saved her from finishing the sentence.

"Yes. I saw it in your eyes. We're a perfect fit." The memory of that moment scorched her to her core as much as his mouth.

"What were you going to tell me?" she asked between kisses. "That night in New Orleans."

He pulled back enough to meet her eyes. "I was going to ask you to marry me."

"No, you weren't."

"Yes…I was," he said, punctuating their words with kisses.

"That's crazy…You hardly knew me."

"I'd worked with you here almost every day for weeks, and before I knew it was happening, I had fallen in love with you… I was in the middle before I knew I'd begun….I knew I wanted you from the moment I tried to kiss you on the set that first day of rehearsals…You were the only woman I wanted."

"But I didn't even like you…I put you in an incestuous relationship."

"I took it as encouragement…I thought you didn't want me kissing Giselle."

"How could we have gotten married? We hadn't even slept together."

"It has been done before…and I did try to remedy that."

"And you thought I would jump at the chance at marrying a movie star."

"I cannot believe my own vanity. I want the chance to redeem myself in your eyes. I want to prove that I have become worthy of your love."

She smiled. "Where have I heard that line before?"

He wound an arm around her and pulled her tight against him as he brought their mouths together and let their tongues tangle.

"Will you?" he said when he came up for air. "Everyone already thinks we're engaged. We shouldn't disappoint them."

As he kissed her again – *Oh, yes, please. Kiss me just like that* – she couldn't believe she actually considered it; but as he kissed her, she couldn't imagine saying no.

"Are you willing to give up being Miss McGillicutty?" The question came out as a rasp, and as he had his way with her mouth, his hands roamed out of her hair to her neck and over her shoulders.

"I have a confession to make," she said against his lips then resumed the kiss.

"Oh?"

"My name is not McGillicutty…That's just my pen name."

"Mmm?...So what's your real name?"

Does he think his kisses will distract me from his unbuttoning my blouse?

"Bristol," she managed to say as she started on his buttons, but the exertion of all this kissing and talking and unbuttoning made them both out of breath.

"And you changed it to McGillicutty?" He pulled her blouse free from her skirt.

"I couldn't think of anything else."

"Alice Bristol McGillicutty, say yes." But how could she speak with his mouth over hers?

"Yes," she said quickly before he claimed her lips again, then he backed her up against the desk, pushed papers to the floor, and tugged at her skirt.

"No more misunderstandings. You will marry me?" He pushed her skirt up as he lifted her to the desk, and she ran her arms around his neck as they continued to kiss.

"Yes."

"I'm willing to wait if you want a big wedding... but after these many months' suspense, I thought we could go to Vegas." His hands slid up her thighs as their tongues whirled around each other. "Today."

"Yes," she said, which incited another frenzied, deep kiss from him.

"And do you know what I'm going to do to you now?"

Oh, yes.

Life is too short and precious for no.

The end

ALSO FROM THIS AUTHOR

Pulse and Prejudice – A tale of love, blood, and desire; the definitive vampire adaptation of the Jane Austen classic.

This compelling paranormal adaptation of *Pride and Prejudice* tells the story of Mr. Darcy, vampire, as he endeavours to overcome both his love and his bloodlust for Miss Elizabeth Bennet.

When the haughty and wealthy Fitzwilliam Darcy arrives in the rural county of Hertfordshire, he finds he cannot control his attraction to Elizabeth Bennet – a horrifying thought because, as she is too far below his social standing to ignite his heart, he fears she must appeal to the dark impulses he struggles to suppress.

Praise for *Pulse and Prejudice*

"Author Colette Saucier has put a fun, thrilling twist to Mr. Darcy in this engaging adaptation. She has obviously done her research and the Regency world inhabited by Elizabeth and Darcy comes vibrantly alive.

—Z Hayes, Amazon *Hall of Fame* Reviewer

"I cannot express enough how sceptical I was upon starting this book. But, within only the first chapter, I found myself strangely drawn to the story. The vampire Darcy weaves his spell quickly."

—Austen Prose

"Saucier's eroticism between Darcy & Elizabeth exploded off the pages."

—Angie Kroll, Goodreads

"Saucier uses Darcy's emotions as a most effective way of expressing his vampire side. His dark desire mixed with his haughty personality and shortening temper make him an extremely exciting character to follow. Once he is rebuffed for his demeanour to Elizabeth and reveals his true self, his demise and subsequent 'rebirth' are written to perfection. It has renewed my faith in the sub-genre."

—Reflections of a Book Addict

"I completely enjoyed this version and fell in love with Mr. Darcy all over again as a vampire. I think all paranormal and romantic fans will enjoy this tale. Excellent read!"

—Close Encounter of the Night Kind

"Saucier's language follows the style of 19th century literature, while adding the necessary imagery to engage the 21st century reader. She also appeals to the modern reader with a more satisfying conclusion in the final section that is all her own—Beyond Pride and Prejudice."

—Stephanie Judice, A Writer's Rest Stop

"Combined the traditional beloved Austen novel with Darcy being a vampire trying to control his thirst for human blood, in particular Elizabeth Bennet's. It followed the novel pretty religiously, while throwing in the Darcy vampire plot line. It bends here and there to accommodate the new paranormal twist and the reader is rewarded with a passionate ending between Darcy and Elizabeth. I loved that I felt like I was re-reading Austen."

—My Little Corner of the World

"5/5 Stars I was truly impressed, and it takes a lot to impress me!"

—The Right Words in the Right Order

EXCERPT FROM
PULSE AND PREJUDICE

Darcy leaned in with his hands on either side of the doorframe and let his forehead fall against the door. He closed his eyes and imagined her lying on the bed, her hair splayed out on the pillow, the eyes that had challenged him so brightly just that evening now closed in repose. What little effort, how few steps it would take, for him to be upon her, taking what he needed, sating his thirst.

He pushed himself away from the door and leaned back against the wall beside, despair filling him. He had stood watch over Elizabeth and her sister for two nights and had come back to do so again, to protect them from the very thing he now ached to do himself. The irony sickened him but did not staunch his desire. Gathering all the resolve he knew it would require to return to his room, he stepped away from the wall.

Darcy turned just as the door opened and Elizabeth appeared. They cried out in surprise simultaneously.

"Mr. Darcy!"

"Eliz-a-Miss Bennet!"

She was dressed in her night-rail and wrapper; and, though more modest than even her day dresses, the sight set his nerves on edge. Her hair hung down as he had imagined. She held one hand to her heart as the other gripped a candlestick.

"Mr. Darcy, you frightened me! What do you mean by all this skulking about in the dark? How can you even see where you are going?"

He steadied himself before speaking. "I seem to

have mislaid my book. I was unable to sleep and thought to read."

"The Lord Nelson? I believe I saw it in the library on the sideboard."

He nodded. "That would be a good place for it."

She smiled. "Indeed. Although if you are looking for the second volume, you may have to wrest it away from Miss Bingley," she said with a glint in her eye. He smiled at that; but then they both became sensible to the impropriety of their current circumstance and their close proximity. "I was on my way to check on Jane."

He knew he should step aside, but he did not. He knew he should look away, but he did not. He held her eyes in his stare, his resistance faltering. Another moment and he might have moved towards her, reached his hand to hold the nape of her neck, pierced her flesh with his aching teeth, pressed his mouth upon her lips; but the light from her candle illuminated his face, and he saw his wan reflection in her eyes. As with all those with his curse, he could not bear the sight of his own reflection, a vision of death itself. Her candle flickered out in an instant, and she gasped and broke her gaze.

Available now in print, audiobook, and all eBook formats.

Alicia's Possession – Will Alicia surrender to the demons that torment her day and night, or to the man who wants to possess her, body and soul?

After recovering from a freak car crash that put her in a coma and left her with no memory of the accident, wealthy socialite Alicia Pageant becomes convinced there is a connection between the mysterious disappearance of her neighbor and a series of bizarre occurrences inside her own house; but everyone – including the detective called to investigate – thinks the woman's head injury has left her unable to distinguish reality from fantasy.

As Detective Mason Crawley investigates this "suspicious incident," Alicia's palpable sadness and vulnerability awaken his instinct to protect her and lead her into the light; but when her story begins to unravel, each new piece of information creates more questions than it answers. He begins to wonder if he is falling in love with a woman who is a witness to a cleverly-concealed crime, dangerously delusional, or a murderer.

Praise for *Alicia's Possession*

"It grabbed my attention and kept me riveted to the end. I couldn't wait to read this work, which offers everything: romance, sex, BDSM elements, crime, mystery, compelling characters, and a gripping plot. I read the novel in just a couple of hours, never putting it down."

— Masquerade Crew

"*Murder, Mystery, love, BDSM, and some great sex*. When I read a book and I can feel the characters emotions, then I know it's a good book. That's what we have here."

—Between the Sheets Book Reviews

"*A good read for both the love story and the mystery*. Saucier has blended together a very interesting mystery with a BDSM relationship in its infancy. As the relationship between Alicia and Mason deepens, and he teaches her about his lifestyle, she is intrigued, but still troubled about losing her mind. In the end, the bad guys are found out, although there is a twist I didn't expect."

— Manic Readers

"*Captivating*: the characters also had that instant connection and you could feel it. There is also murder and mystery involved and keeps you guessing until the last page. I started reading it last night and was done this afternoon."

— Simply Southern Couponers

"A great story. It's got everything—sex, crime, cops, more sex, a twisted mystery, knot tying, and a superb denouement."

— Chuck Hustmyre, screenwriter and bestselling author of THE AXMAN OF NEW ORLEANS

EXCERPT FROM
ALICIA'S POSSESSION

"What do you want?" she asked. "I don't know what you want from me."

Mason gripped her upper arms, forcing her eyes to meet his. He knew he'd made a mistake the moment her warmth bled through the silk of her robe and into his palms, sending a ripple of sensation up his arms and down his body. "Why did you lie about knowing Judith?" he asked, his voice low and gravelly but not in the terse tone he used to intimidate a witness. No, she might not recognize it, but he could hear his lust cradling each syllable.

She squeezed her eyes tight as if to prevent her tears' escape, but instead it forced them down her cheeks. "I wasn't lying. I don't know her. I don't remember her. I don't remember anything."

He lifted one hand from her arm and brushed the tears from her cheek with his thumb before running it across her bottom lip. Her eyes remained closed, and his chest rose and fell in rhythm with hers. He leaned in close enough to inhale her breath.

"Don't," she said without force.

He shuffled his feet forward the few inches required for his body to brush against her breasts. "How can you not remember?"

"Th-the accident."

He brought his mouth down, barely touching hers, his tongue tasting the salt of tears on her lips—those lips he had wanted to kiss from the first moment they'd met

"Please," she said on a puff of air and tried to pull

away from him, but he tightened his hold on her arm.

"Please what?"

"Please...don't kiss me."

"I think you want me to kiss you." When she said nothing in protest, he pressed his lips to hers and gently pulled first her top, then her bottom lip into his mouth. He held her chin between his thumb and fist to lift her face.

Tears still streamed down her cheeks, but she opened her eyes and shook her head. "I...I can't do this."

Mason trailed his finger down her throat to the opening of her robe, stopping just over her heart, and she trembled with a hitch in her breath.

"What do you mean you didn't remember her because of the accident?"

"I have...gaps, memory loss." Her tears had begun to wane.

"I'm going to kiss you again."

"No," she whispered when his mouth hovered mere millimeters over hers. He dropped his hand from her arm to the small of her back and pulled her against him, and she gasped at the unmistakable evidence of his arousal. "I'm not ready for this."

"Because of your injury?"

"Because of the infidelity. My husband. He hurt me." Her words pinched his heart and he nodded. "I can't be with a man—any man. I can't trust anyone. I don't even trust myself to have the sense or judgment to know who can be trusted. I don't know if I'll ever be able to trust anyone again."

Mason laid a soft kiss on her mouth, tugging her bottom lip gently between his teeth. He lifted his face just enough to look at her. In time, he could teach her to trust again, at least to trust him, but it would take patience—and perseverance. He thought she might be worth the effort.

"If you want me to stop," he told her, "if you really mean it, say 'apple.'"

Alicia furrowed her brow and blinked before meeting his stare directly. "But I told you to stop."

"Yes, but you didn't mean it." The color rushing into her cheeks proved him right. "I will only stop if you say 'apple.' Understand?"

She responded with a single, slow nod, never taking her eyes off him. When he covered her mouth with his, he ran his tongue along the seam of her lips, and she opened for him. He wrapped both arms around her then, holding her tight, and she placed her hands on his shoulders. As his tongue swirled inside her mouth, she leaned against him and released a low, moaning sigh. He allowed the kiss to continue and to deepen, in part because he wanted to prevent her from using the safety word, but primarily because he didn't want to relinquish her delicious mouth. Although he would never call himself a connoisseur, he could detect the subtle notes of cherry, chocolate, and plum from the wine on her tongue.

Available now in print, audiobook, and all eBook formats.

(Contains light bondage and elements of Dominance and submission.)

COMING SOON!

Viuda
(The Widow)

In this thrilling, suspenseful, page-turning romance, DEA agent David Alvarez invested four years in deep undercover infiltrating the ruthless Sonora Drug Cartel only to have his primary target gunned down by a rival gang. Now his only hope in salvaging the operation and bringing the largest drug trafficker in the world to justice lies with the man's beautiful, young widow Catherine, whom he cannot bring himself to trust.

Catherine would do anything to break free from the clutches of the cartel, but despite her desperate efforts, she can never escape the mistakes of her past that continue to haunt her.

Even though he cannot deny their mystical, mutual attraction, David must carry out his orders—from both the DEA and the Cartel—catching Catherine in a spider web of duplicity and deceit. How far will David go to bring down the cartel? If he succeeds in winning the widow's trust, would he be willing to risk her life...or his heart?

ABOUT THE AUTHOR

Colette Saucier has been writing poems, short stories, and novellas since grade school. Her interest in literature led her to marry her college English professor, but eventually a love of history encouraged her to trade up to a British historian. Technical writing has dominated Colette's career for the past twenty years, but finding little room for creativity in that genre, she dedicated 15 months traveling to Europe and Britain, researching Regency England and vampire lore and literature, to complete her first full-length novel *Pulse and Prejudice*. (Austenprose Readers' Choice, Top 5 Books of 2012).

Pulse and Prejudice was the 1st Place Winner in its category in the 2013 Chatelaine Awards Romantic Fiction Contest and is listed in Chanticleer's *2013 Best Book Listing*. It has been meticulously researched for historical accuracy and remains faithful to nineteenth century literary conventions and Jane Austen's narrative to create a compelling, thrilling paranormal adaptation of *Pride and Prejudice*.

Colette was selected a "2013 Amazon Breakthrough Novel Award" Semi-finalist and named "Debut Author of the Year" by Austenprose for *All My Tomorrows*—now expanded and republished as *The Proud and the Prejudiced*—which was also chosen Austenesque Reviews "Favorite Modern Adaptation" for 2013.

Colette's latest release, the romantic thriller *Alicia's Possession*, was the publisher's #1 Bestselling Romantic Suspense for 4 straight weeks following its debut in June of 2013 and then again in January, 2014, after being voted a "Top Ten Romance Novel of 2013" (P&E Reader's Poll).

Colette's next release is the romantic suspense thriller *Viuda – The Widow*. She is currently researching and writing a sequel to *Pulse and Prejudice* entitled *Dearest Bloodiest Elizabeth*, which follows the newlywed Vampire Darcy and his bride Elizabeth from Britain to Antebellum New Orleans.

Colette lives in South Louisiana with her historian husband and their two dogs.

CPSIA information can be obtained
at www.ICGtesting.com
Printed in the USA
FFOW02n1917130315
11744FF

9 780986 371806